PRAISE FOR TAMMY L. GRACE

"I had planned on an early night but couldn't put this book down until I finished it around 3am. Like her other books, this one features fascinating characters with a plot that mimics real life in the best way. My recommendation: it's time to read every book Tammy L Grace has written."
— *Carolyn, review of Beach Haven*

"*A Season of Hope* is a perfect holiday read! Warm wonderful and gentle tale reflecting small town romance at its best."
— *Jeanie, review of A Season for Hope: A Christmas Novella*

"This book is a clean, simple romance with a background story very similar to the works of Debbie Macomber. If you like Macomber's books you will like this one. The main character, Hope and her son Jake are on a road trip when their car breaks down, thus starts the story. A holiday tale filled with dogs, holiday fun, and the joy of giving will warm your heart.

reveals their hidden secrets—an absorbing page-turning read."

— *Jason Deas, bestselling author of Pushed and Birdsongs*

"I could not put this book down! It was so well written & a suspenseful read! This is definitely a 5-star story! I'm hoping there will be a sequel!"

—*Colleen, review of Killer Music*

"This is the best book yet by this author. The plot was well crafted with an unanticipated ending. I like to try to leap ahead and see if I can accurately guess the outcome. I was able to predict some of the plot but not the actual details which made reading the last several chapters quite engrossing."

—*0001PW, review of Deadly Connection*

LONG WAY HOME

LONG WAY HOME

HOMETOWN HARBOR SERIES BOOK 8

TAMMY L. GRACE

LONE MOUNTAIN PRESS

LONG WAY HOME
A novel by
Tammy L. Grace

LONG WAY HOME is a work of fiction. Names, characters, places, and incidents either are products of the author's imagination or are used fictitiously. Any resemblance to actual events, locales, entities, or persons, living or dead, is entirely coincidental.

LONG WAY HOME Copyright © 2024 by Tammy L. Grace

www.tammylgrace.com
Facebook: https://www.facebook.com/tammylgrace.books
X(Twitter): @TammyLGrace

Published in the United States by Lone Mountain Press, Nevada

ISBN 978-1-945591-72-3 (paperback)
ISBN 978-1-945591-71-6 (eBook)
FIRST EDITION
Cover by Elizabeth Mackey Graphic Design
Printed in the United States of America

Christmas Surprises: Soul Sisters at Cedar Mountain Lodge

GLASS BEACH COTTAGE SERIES

Beach Haven

Moonlight Beach

Beach Dreams

WRITING AS CASEY WILSON

A Dog's Hope

A Dog's Chance

WISHING TREE SERIES

The Wishing Tree

Wish Again

Overdue Wishes

One More Wish

SISTERS OF THE HEART SERIES

Greetings from Lavender Valley

Pathway to Lavender Valley

Sanctuary at Lavender Valley

Blossoms at Lavender Valley

Comfort in Lavender Valley

Reunion in Lavender Valley

Remember to subscribe to Tammy's exclusive group of readers for your gift, only available to readers on her mailing list. **Sign up at www.tammylgrace.com. Follow this link to subscribe at https:// wp.me/P9umIy-e** and you'll receive the exclusive interview she did with all the canine characters in her Hometown Harbor Series.

Follow Tammy on Facebook by liking her page. You may also follow Tammy on book retailers or at BookBub by clicking on the follow button.

"When we lose one blessing, another is often most unexpectedly given in its place."
—C.S. Lewis

CHAPTER ONE

Amelia slipped a popular children's book from the shelf and handed it to the woman who was searching for a birthday gift for her niece. The woman smiled. "Oh, this is perfect for her. Thanks so much."

As Amelia watched Mel at the counter as she wrapped the book in tissue and put it in a festive bag with ribbons, she glanced around Books by the Bay and felt a sense of accomplishment. Even a bit of pride.

Over the last nine months, she'd transformed the old building into a cheerful and welcoming store filled with volumes of books, along with comfy chairs and rustic tables, and a smattering of bookish giftware. The complimentary beverage station was a huge hit with customers, who often liked to sip tea or coffee, or whatever infused water Amelia felt like making, while they browsed or read books.

She loved her store, and it was even more than she imagined when she first visualized the idea. She whispered her thanks to her dad, who pushed her to get a degree in business when she was in college. She could almost hear his voice reminding her that she never knew what the future would hold, and a business degree was something that could benefit her no matter what.

She hadn't worked when she and Ron were married, but she loved the feeling of being her own boss and accomplishing so much on her own.

Cyndy from Bayside Gifts had welcomed her to the retail district in Driftwood Bay with open arms. She even shared her talents when it came to decorating and helped Amelia bring her dream of a coastal and relaxing style to the brick walls and wooden planked floors that made up the bones of her store.

Cyndy introduced Amelia to Lily and Mel and with Mel's love of reading and books, it didn't take Amelia long to hire her as a manager.

It had been one of her best decisions.

Mel was terrific with the customers, and Amelia never had to worry about her being late or not showing up. She handled the computer with ease, and her daily reports were always accurate.

Mel was almost the same age as Amelia's daughter Natalie, but she seemed much more mature and serious. Lily once told Amelia Mel was an old soul, and the more time Amelia spent with the young woman, she had to agree.

With Lily's encouragement, Mel shared her childhood trauma and losses with Amelia and after learning about her early years and abandonment, being homeless as a teenager, and the constant struggles, Amelia was even more impressed with the young woman who ran her store like a well-oiled machine.

Amelia loved having Mel around. It helped ease the pain of missing her daughter. She and Mel also shared a bond over their family situation, although Amelia had it far easier.

Amelia had no real memory of the first two years of her life, which had been less than ideal. She was adopted by a loving couple and had a wonderful childhood and parents who always put her first and prepared her for life as best they could.

As her thoughts drifted to her parents, tears filled her eyes. She'd lost her father a few years ago and her mother just last year. On the heels of her death, her now ex-husband Ron asked for a divorce.

Amelia let out a long sigh.

The last year had shaken her to the core. Natalie was in college, and that was the catalyst that pushed Ron to ask for a divorce. He confessed he'd been unhappy for years but didn't want to abandon his daughter. In her second year, he was confident it wouldn't impact her.

He was, however, perfectly fine with abandoning his wife.

With no parents, no husband, and her daughter over a thousand miles away, Amelia needed a purpose. She found it in an advertisement she saw online for the building she and the bank now owned in Driftwood Bay.

After growing up in White Rock, just over the border in Canada, Amelia attended the University of Washington and met Ron when she was a junior. Ron pursued his dream and became a successful lawyer. They married and built their life together in a Seattle suburb, where they welcomed Natalie twenty years ago.

Now, Ron lived in California. He transferred from the law office where he worked in Seattle to their San Francisco office. She and Ron communicated when it came to Natalie but other than that, they didn't speak often.

She missed that sense of a partnership and the companionship more than she thought she would.

With school just getting out, Ron was making the trip

down to San Luis Obispo to drive Natalie back to his place to spend the first half of summer. She'd be coming to Driftwood Bay later in July.

Amelia couldn't wait to wrap her in a hug and spoil her rotten. Ron had paid for Natalie to fly up to Washington and spend Mother's Day weekend with Amelia only a few weeks ago, and they'd had a fun, but much too short, visit.

As she thought about all the things she wanted to show Nat when she arrived later in the summer, Amelia kept busy checking in a large book order and getting them ready for the shelves.

The one bright spot over the last year was her long-lost sister Georgia. She was ten years older and while Amelia had been adopted, Georgia had been in foster care. Georgia found Amelia last year and reached out to connect with her. It had been such a blessing. She even invited Amelia to spend the holidays with her and her new husband at their house in the San Juan Islands.

Amelia wanted to go, but her daughter was due to visit Driftwood Bay over Christmas. As it turned out, at the last minute, Natalie opted to spend the holidays last year with Ron, which only made the crack in Amelia's heart deeper, but she kept busy with the store and the rush of holiday shoppers. This year, Nat promised to spend her Christmas break with Amelia in Driftwood Bay.

She finished adding the last of the order to the shelves when Mel walked toward her, her bag slung on her arm. "I'm taking off, Amelia. I left the report on your desk, and I'll drop the deposit at the bank on my way."

"Sounds great. Thanks so much, Mel. See you in the morning."

Amelia waved goodbye as she locked the front door behind Mel. After she finished straightening her desk, she opted to brew a cup of tea and take a book outside on the front deck.

The weather was perfect, with the sun shining and a gentle breeze coming from the bay. Amelia breathed in the hint of salt in the air and smiled. She loved living in the quaint little town on the edge of the water. Now with the store up and running, she vowed to spend more time enjoying the beach.

Between greeting people walking by and saying hello, Amelia managed two chapters in the latest mystery she was reading and finished her tea.

As she gathered her things, Nora, the policewoman Lily introduced her to and who often shopped at the store, came up the walkway.

"Hey, Nora. What brings you by so late?"

Nora, in her dark uniform, stepped onto the deck. "Amelia, I'm afraid I've got some bad news to deliver. Could we go inside?"

Amelia's pulse quickened. Her entire head tingled as she tried to process what Nora was saying. "What? What do you mean?" Her voice cracked.

Nora took the things from the table and guided Amelia through the front door to an oversized chair.

Amelia sat and looked up at her, filled with worry.

Nora placed a hand on her arm. "There's no easy way to tell you this. We received a call from Santa Clara County in California. There was a multi-vehicle accident on the 101. Ron and Natalie were involved in the accident."

Amelia gasped and brought her hand to her pounding chest.

"Amelia," said Nora, in a quiet tone. "They didn't make it. They both died at the scene."

"No, no," Amelia wailed. "That can't be. Are you sure?"

As Amelia sobbed, Nora wrapped her arms around her. "I'm so very sorry, Amelia. Is there someone I can call for you?"

Amelia couldn't breathe. She gasped as her heart continued to race. She managed to whisper, "My sister Georgia," before she saw only black and crumpled to the ground.

CHAPTER TWO

Amelia woke on the day of her daughter's funeral and couldn't make herself get out of bed.

None of this seemed real. It had to be a bad dream. Her beautiful daughter couldn't be gone. She didn't even get to say goodbye.

She had so many plans. They were going to visit Olympic National Park when Nat came later in the summer. Amelia arranged for them to go out on a boat with a local. Cyndy wanted to host them for a dinner party.

She couldn't bear the thought of Christmas. Amelia was so excited to have Natalie all to herself for the holidays this year. The idea of spending them alone made her gag on the bile in her throat.

She shut her eyes and willed herself not to throw up again. She hadn't been able to keep anything down since the night she got the news.

The days since Nora came to the bookstore to notify her about the accident had gone by in a blur. Dale and Georgia rushed to Driftwood Bay to take care of Amelia and help her go through the motions of dealing with the authorities in California and getting Natalie to Driftwood Bay.

Ron's brother in Seattle, Bob, who was also an attorney, traveled to California and handled the worst of it. He dealt with the police and medical examiner and was instrumental in getting both Ron and Natalie transported. He organized a service for Ron in Seattle, where he would be buried next to his parents.

She had a vague memory of talking to Bob on the phone. He explained that the accident was caused by a small car cutting off an eighteen-wheeler, who swerved to avoid it and ended up tipping over and causing a massive pileup. Six other people had died, and several were injured.

The details didn't mean much. The horrible result was all that mattered.

Amelia struggled with where to bury Natalie. She never imagined having to make such a horrible decision. Natalie had lived her entire life in Seattle, so Amelia thought she should rest there with her dad and grandparents.

On the other hand, Amelia longed to have her beloved daughter close by, so she could visit her whenever she wanted. She didn't want to trek back to Seattle.

But Nat didn't have a connection to Driftwood Bay. Amelia wasn't sure she'd live in Driftwood Bay forever. She was torn.

She was angry that she had to even consider such a choice.

Georgia held her hand and comforted her as she struggled to come to terms with an impossible decision. Outside of the military cemetery, there was only a small, but beautiful one in Driftwood Bay.

The last few days, Amelia felt like she was underwater. Words and sounds were muffled. She didn't understand much and when her eyes were open, they were always watery. She made out the shapes of Georgia and Dale and had a vague recollection of other people in her house, but she paid little attention.

It was like she'd been drugged, and sometimes, she thought she was dreaming.

Tears leaked from Amelia's eyes as she remembered Georgia's kind words assuring her that having Natalie close by was most important and having her in Driftwood Bay made the most sense. Amelia had no plans to leave and would take comfort in being able to visit her grave whenever she wanted.

Anger bubbled to the surface as Amelia lay in bed. It wasn't fair that she even had to make a choice on where to bury her daughter. She hated everything about it.

Georgia helped her pick a casket and guided her on the choices the funeral director offered. Amelia worried that Natalie's friends wouldn't come to her service if it weren't in Seattle. With her steady counsel, Georgia assured her that their old friends from Seattle would have no problem making the one-time trip, and it would be much easier for them to do that than for Amelia to worry about traveling to see Natalie.

Amelia shook off her doubts and dragged herself from the bed. After a shower, she slipped the black dress Georgia bought for her over her head. It hung on her thin body. With a glance in the mirror, Amelia shook her head. She looked as awful as she felt.

The small scar at the edge of her forehead, courtesy of a fall and stitches after a roller-skating mishap when she was nine, was more pronounced. Whenever she was tired or stressed, it darkened. The crow's feet at the corners of her eyes she always worried about were deeper and heavier than they'd been just a few days ago. They no longer mattered. No amount of concealer could fix what was wrong.

A soft knock on the door interrupted her gaze in the mirror.

Georgia cracked it open and greeted her with a smile. "I came to see if you needed some help getting ready."

Amelia sat on the edge of her bed, her chest tightened, holding in the sobs that threatened to escape. If not for Georgia, she wasn't sure she could have done anything these past few days. While she was so thankful to have her and even more grateful that Georgia had found her and reached out to her last year, Amelia couldn't help but feel sad knowing that Natalie never got to meet her in person. Georgia had been a part of Amelia's life for such a short time, and they'd missed out on so much.

Georgia ushered Amelia into the bathroom, where she had her sit on the closed toilet. When Georgia opened the drawer with her makeup, Amelia shook her head. "I don't want to bother with it. My face will be a mess by the time this is over."

Her big sister nodded and plugged in the curling iron at the end of the counter. She took a brush from the drawer and picked up the blow dryer.

Amelia closed her eyes, letting tears run down her face as Georgia, with gentle strokes, dried and brushed her hair. With the noise from the dryer gone, Amelia opened her eyes and looked in the mirror. Her long, blond hair needed a color touchup, but she was past caring what anyone thought of her today. She just wanted it to be over.

Except part of her didn't want it to be over.

Once she saw her daughter placed in the ground, she couldn't pretend this wasn't real.

Georgia took her time curling strands of hair and when

she was done, she put her hands on Amelia's shoulders. "How's that?"

Amelia reached up and covered Georgia's hand with hers. "Thank you."

Georgia turned her hand and gripped Amelia's, squeezing it tight.

After a long sigh, Amelia used the tissue crumpled in her hand to swipe at her eyes. "I'm not sure I can do this, Georgia."

"I know, dear. This isn't how things are supposed to go. My heart is breaking for you, but Dale and I will be by your side the whole time. You're stronger than you think."

She urged Amelia into the kitchen for a cup of tea before they had to leave.

Dale was outside, giving them space and admiring the job he did mowing Amelia's lawn, making sure every stray blade of grass was swept from the sidewalk.

When Amelia sipped the last of her tea, it was time to go. As she walked toward the car, her feet got heavier, like she was sinking into mud. She didn't want to go. She didn't want to be here.

Dale drove them the short distance to the chapel. As she made her way to the front, Amelia caught sight of Cyndy, Mac, and Lily, plus her sister Wendy, Mel, and several other people from town she recognized. She also spotted several of her old friends from Seattle. She couldn't make eye contact for fear she wouldn't be able to continue. Right now, she was focused on getting to the front row.

Once she was seated, the pastor, who she'd only met a handful of times when she came to church with Cyndy, started with a prayer.

Amelia stared at the casket, covered in beautiful pink and white flowers. She couldn't concentrate on the words coming from the pastor's mouth. She only heard the rush of blood in her ears. She was slipping back underwater.

Her beautiful girl shouldn't be in that box. No matter how pretty it was. The bouquets of flowers surrounding it were gorgeous, but they couldn't make up for the loss of her one and only daughter.

She felt like she was sleepwalking or watching from a distance. Like she wasn't part of the proceedings.

When the ceremony concluded, Georgia reached for her arm to lift her from her seat. Amelia hadn't heard a word of what had been said. She had no memory of the songs sung or the kind words spoken from those in attendance.

She stood and shook hands with people she knew. She had no words to offer, only murmuring the same to each of them. "Thank you for coming."

When the last of the guests passed by her, Cyndy appeared. "I've got all the food set up at the Water Street Building. Everyone has been told where to go, so just take your time."

Amelia squeezed her hand in reply. She'd opted for a private burial at the cemetery, with just Georgia and Dale and Ron's brother and his family. He had called and asked if they could attend Nat's service, and she assured him they were welcome.

She didn't have the strength to go to Ron's, but Bob told her he understood.

The small group followed behind the hearse and took the short ride to the cemetery. Amelia stood between her sister and Dale, leaning on them for fear she would collapse as she watched the funeral staff lower the casket into the ground.

A horrible sound, a howl, startled her.

Then she realized the awful wailing noise was coming from her. She sounded like a wounded animal.

She was wounded, and it was a wound that would never heal.

She stood at the edge of the grave for what seemed like hours

This was it.

It was real.

She would never see Natalie smile again.

Never see her graduate college.

Never see her married.

Never have grandchildren.

She stood there through her tears until she couldn't see anything but the watery outline of the cemetery. Her stomach was in knots, and her ribs were sore from the heaving sobs that racked through her during the service.

Georgia gripped her arm tighter. "Are you ready to go? We can come back later."

Amelia nodded and tried to take a step but collapsed at the edge of Natalie's grave. Ron and Dale helped her up and carried her to the car.

She stood, leaning against it while Ron and his wife hugged her and whispered their love and condolences in her ear.

She slipped into the backseat of the car and steeled herself for the reception. She had to make an appearance, but all she wanted to do was crawl back into bed and never wake up.

How would she manage?

CHAPTER THREE

Two days after the funeral, Amelia emerged from her bedroom. She'd slept most of the last forty-eight hours. If you could call it sleep.

She dozed between nightmares and memories.

The first thing she saw when she woke was the picture of her and Natalie on her bedside table. There was another one with all three of them, years ago when Natalie was little and their world had been perfect.

A sob escaped her mouth and along with it came the urge to vomit. She clamped a hand over her mouth and breathed deeper. She had nothing left to purge.

She focused on the photos. It was all she had left.

Ron and Natalie were gone forever.

She padded into the kitchen and found Georgia at the stove, making soup. Surprised that the aroma actually smelled good.

Amelia stepped up behind her and wrapped her arms around her sister. "Thank you for staying with me. I'm sorry I've been such miserable company."

Georgia turned from the pot she was stirring and hugged Amelia. "Nonsense. You have no reason to be sorry. This is a horrific situation you're in. There are no easy answers."

Georgia sighed. "I feel quite helpless but thought some soup might be good. Will you eat a little for me?"

Amelia nodded. She had to admit the scent made her hungry, and her stomach was begging for sustenance.

Georgia joined her at the table, and they ate soup and fresh bread from the bakery. "Where's Dale?" asked Amelia.

"He went back to Lake Stevens. He said to tell you goodbye, and he'd see you soon. He had to get back to take care of our dog Suki, the yard, and a few things."

Amelia nodded and finished off the soup. The chicken and rice with a hint of lemon was perfect.

Georgia cleared her throat. "Cyndy and I made a couple of executive decisions while you were resting."

Amelia raised her brows. "I'm sure whatever you did is perfect. I can't tell you what it means to have you here. I couldn't have made it through the service without you and Dale."

"Of course, dear. We're happy to help." She took a sip of tea. "Mel is going to handle the store for you until you're ready to go back. No rush at all. Cyndy is pitching in to help, and so is Lily. So, it's all under control."

Amelia helped herself to another bowl of soup. "That's for the best. I haven't given the store a thought."

"Dale paid for a yard service to take care of your lawn and plants until the end of the season. He didn't want you worrying about it."

Amelia's lip quivered. "He's such a good guy. You really hit the jackpot with him."

Georgia chuckled. "You're telling me. He's my knight in shining armor."

She pointed at the notepad on the counter. "Yesterday, Bob called. He wanted you to know that Ron hadn't changed his life insurance or will. He also said Ron had confessed to him not long ago that he'd made a huge mistake in asking you for a divorce. He was sorry and missed having you in his life. Bob said Ron still loved you."

Tears welled in Amelia's eyes,

"Anyway, Bob is his executor and wanted you to know that along with the insurance money, you'll receive other beneficiary benefits from the firm and will inherit Bob's house and property in San Francisco. He said he can handle selling it if you'd like him to. At no charge to you, of course. He's sending an email with the details."

"Wow," said Amelia. "That's a huge surprise. It makes me sad we ended up this way and that he couldn't talk to me about things. He hurt me so much, I worked hard to keep him from my mind. I concentrated on Natalie and focused all I had on her."

Before she knew it, sobs escaped from her mouth.

Georgia reached across the table for her hand. "I know none of this is easy. I don't want to stress you further, but I have an idea. What would you think about the two of us going to Friday Harbor for a bit? I think you could do with a change of scenery. We can stay at my house, just relax."

Amelia used a napkin to dab her cheeks and eyes. "I don't know. It sounds nice, but…"

"Think about it. No pressure. It's a lovely and quiet place, and I've already got a great group of friends there. You'd like them." She paused and added, "Grief isn't easy or predictable. I'd like to tell you time heals, but it really doesn't. The pain becomes less pronounced, less biting. You'll get to a point where you don't think of Natalie every minute. Then, you can work on expanding those moments into longer periods of time. Your heart will be forever scarred, but the excruciating pain will dull and transform into just being a part of who you are."

Amelia's heart swelled at her sister's words. The tears in Georgia's eyes made Amelia reach out and hug her sweet sister. Despite all the tragic events in her life, Georgia was happy and kind. She was a true caretaker. A nurturer. Amelia was lucky to have her.

"Try not to think too far ahead. Just do your best to live in the moment and remember nothing is permanent. Not sadness. Not happiness. There's an ebb and flow to life, like the tide on the beach." Georgia collected the dishes and tidied the kitchen while Amelia sipped on her tea.

With each sip, she warmed to the idea of a trip to Georgia's house on the island. She could wallow there as well as here; maybe something new would be good for her. The bookstore she dreamed of and loved meant little now. It didn't hold the same appeal as it had for the last nine months.

Going somewhere new, where she hadn't thought of Natalie or Ron, and they hadn't visited together, might be good. Not that she wouldn't think of her daughter every waking moment, but, like Georgia said, she could find a few minutes each day where the loss wasn't at the top of her mind.

As Georgia dried the last of the dishes, Amelia brought her empty teacup to the sink. "Let's go. I think you're right. A change might be good."

Georgia hugged her close. "I'll get things arranged."

After a lovely evening at Cyndy's, with Lily and Mac, Mel, and Wendy, Georgia and Amelia were up early, ready to hit the road and the ferry terminal.

Amelia didn't trust herself to drive and gave Georgia the keys to her SUV. Mac had loaded their belongings in it last night after the delicious send-off meal Cyndy hosted.

Everyone was so kind and helpful. It made Amelia's lips quiver as she thought of all of them.

It didn't take long to reach the first ferry, which would take them to Coupeville. They opted to stay in the SUV for the short crossing and with the sun shining through the window and oldies playing on the radio, Amelia dozed in the passenger seat as Georgia made her way to the next ferry terminal in Anacortes.

She managed to sleep until Georgia stopped the car in the line for the final ferry they would board to take them to Friday Harbor. Amelia sat up and took in the bustling terminal with the lines of cars waiting to make their way onto the ferry. She rolled down her window and let the breeze, filled with the scent of flowers that were planted along the edge of the lanes, drift over her. It wasn't long before they were onboard and parked on the vehicle deck.

The crossing took just over an hour, and they climbed the stairs and sat at one of the tables with a window and watched the blue waters as the ferry made its way through the channels of the San Juan Islands.

The gentle motion and hum of the ferry comforted Amelia, like a gentle rocking chair. Ferry travel was always relaxing, and it had been a long time since she'd been on one. There was nothing hurried or rushed about it. People visited, played cards, read books, or just enjoyed the gorgeous view.

There was no frantic pace, like in airports. Things were simple and easy. Exactly what Amelia needed right now.

Soon, the captain's voice announced that they were approaching Friday Harbor, and he asked passengers to make their way to their vehicles.

In no time, Georgia steered the car across the metal apron and onto Front Street along the harbor. "It's such a cute place. I can't believe I haven't been here before," said Amelia, taking in the colorful buildings lining the waterfront.

Georgia smiled as she guided the car through town. "We love it here. Dale's house in Lake Stevens is lovely and so spacious, but I like this smaller house here. I think it suits me."

As she made the turn for the golf community, she pointed across the road. "Along with the walking trails throughout the golf course, there's a nice path just off the road that goes down to the beach. It's for the residents of the area, so nice and private."

"It's beyond beautiful here. I can see why you like it so much. I wish I could have come and spent Christmas with you."

Georgia reached over for Amelia's hand and squeezed it. "We can make that happen this year."

After a couple of turns through the neighborhood, Georgia pulled into the driveway of a quaint Cape Cod style house, gray with white trim. Amelia pointed at it. "I love those weathered shingles. It looks so beachy."

Georgia smiled. "And the best part is that they're made of some composite, so they look weathered but will last forever. It's a maintenance-free property, which I like."

They made their way up the sidewalk to the covered porch, where gorgeous peonies, in various shades of pink, bloomed. Georgia opened the blue front door and motioned Amelia inside her home.

"It's only two bedrooms, but they're generous. I want you to take the master suite."

Amelia shook her head. "No, I'll be fine in the guest room."

Georgia pursed her lips. "My house. My rules. I want you to have all the space and privacy you need. I insist." She led the way through the living area, where a gorgeous bouquet of white and blue flowers graced the coffee table and into the kitchen. Another vase of flowers, in purple tones, stood atop the island.

"Your house smells wonderful with all the fresh flowers."

Georgia beamed. "That's thanks to my lovely friend, Linda. She owns the local nursery and the floral shop downtown. She is beyond talented and helped us with all the plants you'll see around the outside."

Georgia pointed at the bottles of wine on the island. "Izzy, my friend who lives just around the corner, her family owns a winery, and her brother Blake moved here to run the one on the island. These are from their vineyards."

Amelia's eyes widened. "How wonderful and nice of them."

Georgia turned down a short hall. "Now, let's get you settled in the master. It's right down here."

She led her to a serene space, done in shades of blue, ivory, and gray. Watercolor prints of shells, coral, and seaweed graced the barely blue and neutral walls. The white bedspread was decorated with textured throw pillows in muted blue and ivory. Amelia rested her hand on the weathered wooden dresser. "This is lovely, Georgia."

Her sister waved her hand across the space. "I'm no decorator, but my friend Kate is top-notch. She has a lovely antique store downtown, and she worked her magic on this place. We bought it furnished but ended up replacing much of the furniture and let Kate put her signature style on it."

Amelia pointed at the vase of white and ivory ranunculus on the nightstand "I see Linda's handiwork again."

"Oh, yes. I let them know we were coming, and they all pitched in to get things ready. I'm sure we have a stocked refrigerator and enough food to feed us for a month. Not to mention the lovely flowers."

As Georgia pointed out the amenities in the master bath, where the scent of lavender filled the air, Georgia's cell phone chimed.

After a short conversation, she disconnected and slid the phone back in her pocket. "That was my friend Izzy. She lives a couple of streets over. She's dating the manager of the golf club, Colin. He's on his way to unload the car for us."

"Wow," said Amelia. "This place is a like a five-star resort."

Georgia wrinkled her nose. "Even better."

Colin arrived, greeted them with a warm smile, made quick work of his task, and left the ladies to relax.

Amelia stood at the windows of the sunroom off the kitchen, taking in the view, while Georgia retrieved some glasses from the cupboard. She opened the fridge and pulled out a pitcher of iced tea, while she eyed the food her friends had provided.

"How about some lunch?" she asked, handing Amelia a glass of iced tea. "It looks like we've got some yummy chicken salad from Izzy, and I saw some fresh croissants from the bakery on the counter. How does that sound?"

"Actually, it sounds good. I'm hungry."

In no time, Georgia had their sandwiches plated, and she carried them out to the patio. Amelia brought their iced teas, and Georgia added a box from Sam's shop for dessert.

A short vase of blue hydrangeas decorated the patio table, and Georgia made sure Amelia sat in a chair that would give her a nice view of the greenbelt surrounding the golf course.

As they ate, they were quiet. Amelia stared at the peaceful view, interrupted only by the flutter of a few birds and butterflies.

When they finished their sandwiches, Georgia opened the box and tempted Amelia with a fresh brownie, slathered in a thick, fudgy frosting and sprinkled with walnuts.

"Oh, my," said Amelia, with a hint of a smile. "Those look sinful."

Georgia laughed. "They are. You'll love them. Sam, who owns the coffee shop down by the harbor, loves to bake. She and Jeff are the couple who hosted Dale and me when we came to visit. When you're up to it, she wants to have us over soon."

Amelia took a bite and groaned. "Oh, my goodness, these are so yummy. You've got a wonderful bunch of friends, Georgia. That's something to treasure."

"Believe me, I do treasure them. In Boise, my friends were always affiliated with work or sometimes church, but this is the first time in my life I've had a circle of friends that I've cultivated on my own. Well, sort of. They visited Lavender Valley, and I met them there, but like my newfound foster sisters, I felt like we're all sisters of the heart."

Georgia reached out and gripped Amelia's. "I'm also very blessed to have found you and have you as my sister."

Amelia nodded, her throat suddenly dry and her voice gone. Tears slipped down her cheeks. She was beyond grateful for Georgia and the comfort and steadiness she offered.

Today had been a better day than yesterday. Like Georgia

suggested, Amelia wasn't thinking too far ahead to tomorrow. She vowed to enjoy each minute as it happened, knowing her grief could appear at any moment. Like the tide along the beach, without warning, it would sweep away the calm she felt.

CHAPTER FOUR

O ver the next week, Amelia suffered intense periods of sorrow, spending hours lying in bed or staring out from a chair on the patio, but with Georgia's help, each night before they went to bed, Amelia recounted the bits of happiness she experienced each day.

On Saturday, Izzy invited them to her house for a small welcoming celebration she and Colin wanted to host for Amelia. She invited the group of six other couples who had all become close friends and spent most of their time together and promised it would be casual and low key.

Accustomed to dressing up for events she attended with Ron for all of their married life, Amelia was self-conscious to show up in the shorts and t-shirts she'd packed for the trip to the island. Georgia assured her nobody would give her a second glance, and they were all used to shorts and jeans. It wasn't a high-power party, just a fun group who wanted to meet her.

She did manage to fix her hair, although it was way past its prime. Her graying roots had a growth spurt over the last couple of weeks and looked horrible. She didn't bother with makeup. It didn't go well with a face that crinkled and burst into tears whenever someone mentioned Natalie or the accident. At least that didn't happen on the island where nobody knew her or her situation. In reality, nobody even had to mention her; all Amelia had to do was think of Nat.

She finally settled on her navy-blue shorts that looked the least casual, paired with a light-blue tank top and a lightweight cardigan that matched it. Georgia wore jeans and a blouse she'd made in a pretty red fabric. She took out the fruit salad she and Amelia made after visiting the farmer's market in the morning, and they set out to walk to Izzy's.

Izzy met them at the door of her house, which was the same style, just larger and a darker color of gray than Georgia's. She hugged Georgia hello and reached out a hand to Amelia.

"I'm so glad you're here, Amelia. Come on in, and I'll introduce you to the others and get you something to drink." She led the way through the entry and her large kitchen to the dining area and patio beyond.

"Everyone is out here enjoying the lovely weather. We've all been so excited to meet you since Georgia told us she found her sister. She and Dale are such sweet people."

Amelia felt at ease with Izzy at her side. "Yes, I was so happy to connect with her and, now more than ever, am thankful to have her in my life."

Izzy stepped over to the table where everyone was gathered. "Amelia has arrived," she announced.

She pointed at the group and glanced over at Amelia. "Okay, I'll go through and make introductions. Don't worry, we won't be testing you when we're done."

"You've met Sam at her coffee shop already, and next to her is her husband, Jeff. He watches over the family hardware store with his son." Jeff took a few steps toward her and extended a hand.

He had kind eyes and a warm smile.

Izzy continued around the table and the edge of the patio, introducing Linda and Max. "Linda is responsible for all the gorgeous flowers in the yard, and Max is a semi-retired doctor, who spends lots of time out there on the green." They both greeted Amelia with hugs.

Kate turned from arranging a bowl of salsa and smiled at Amelia. "I'm Kate and so happy to meet you." She put her hand on the shoulder of a man with gray hair and striking blue eyes. "This is Spence."

He stood and shook Amelia's hand. "Great to meet you."

Izzy smiled and added, "He's a retired detective from Seattle and has some of the best stories."

Next came Ellie and Izzy's brother Blake, whom she put her arm around when she explained she was his older, wiser sister.

Amelia smiled when she shook both of their hands. "Georgia tells me you run a vineyard here. That sounds fun."

Ellie chuckled. "Fun and busy, especially now in the tourist season. You'll have to come out and visit."

Jess, who Amelia met when she and Georgia were on a walk one morning, stepped over to her and hugged Amelia. Izzy pointed at the man sitting next to Jess' empty chair. "This guy with his handsome service dog, Rebel, is Dean. He and Jess are newcomers to the island, and we love having them here."

Izzy put her hand on Regi's shoulder. "This is Regi and her husband Nate. Regi works at the high school, and Nate runs a delivery service. His dad is in real estate, and Dean works for him doing graphics and photography."

As she was talking, a tall man and a golden retriever

came from the house. "Ah," said Izzy. "This is my beau Colin, who manages the golf club and my sweet girl, Sunny."

Amelia bent down to pet the dog's head and returned Colin's greeting, who was doing his best to get Sunny's attention. She was planted firmly next to Rebel, sitting calmly next to his master.

Izzy put her hands on her hips. "Now, I won't confuse you by telling you all of our dogs' names, but everybody here has at least one. Sunny is here because she lives here, but she's on her way over to Colin's to play with his dog, Jethro, and Ruby, who belongs to Jess. Rebel is always with Dean, but the others are sitting this one out tonight. I think the rest of them are having a playdate at Sam's."

They all greeted her with such warmth, it was easy to see why Georgia loved them and wanted Amelia to meet them.

Izzy made sure she had a glass of wine and pointed out the two empty chairs near Kate and Spence. As she sat, Spence winked at her. "Our dog is named Roxy. She's at home. We live in town, near the harbor. She's a retired, or I guess rejected police dog that I was able to adopt. She enjoys her alone time."

Amelia chuckled and took a sip from her glass. "I'm never going to remember the names of all these dogs. I bet it's a zoo when they all get together."

Spence nodded. "We usually save that for Sam's place or Linda's. They both have huge yards with space for them all to play. Our yard couldn't begin to handle them."

Amelia chatted with everyone while Izzy, Linda, and Sam toted dishes out of the house and set up a buffet. Soon, Izzy whistled and announced dinner was ready.

As they all stood, she pointed out the stacks of plates and utensils. "This is casual tonight. Help yourselves to whatever you like and if you need something you don't see, just let me know."

Once everyone had filled their plates and gathered around the large table made up of smaller tables pushed together, Max stood. "I'm always the one to kick off a toast and am so pleased to be able to welcome Amelia. Georgia, as I'm sure you know, is a happy and upbeat person. Since she told us about finding you, that little light in her shines even brighter. We're overjoyed that you're here to spend some time with her and us. We want you to know we're here for you, whatever you need."

He looked around the table and continued, "I've been Sam's best friend since we were kids and came to visit her and fell in love with this place." He glanced over at Linda. "Not to mention this lovely woman. Just know you're surrounded by a group of loving and kind people, who have had our share of hardships and trials. Whatever you might need, you can count on this group to help, even if it's just to listen."

He held his glass higher. "Here's to Amelia and Georgia."

The group of friends clinked glasses, and, through fresh tears, Amelia did the same and took a long swallow from her glass.

Over the next few days, Georgia and Amelia walked with Izzy and Jess most mornings. Their two goldens, Sunny and Ruby, tagged along with the women and swished their tails while the ladies chatted. It was nice to have the company and listen to them talk about current happenings on the island and trying to avoid the busiest tourists areas downtown.

As they walked together, Amelia learned Jess would be a

first-time grandma in July. She was excited about the prospect, especially since her rocky and estranged relationship with her son. Just last year, they'd finally spent time together, and she beamed with pride when she spoke of him and his wife.

She and Dean were planning a trip back to Maine so she could see the baby and spend time with all of them.

Izzy was still working part-time, but she enjoyed helping Blake and Ellie at the winery during the busy season. With the summer season upon them, they were booked for weddings and parties in the barn and at their outdoor venue.

Georgia chuckled. "Dale and I are the slackers of the group. With both of us retired, we don't have to do anything, and we like that. Dale does enjoy golfing, and he can always find a partner with Max or Spence, or even Jeff, if he can get away from the store."

Izzy chuckled. "I seem to remember you and Dale coming to the rescue when Regi and Nate needed someone to watch little Emma."

"Oh, yes, that's true. We're excellent babysitters. She's a cutie."

Izzy explained that Regi and Nate adopted a little girl, who was connected to an old friend of Kate's. "I'll let her tell you the story. It's tragic and sad but has a happy ending for sweet Emma."

As they were on the first leg of their second loop around the golf course, Jess turned to Georgia. "I forgot; you probably haven't heard the news about Margaret." She took a few minutes to explain to Amelia that Margaret was her niece. A niece she never knew until she showed up on her doorstep right after she came to the island last year.

Amelia noticed the sadness in her eyes when Jess explained that her sister, who was rebellious and estranged from the family, had a daughter and never told anyone. The daughter was adopted, and Jess' sister passed away over eight years ago.

"Margaret is a bit of a handful," she said with a chuckle. "Anyway, I helped guide her into becoming a substitute teacher here on the island. She was lost and unsure what to do. She lost her mother right before she came here to find me, and her mother urged her to get a teaching degree so she'd always have a way to support herself."

Amelia nodded. "Smart mom."

"Well, she was a long-term sub this last year, and Sam was kind enough to let her live in the apartment above the coffee shop. That was a huge deal for me. I was about ready to go crazy having her at my house. I'm officially too old for the twenty-somethings."

Georgia laughed. "Yeah, I second that one. I've been too old for that crowd for decades."

Izzy shook her head. "Don't even talk to me about that age group. My own daughter and I can hardly be in the same room with each other." She glanced at Amelia. "Sadly, we've been estranged since my ex and I divorced. She chose him and believed all of his drivel. She's living with him in California, last I knew. He's got a load of money and isn't afraid to use it, if you know what I mean."

"I'm so sorry, Izzy. That can't be easy for you." Amelia saw the flash of sadness in Izzy's eyes, but only for a moment, before she covered it with a wave of her hand.

"I've learned to accept it."

Georgia stopped walking and met Jess' eyes. "So, what's going on with Margaret? What's the news?"

Jess raised her brows. "It's actually great news. With help from the principal where she subbed here, she put in for a permanent teaching job on Orcas Island and got it. She's moving over the summer and will teach second grade in the fall."

Georgia clapped her hands together. "That's wonderful news. I'm a little surprised since she talked so much about moving to Seattle or Portland."

Jess shrugged. "I know. I was shocked, but I think she started to see the advantages of small-town life. This is just a one-year position, so she might decide to move on after it. I do think the dream of being a musician is fading for her. It was a fad, I think."

As they turned the corner and Izzy's house came into view, she said, "It'll be great for her to be on her own but still close enough that if she needs you, you can be there for her. It's a great way for her to spread her wings a little."

Jess nodded. "That's what I think, too. She's a bit immature and losing her mom really had an impact on her. I think a slower pace and a small group of supportive coworkers will be great for her. I also like having her close, and I don't think she can get in too much trouble on the island."

Izzy chuckled and wished them all a good day before taking off for her yard.

Soon, Jess did the same, and Amelia and Georgia walked the rest of the way back to Georgia's house.

They came through the backyard. As they walked onto the patio, Georgia pointed at a box on the outdoor table. "What do we have here? A box from the bakery is always fun."

She hurried to it like a kid on Christmas morning. "Aww, it's from Max. He said enjoy breakfast and hoped we have a great day."

"What a nice guy," said Amelia.

Georgia grinned. Let's brew some tea to go with these

lovely pastries, and we can enjoy the morning out here on the patio.

As Amelia sipped the Earl Grey Georgia made for her, she sighed. Listening to the ladies while they walked and visiting with everyone at Izzy's the other night, she appreciated how genuine and sincere they all were. They'd all had some tragic times in their lives, lost people they loved, and they were living. Not just living but thriving.

They gave her hope that one day, she might do the same.

By the end of the week, she noticed she had more happy moments to highlight than she had on her first day in Friday Harbor. Georgia made a point of writing them all down on a little tablet on her bedside table. Each night before they turned in, they'd discuss the day and their favorite parts or things they enjoyed.

Meeting the friends Georgia told her about was uplifting and healing. None of them dwelled on the tragic loss Amelia suffered. They treated her like anyone else. They were willing to listen if Amelia wanted to talk about Natalie, but they didn't focus on it.

The kindness in Kate's eyes spoke volumes. She understood Amelia's pain more than anyone. Earlier in the week, Georgia explained Kate's daughter had died years ago when in college, and Kate still struggled with it. She suggested that Kate would be someone she could confide in. Someone who would understand what she faced.

Last night, at the girls' night Sam hosted at her house, while Amelia sat on the deck watching the water, Kate placed a gentle hand on her shoulder. She let her know if she ever needed to talk, she was happy to listen.

All of the ladies were so kind and friendly. Amelia could see why Georgia loved spending time on the island. Amelia gained a little strength each day, and even though she still had bouts of tears and heavy grief, they were less in duration and further apart than the first days she spent at Georgia's.

Her thoughts drifted to the store and going home, but as Georgia often reminded her, the store was in capable hands, and Amelia's priority was only herself.

She had to go back to reality someday but not today.

CHAPTER FIVE

Thursday morning, two weeks since they arrived, Amelia carried two cups of tea to the patio, waiting on Georgia to join her.

When Georgia came through the doorway, Amelia looked up and noticed her sister's pale face, etched with concern and worry. "What's wrong, Georgia?"

"Dale just called. He's at the emergency room. He took a fall, and they suspect he might have broken his ankle." She sighed and slipped into the chair next to Amelia.

After a long sip of tea, Georgia met Amelia's eyes. "I hate to do this, but I have to get back to Lake Stevens. Dale will need help. He's left Suki with the neighbors until I can get there."

Amelia nodded. "I understand. I'm so sorry, Georgia."

"I'm sure he'll be okay. It's just a bump in the road. I want you to stay here, as long as you like. I was going to leave at the end of June anyway, so I could help with the festival in Lavender Valley. This just accelerated my departure." She chuckled. "Although, I'm not sure a trip to Oregon will work now either."

Amelia wrinkled her brow. "I don't have to stay. I can just go back to Driftwood Bay."

Georgia shook her head. "No, no. I think this is where you need to be. You don't need to disrupt your time. You've got Jess and Izzy just down the street, and all the others will be around if you need anything. Just relax and enjoy the island. It's a wonderful place to heal. I just need to trouble you for a ride to the ferry dock." She glanced at her watch. "I should be able to make the eleven o'clock crossing."

In no time, Georgia had her suitcase ready, and Amelia drove her to the harbor. As they drove, Georgia kept apologizing, "This timing is so unfortunate. I'll call you when I know more and see if I'm able to come back, but realistically, I don't see that happening until late July, since I committed to help at the farm."

Amelia pulled into one of the few parking spots close to the dock and turned off the engine. "Please don't worry about me. I'm going to stay for a few more days, give it some thought, and see if I'm up to returning to the store. I feel a bit guilty not working, but I realize I need some time. I'm not ready to face everyone with their sad eyes, and it's easier not to think about it here."

Georgia patted her hand. "Yes, exactly. You rest and take as long as you need. In the short time I spent with Mel, I can tell she is more than capable of running things for you. With Cyndy and Lily helping, you have no reason to rush back or worry about a thing. Just call them and check in if you feel you must, but don't hurry back just because of this mishap."

Tears clouded Georgia's eyes. "I wanted nothing more than to give you a quiet place to recover and regain your strength at your own pace. I wouldn't leave you on your own if I didn't know all the ladies who've been so kind to me, will be there for you. In fact, I texted Kate to share the news, and she's already planning to stop by with dinner tonight. Plus, she let the others know. You might be overrun with company."

Amelia reached across and hugged her sister. "You're the best big sister in the world. I'm so glad we found each other."

They stepped from the SUV, and Amelia retrieved Georgia's suitcase for her. As they stood on the sidewalk, Georgia pointed at the ferry. "I hate to rush off. I'll call you as soon as I can. Please make yourself at home. If you need anything, call Izzy. She's close by and can organize an army. You've got all their numbers, right?"

Amelia nodded and grinned. "Yes, I've got everything I need. Don't worry about me. Give Dale my love and let me know the outcome when you get home."

They hugged again, and Georgia hurried to the terminal.

Amelia leaned against her SUV, her eyes focused on the ferry. After a few minutes, she spotted Georgia standing on the outdoor deck, waving at her, as the ferry inched away from Friday Harbor.

A hint of sadness and worry crept over her. She felt stronger when Georgia was there, but she didn't want Georgia to worry and told herself she could handle things on her own.

She was still waving when Sam walked up next to her. With a warm smile, she handed Amelia a latte. "Vanilla, right?"

Amelia's heart filled as she took the cup. "Yes, that's so sweet of you. Georgia assured me her friends would take good care of me and look, here you are already."

Sam shrugged. "Kate let us know about Georgia having to leave to be with Dale. We're all more than happy to help with anything you need, but if you want to be alone, we understand that too."

"Thank you. That means so much." She took another sip and sighed. "Honestly, my emotions are all over the place. My days are a mixture of quiet and often sad times and then happier moments when I'm sharing a meal or conversation with Georgia. We've taken to walking each morning and evening, and I like doing that."

Sam laughed. "Well, you have no shortage of dogs who love to walk. I know Jess and Izzy walk all the time around those trails. You can get down to the beach easily too, which is a lovely spot. You have a standing invitation to join us at our house for dinner anytime you want, and I know the others would offer the same. I'm usually working during the day, but you can always pop by, and we can do a quick lunch together."

"Oh, that would be wonderful. Georgia said Kate is coming over with dinner tonight, but I might take you up on your offer another evening. You have such a gorgeous home, and I think I could sit on your deck and watch the water for days."

"Anytime, Amelia. You are welcome anytime. You don't even have to call ahead. Just show up and help yourself to a lounge chair."

Tears leaked from Amelia's eyes. "You're all so kind. I appreciate it."

Sam put an arm around her shoulders. "Each of us has endured struggles and loss. We understand it takes time and lots of patience to get through the trauma you're experiencing. The best thing to remember is you're not alone here. Between the seven of us and our significant others, we've got you covered."

Amelia surprised herself when she engulfed Sam in a

tight hug. She wasn't one to hug people she barely knew, but she wanted Sam to know how much her kind words meant to her. "I really appreciate that. I promise to reach out and come by to visit."

Sam squeezed her back. "We've all been there. Sometimes it's a long way home, but with the help of supportive friends, who are more like family for me, I found happiness and a home, not to mention the man I love here. This place has a way of healing the most shattered hearts."

Amelia released Sam and used the napkin around her cup to dry her cheeks. "I already sense that. As Georgia said, I'm having a few more happy moments each day."

Sam smiled at her. "We'll have to see what we can do to increase those moments for you." She pointed across the street. "I need to get back to the shop. You're welcome to hang out if you want."

"Thanks, but I think I'm going to head back to the house. I need to get my walk in before it gets any later in the day. I'll make a point to stop by in the morning though."

"Sounds great. I'll hold you to it." Sam waved as she hurried across the street.

Amelia finished off her latte before she climbed behind the wheel and headed back to Georgia's house.

The house was quiet and felt empty without the happy sound of Georgia's voice. Amelia brushed away the trace of anxiety the silence brought and made sure she put the house keys in her pocket before trekking out of the neighborhood to the beach.

She made her way down to the large piece of driftwood she and Georgia had commandeered as their bench and took a seat. The rush of the water toward the shore and the slap of it against the sand relaxed her mind. She focused on it and let her anguish flow out to sea with each wave.

Along with the power of the ocean and the constant movement, there was a stillness to the beach. It mirrored her own emotions. The sea could sometimes be quiet and reflective and other times savage and unrelenting like her grief.

Back in Driftwood Bay, Lily invited her to walk on the beach below her property. She told her how much it had helped heal her broken heart when she first arrived, mourning the loss of her husband and their life together.

Amelia didn't really understand her suggestion and hadn't been in a frame of mind to give it much thought, but now she understood. There was something to the gentle motion, the vast size of the sea, the sound of the soft edge of the wave against the sand, and the power of the rushing white water as it came to shore. The scent of salt hung in the air, and the breeze ruffled her hair. It all worked together to remind her she was alive and that there was something bigger than her, something that transcended time and space.

As she sat and pondered, she imagined the thousands of people who had sat like her. Some hundreds of years ago. Some last week. She wondered what they'd thought when they looked out at the expanse of water and sky. Some, like her, were no doubt grieving and looking for answers, at least respite.

She vowed to spend her mornings on the beach when she returned to Driftwood Bay.

As she studied the shore, she noticed a man walking in the distance with his dog. The man threw a stick, and the dog rushed into the water to retrieve it. She watched as they went through the motions of the game dozens of times.

The dog looked so proud of himself as he returned the stick, sporting a patriotic bandana that was getting soaked from the seawater.

Finally, the man quit throwing, although the dog looked like he was ready to fetch for at least a few more hours. They made their way toward her and turned at the worn path leading up to the road. The same path she'd taken.

The man glanced over at her as they climbed the sandy trail, touching the brim of his hat, covering his salt and pepper hair. She gave him a quick wave and turned her attention back to the shoreline.

After another thirty minutes, she climbed the path and crossed the road. As she approached Izzy's property, she took the pathway to the longest trail that wound around the golf course. She needed the exercise, and the idea of going back to Georgia's quiet house held little appeal.

The weather was pure perfection with the sun shining, but not too hot to make walking difficult. A lovely breeze cooled the air and carried the scent of the wild pink roses tucked into the landscaping throughout the trail.

She was about a quarter of a mile from Georgia's house when she spotted a golden retriever in the backyard of a house. It had the same flag-themed bandana of the dog she'd seen at the beach.

As she got closer, she studied it. She doubted it was the same dog. Patriotic bandanas were popular and with the upcoming Fourth of July holiday and Memorial Day having just passed, she imagined lots of dogs wore them. As she convinced herself it couldn't be the same dog, a man emerged from the house.

Her eyebrows arched. It was the same dog. She recognized the man, dressed in jeans and a blue shirt, wearing the same hat he'd worn at the beach. He must have sensed her staring and turned his head toward her. He focused on her for what seemed longer than necessary, but then waved.

She waved back and kept walking, averting her eyes and concentrating on the pathway. She didn't want him to think she was following him. The way he'd looked at her made her self-conscious.

On the way to Georgia's, she chastised herself. She was the stranger in the neighborhood. The island was one of those places where everyone knew their neighbors and chances are, he didn't recognize her. Or he remembered seeing her at the beach and wondered what she was doing in his backyard.

This was silly. Everyone was friendly in the community. A few people had waved and said hello when she and Georgia walked earlier in the week. He just looked so intense when he stared at her.

With only a couple of hours before Kate was due, Amelia gulped down a glass of iced water and opted to take a nap. She wasn't a napper, but since losing Natalie, the emotional drain exhausted her, and she found herself napping each afternoon.

Georgia assured her sleep was required for healing and urged her to listen to her body and rest. She settled atop Georgia's bed, breathing in the sweet and delicate scent from the ranunculus on the bedside table.

Ninety minutes later, Amelia's phone alarm beeped. She opened her eyes, refreshed from the peace sleep brought her. At least she could sleep here. It had been elusive at best, at home.

She noticed she had a text and smiled when she read that Georgia had arrived safely and would call her later tonight when she knew more about Dale.

Amelia changed her shirt from the wrinkled one she wore and did her best to make her hair presentable. Sam set her up with an appointment with Jeff's sister Jen, for tomorrow. It couldn't come quick enough.

After checking the fridge and finding the pitcher of tea almost empty, Amelia brewed a fresh batch and stuck it back in the fridge to cool. Minutes later, the bell rang.

She opened the door to Kate, who held takeout bags from Soup D'Jour. "Hi, Amelia," she said, stepping over the threshold. "I picked up a variety of soups and salads for us."

Amelia helped her unload the goodies in the kitchen.

Kate unearthed a bakery box and wiggled her brows. "Sam sent us some treats from her shop. Pie and brownies."

Amelia grinned. "I'm going to have to walk double this week to keep up with all the yummy treats."

Amelia took down some plates and retrieved silverware. "Are you up for eating on the patio?"

Kate nodded. "Sure. It's lovely outside, and you've got a nice view."

Between the two of them, they carted out the food and iced tea. As they ate and enjoyed the early evening, with glimpses of golfers passing by, Kate shared her story with Amelia.

By the time she finished, they were both in tears. Kate dabbed her eyes and met Amelia's. "Like you, I thought I wouldn't survive losing my sweet girl. If not for Spence and his unwavering support, I might have lost the battle. Honestly, I still struggle. Especially around important dates like Karen's birthday, Mother's Day, Christmas. It's gotten easier, but that immense sadness and the regrets that come with missing her are always there."

Kate took a sip from her glass before she continued, "The pain changes. It's not fresh and sharp. Now, it's just something that's always there. Things started to change when I could remember Karen and smile instead of cry, but that took a long time. Of course, I had to leave her when I moved here. Linda helped me design a memorial rose garden in my yard, and I spend time there every morning. Sometimes, I feel her there. Many times, I pretend she's there; it makes me feel better."

Fresh tears sprung from Amelia's eyes. "You give me hope, Kate. I never would have imagined you endured such a loss. There are so many days, I don't even want to wake up. I'm not sure I can do this."

Kate placed her hand atop Amelia's. "That happened to me for a very long time. Sometimes, it still happens. I try to shift my thoughts and focus on being grateful for all I have. It's a mindset that helps. Instead of concentrating on all I lost, I made a purposeful effort to write down things I was thankful for each day. It might help you, too."

Amelia nodded. "Georgia and I were doing a similar thing. She had me recall moments of happiness each day. It did help and I saw a little progress. It's easy to shift into a negative state of mind."

"Oh, yes," said Kate. "It can happen in an instant. The old adage that nothing is permanent is a good reminder. The immense despair and hopelessness you feel now won't be forever. The loss and sorrow will always be there, but it won't be the focus of your thoughts. Slowly, over time, it will diminish, and you'll experience a day when the loss of Natalie doesn't dominate every moment. It just takes time."

As they chatted, Kate's eyes widened. "I have to warn you, as much as you can't imagine it right now, there will be a time when you realize you haven't thought of Natalie. You're happy or excited about something. It sounds terrific, but what happened to me more than once was a horrible feeling of shame and guilt. How could I be happy with my daughter dead? It's really hard to come to grips with and can cause you to slip back into the grief. All I can tell you is that you deserve to find happiness again. Remember that."

They talked for hours. Kate told her more about her business, and Amelia talked about her new bookstore and how scary it was to start a venture like that on her own. "The divorce was a real shock to me. I was in a fog after losing my mom and then with an empty nest, it wasn't easy. Sadly, Ron had also lost his mom the year before and his dad prior to that. We were both struggling. Looking back, I think that might have been the reason. Ron wanted a change, and our marriage was the target."

Kate sighed. "My divorce was also very traumatic. For different reasons, but that's a story for another day. I'm lucky though. My best friend and the man who has stood by me forever, is now my one and only. Spence is my rock. I'm the luckiest gal to have him in my life."

"He looks at you with such adoration. I would say he feels the same."

Kate gripped Amelia's hand tighter. "Speaking of Spence, I best get home to him. You promise to call me if you need to talk. I'll always make time for you."

Amelia stood and hugged Kate. She was the wise woman she needed in her life right now and was beyond thankful to spend her first evening alone on the island with her.

CHAPTER SIX

Amelia woke early the next morning, feeling better than she had since Natalie's death. She didn't bother with her hair since she had an appointment in a few hours with Jen. Instead, she donned one of the baseball caps hanging by the back door she was sure belonged to Dale and set out for her morning walk around the golf course.

She was about halfway through the longest trail when she decided to take a break on the bench that rested among the vibrant pink rhododendrons. The cool morning area refreshed her, as did gazing at the gorgeous blooms. She noticed the dog waste bag station and a big bowl of water stationed next to the bench.

As she studied the flowers, something brushed against her leg. She looked up to see the same golden retriever she saw at the beach yesterday. He was still wearing his flag bandana.

She thought he must be there for a drink from the water bowl, but he sat in front on her, his pink tongue peeking out from his smiling mouth. His warm, brown eyes rested on Amelia, and he raised a paw in greeting.

She laughed and reached out to shake it. "You're quite a handsome guy and so polite."

Amelia let go of his paw and reached out to pet his head. He leaned closer to her and shut his eyes as he let her massage it. He was beyond cute.

Moments later, a man came around the corner from the opposite direction that Amelia had traveled and shook his head. "Goose. What are you up to, my friend? Have you found someone new to pet you?"

Amelia laughed. "He's quite the guy. What a love."

The tall, slender man, with his sunglasses and hat, was hard to discern. He had a nice voice. Deep, but gentle. His gray shirt matched the streaks of gray in his otherwise dark-brown hair.

"Sorry about Goose. He loves people and thinks everyone is a fan."

"No need to apologize. He's exactly what I needed this morning. I think I saw you two on the beach the other morning?"

The man nodded and extended his hand. "Yes, sorry. I'm Noah, and this is Goose."

Amelia shook his hand. "I'm Amelia. I'm staying at my sister's place here on the golf course."

Noah reached for his calf and gritted his teeth.

She motioned to the empty space on the bench. "Have a seat."

He stepped over to it and sat on the end opposite Amelia. "Thanks. I tripped and fell the other day, and my leg has been bothering me. I'm trying to walk it off."

She glanced at his leg. "Oh, that's not good. I hope it gets better." She focused on his face. "So, do you and Goose live here in the golf community?"

He removed his sunglasses, revealing blue eyes. "I'm renting a place for the summer."

"It's lovely here. So peaceful."

He sighed. "Yes, exactly what I was looking for." He wiggled the leash he held in his hand. "I better get this back on Goose, since he's proven to be a bit untrustworthy today."

"Aww," she said, reaching to scratch Goose's chin. "He's just friendly, and you can't help but smile when you see him."

"His cuteness keeps him out of trouble most of the time." He stood and attached the leash to Goose's collar. "He's also got an affinity for beautiful ladies. He always seems to gravitate to them." He chuckled and stepped back toward the trail. "Have a good day, Amelia. Nice to meet you."

Color rose in her cheeks at his compliment. She waved at them. "Nice to meet you and Goose. I'm sure I'll see you two again in the neighborhood."

"Looking forward to it," he shouted, as he guided the dog to the pathway.

Amelia rose and set out to finish her loop. It was the first time since her divorce that she'd interacted with a man she didn't know. Goose was a gorgeous dog, and Noah seemed like a nice guy. Most guys who owned goldens were, right?

It wasn't until she walked into the house and saw her reflection in the mirror hanging in the entryway, that she remembered she hadn't even combed her hair. She looked like a complete mess. No makeup to hide her lines and wrinkles, her hair a disaster, and her old exercise clothes were less than flattering.

She shrugged. "I guess if he commented I was beautiful when he saw me like this, he's got to be a good guy."

After a quick shower, she headed downtown to the salon. Jen was at the counter when she arrived and introduced herself as she led Amelia to her station. "Sam told me you and Georgia are sisters but were separated and just found each other last year. That's such an awesome thing that you reconnected."

Amelia felt at ease with Jen. She had the same easy way about her as her brother Jeff. As she applied color to Amelia's long hair, she chatted about life on the island, her deep love for her brother and Sam, and how much she enjoyed growing up and living in Friday Harbor.

Jen asked how Dale was doing.

"I talked to Georgia last night. He has a hairline fracture, so not horrible. No surgery will be required, but he has to stay off it and curtail his usual activities."

"Oh, that's good news. I've only known Georgia a short time," said Jen, folding one of the last pieces of foil atop Amelia's head. "She's a sweetheart and such a kind person. Everybody just loves her and Dale and were so excited when they bought a place here."

"She's definitely a sweetheart, and I'm so lucky to have her. Especially, now. She's been a huge help."

Jen shook her head and rested a hand on Amelia's shoulder. "I can't imagine your pain. I have a daughter and would be totally destroyed. I'm so very sorry, Amelia."

As tears filled her eyes, Amelia nodded. Jen handed her a box of tissues and retrieved a glass of lemon-infused water for her. "You just sit back and relax. I've got a huge pile of magazines if you'd like me to bring you some."

Amelia pointed out the window that looked out on the street. "I think I'll just sit here and people watch."

Jen turned her chair so it faced the window and squeezed the top of her shoulder. "I'll be back to check on that color in a few minutes. If you need anything, just give a shout."

Amelia took a sip of the citrusy water and settled back

against the comfy chair. People wandered down the sidewalk. Lots of tourists lugging their bags from the ferry made their way up the street.

She spotted a man and woman with a young girl between them. They held her hands and picked her up every few feet. All of them laughing and smiling as they walked by the shop.

Fresh tears spilled from her eyes at the sight of them. It reminded her of days long ago when she and Ron would do the same with Natalie. When their world had been happy, Amelia never would have imagined losing either of them, much less both of them.

She spotted a stray golden hair stuck to her shoe. Her thoughts drifted away from the memories and sadness and to Goose. When she moved to Driftwood Bay, Lily and Mac had done their best to try to convince her she needed a dog for a companion.

She toyed with the idea but was so busy getting the building transformed into a bookstore, she didn't think she'd have time and decided it wouldn't be fair to the dog. Now, she thought having a furry friend might be a good idea.

Since losing Natalie, the silence in her own house and now Georgia's was unsettling. It gave her mind the freedom to wander, and it wasn't good. She needed something to fill the emptiness.

While she was still brooding and considering the pros and cons of dog ownership, Jen returned and checked her hair. She pronounced it done and went about removing the foil before shampooing it.

Amelia did her best to live in the moment and relax as Jen's expert fingers massaged her scalp. In no time, Jen had her hair trimmed, dried, and styled.

When Jen removed the cape from around her neck, Amelia felt like a new woman. She glanced in the mirror and smiled. Her hair looked the best it had looked in a long time, with soft, beachy waves framing her face.

"It's fabulous," she said, reaching for her purse. "Thanks for getting me in on short notice."

Jen grinned. "I'm glad you like it. I'd do anything for Sam, and I had an opening, so it was easy." She wagged her finger at the wallet Amelia extracted from her bag. "No charge today. Consider it a welcome to the island gift."

With a quick move, Jen embraced Amelia in a hug. "You take care of yourself, and I hope to see you at Sam and Jeff's soon."

With a suddenly dry throat, Amelia whispered her thanks.

She left the salon and wandered over to Sam's shop. The deck was filled with people, seated under the cheerful umbrellas enjoying the day. She went inside and spotted Sam behind the counter, waiting on a short line of customers.

The place was bustling with people, some fresh from the ferry, looking for refreshments. When she stepped up to the counter, Sam greeted her with a happy smile. "Your hair looks gorgeous, Amelia. I told you Jen was a magician."

"You were right. She did a fabulous job, and she's so kind. I really appreciate it."

"If you're in the mood for something cold, I've got a popular Arnold Palmer along with a yummy blackberry lemonade."

"Oh, those both sound great but let me try the blackberry lemonade."

Sam returned with the cup, filled with a deep purple-colored lemonade. "We're packed right now, but I think there's room over near the bookcase on the far side of the shop. It will clear out soon once the new arrivals move along. I'll pop over and visit when I get a chance."

Amelia took the lemonade and wandered through the tables to the quieter side of the shop, where bookcases lined the walls, and there were only two small tables, along with a couple of comfy chairs.

As soon as she gazed upon the corner, Goose raised his head from the floor. She eyed the chair next to him and saw Noah focused on the open laptop in front of him, his fingers tapping away at the keyboard.

Goose looked at his master, begging for permission to leave his side, but Noah wasn't paying attention.

Amelia stepped closer, near the table next to the chair. She slid into the seat and, with her eyes, motioned Goose to her. He army-crawled the couple of feet to her, no doubt hoping Noah wouldn't notice if he stuck close to the ground.

As soon as he reached Amelia's chair, she rewarded him with a neck rub and chin scratch. He handed her his paw and let her continue.

With what she thought was a quiet tone, Amelia told Goose what a pretty boy he was, and his tail swished back and forth across the floor.

The movement caught Noah's eye, and he turned from the screen. As soon as he saw Amelia with Goose, he smiled. "There he goes again. Picking up on the ladies."

Amelia lifted her brows. "Actually, I picked up on him."

Noah laughed and shut his laptop. "Sorry, I didn't even see you. When I'm writing, I get in a zone, and the world around me ceases to exist."

"Ah, you're a writer. Have you published anything I would know?"

He grinned and shrugged his shoulders. "I've written over forty books. Have you heard of Noah Preston?"

Amelia's eyes went wide. "*The* Noah Preston. The bestselling author who writes those epic spy novels? Have I heard of you? Yes, yes, I love your books. I can't believe I didn't recognize you."

"My cover jacket photo is a bit dated. I've aged a little since then." He pointed at his head of salted hair.

She laughed. "Wow, this is so exciting. I own a bookstore, so meeting a famous author is my idea of a dream."

He tilted his head. "Don't be too impressed. I'm nothing special."

"I planned to host author signings and talks at the bookstore I just opened in Driftwood Bay. Can I convince you to do a talk there?"

He sighed. "Right now, I can't promise much. My whole focus is to finish up this series under contract. Then..." His smile disappeared. "I'm not sure. The future is murky, at best."

"I can relate. I'm trying not to think too far ahead myself."

She reached down and rested her hand on Goose. "How old is this guy?"

Noah smiled at Goose. "He's three. I got him after I lost my last golden about four years ago. I wasn't sure I was ready for another dog, but my house was just too quiet. He's a rescue I adopted when he was very young. He's the best friend I could ask for."

He reached out to pet him and brushed his hand against Amelia's. "He keeps all of my secrets, too."

Her brows rose, and she met his eyes. "Sounds like you have a story to tell."

"It's a long and complicated one. Best saved for another day."

She nodded. "I've got a long and complicated one myself."

Sam appeared at the table with another iced tea for Noah and a second lemonade for Amelia. She glanced down at Goose. "How's your water bowl doing, big fella?"

"He's got plenty. Thanks, Sam," said Noah, reaching for the tea she offered.

"Amelia here was just about to tell me her story."

Sam smiled and put a hand on her shoulder. "Don't let me interrupt. You two enjoy."

Amelia took a long swallow her lemonade and sighed. "Here goes nothing."

CHAPTER SEVEN

Amelia explained about losing her mother, her daughter going to college, and then her husband asking for a divorce. That was all bad enough. She took a deep breath and started to tell him about Natalie but couldn't do it.

Even without spilling out the worst and her recent loss, the tears flowed.

She used napkins to pat her face dry.

Once done, she took a long sip of blackberry lemonade and shrugged. "Sorry, I'm a bit of a mess."

Noah's gray eyes, full of understanding, were wide. He reached over and put his hand over hers. "Amelia, I'm so very sorry about your situation and your loss. I know what it's like to lose your parents. I was gutted."

She nodded. "Georgia suggested a change of scenery, and I do feel a little better here. She's got this great group of friends, Sam being one of them, and they're all watching over me while she's away. They're all quite kind and lovely."

He nodded. "I haven't met many people, but Sam is a gem.

I come here most days to do some writing. I spend most of my time alone, so it's good for me to get out for a few hours of the day. Otherwise, it's just Goose."

Noah bent and patted the top of his head. "Honestly, he's way more of a people person than I. He's usually how I meet new people. Like how we met."

Amelia gazed at the handsome dog with his gentle brown eyes. "He's convinced me I need a dog. I've been considering it, but now, with nothing but my thoughts to keep me company, I think I could use a loyal friend and a distraction."

"I understand that. Goose is a true friend. No matter how dark my day might be, he's happy to sit beside me. He never judges and is a huge comfort. Goose does a good job of keeping me on my toes, too. If not for him, I'd probably never go outside." Noah chuckled.

Sam was busy wiping down the other table and stepped over to Amelia's. "I couldn't help but hear you mention you might be inclined to get a dog. As you know, most of my friends have dogs, and I'm connected to the local golden retriever community here. I just got a text this morning that there's a young golden in need of a forever home. Can I interest you in taking a look at her?"

Amelia raised her brows. "Wow, I'm not sure. I mean the idea of it sounds good, but I'm not sure I'm ready. I don't want to mess up."

"We could just take a look at her. You could see what you think. Get to know her. Maybe start with fostering her for a bit and see if you're a good fit together."

Noah grinned. "As sweet as Sam is, I think she might have a little used-car salesman streak in her. She's making you quite the deal."

Sam giggled. "I just think sometimes things like this happen for a reason. Call it destiny."

Amelia shrugged. "Well, I definitely need a purpose. A reason to get out of bed in the morning. After…" She glanced at Noah, still not ready to talk about her daughter. "I just don't want this to be a knee-jerk reaction, and then I end up failing as a dog parent."

Sam smiled at her. "That won't happen. I promise. I think the timing is perfect. While you're here, you'll have all us of to help support you and guide you. The puppy will have lots of dog friends, and she needs a home. The woman who bought her from the breeder I know, passed away suddenly, and the poor dog needs someone who will love her."

Tears swelled in Amelia's eyes. "Okay, I can't resist that. Let's go see her."

Sam clapped. "I'm thrilled. Let me work out the arrangements, and I'll be right back."

Amelia glanced over at Noah. "Do you think I'm making a huge mistake?"

He shook his head. "Not at all. There are a few things in life that are always the right answer. Dogs. Chocolate. Coffee. The beach." He smiled. "Like Sam said, I think you two might be exactly what you both need right now. I know my life would be much smaller if I didn't have Goose."

With a sigh, Amelia reached for her second lemonade. It was delicious and refreshing. She swallowed several sips and looked up to see Sam, sporting a wide smile, walking toward her.

"We're all set. We can go and visit this afternoon. Erica, she's the breeder, said she'll have Faith all set to meet you."

"Faith?"

Sam nodded. "Yes, that's her name. She's housetrained and already knows lots of commands. She's just grieving and needs comfort and stability."

Amelia's eyes blurred with tears. "I can relate to that. I'm starting to agree with you. I think it might be meant to be."

Sam looked at her watch. "I'll pick you up at your place in about an hour."

"I'll be ready," said Amelia, finishing off the last of her lemonade.

Noah reached for his cell phone. "Goose would like nothing more than to meet a new golden friend. I'll give you my number and if you end up getting Faith, let me know. We can meet you for a walk at the beach."

Amelia pulled her phone from her pocket, and they traded contact numbers. "I like the idea that she's already housetrained. I'm not sure I'm up for a brand-new puppy."

"Yeah, they're a ton of work. Like having a newborn. Well, a newborn that bites with teeth like razors. I still remember those days with Goose."

At the sound of his name, the dog looked up at his master.

Amelia laughed. "From that look he's giving you, I'm not sure he appreciates you talking smack about him."

The moment Noah reached out his hand, Goose put his head under it. "That's the best thing about dogs. They never judge and are quick to forgive our mistakes. Goose here wants nothing more than to make me happy. Right now, I need all of that I can get."

The tired look in Noah's eyes made Amelia want to ask what he meant, but she opted to let it go. He'd mentioned his story was long and complicated. Someday, she hoped to learn more about him. Someday, she'd tell him about Natalie.

She was fascinated that he was an author she'd read.

As she imagined his story, he stood, slung his laptop case over his shoulder, and took hold of Goose's leash. "I need to get back home but be sure to let me know how the puppy visit goes. Regardless, Goose and I walk every morning. We'd be happy to have you tag along, with or without a dog."

"I'll be sure to let you know and meeting up tomorrow morning is perfect. I've been walking with Jess and Izzy, who live in the neighborhood and are friends with Georgia, but they're both busy tomorrow."

"We're up early. Does six thirty or so work? We can meet at the entrance to the long loop at the golf course and then venture down to the beach."

"It's a date." The moment the words left her mouth, Amelia felt the warmth in her cheeks. "I mean, not a date-date. Just, yeah, I'll meet you there."

He chuckled and led Goose toward the door. "I understand. It's an agreed upon meeting time." He smiled. "We'll see you in the morning." After waving at Sam, the two of them disappeared down the street.

Amelia gathered her bag and said goodbye to Sam, promising she'd be ready within an hour.

Once at Georgia's, she looked around the outside and was happy to find a fenced area. Suki no doubt used it when she was here and if she decided to take the puppy, Faith would have a safe place outside.

Since Georgia and Dale had Suki, she was sure they wouldn't object to her having a dog in the house, but she texted Georgia to make sure.

It didn't take long for her phone to chime with an answer. Georgia was excited and fully supportive of the idea of Amelia adopting a furry companion. She assured her the house would survive the puppy.

Amelia smiled when she replied, sending a graphic of a golden retriever.

As she finished the text, it suddenly hit her. Since Sam mentioned the golden who needed a home, she hadn't thought of Natalie. Despite the initial parallel to the dog grieving a loss, she was focused on how she might make it work. Her mind was busy with a new task and one that brought her joy.

Guilt washed over her. She shouldn't be happy about anything. Not with Natalie gone.

She remembered Kate talking about those feelings she experienced when they had dinner. Amelia's eyes blurred. She would never get on top of her grief if each time there was a glimmer of happiness, she squashed it.

It must come from all the years of putting herself last. Without thinking, she put Natalie's needs at the top of her list, always sacrificing her own interests to be there for her. She did the same with Ron, too. She never resented it or even gave it a thought. It was natural to her.

Ron made plenty of money. Amelia didn't have to work, so she viewed her job as taking care of the two of them, the house, and making sure life ran smoothly. She remembered a few times when she tried to plan something to do on her own and each time, her plan was foiled with a request from Natalie or Ron. Treats were needed for a school event, or she had to chaperone a field trip, or Natalie needed her cheerleading uniform washed and forgot to do it. Ron committed them to dinner with colleagues or even worse, invited them over for dinner, or he needed a suit cleaned or new socks or any number of mundane things.

Mom to the rescue.

That was Amelia's purpose.

At least it had been.

It was bad enough when Nat went to college, and Amelia's main focus in life was gone. She had to adapt to chatting with Nat on video calls or via text when her daughter had a spare moment. Over time, those moments diminished, and Amelia consoled herself, knowing her daughter was spreading her wings. She was doing what she'd raised her to do. But it didn't hurt any less.

Amelia lived for school breaks and visits.

After the surprise divorce and the forced sale of their home, Amelia opted to move so she'd have fewer reminders of their life and a new beginning in a place that had a lower cost of living. The bookstore had been a godsend. It kept her occupied and busy with less time to grieve the loss of her mother, her marriage, and her empty nest.

Amelia closed her eyes and tried to reframe her thoughts. Natalie wouldn't want to see her suffering. Like all young college students, she was focused on her own life and was going through the selfish phase most teenagers go through as they morph into young adults. Despite all that, she loved Amelia and when they did chat or text, that love always came through.

Now, Amelia would never hear her voice again or get a funny emoji text from her.

Amelia forced herself to think about Nat and imagined her watching her from above. Nat wouldn't want her mother to be sad for the rest of her days. She'd want her to be happy and share her love, even if it was only with a golden retriever who was in desperate need of a new home and new owner.

As Amelia did her best to drag her mind away from the negativity and guilt, she went into the master bathroom and splashed some water on her face. She hadn't worn makeup since Nat died. As she patted her face dry, she examined it, crow's feet and all. The tiny lines were growing on her.

It had been years since she'd dared to leave the house without fixing her hair and making sure her face was perfect. These last weeks, what seemed so important before, wasn't even in her top ten. She embraced her new, natural look.

One thing about meeting new people, they had no preconceived ideas or expectations. All of them accepted Amelia as she was. It was something positive that came from the devastating loss.

She added a squirt of lotion to her hands, breathed in the scent of lavender, and noticed the lotion was from the lavender farm where Georgia and her foster sisters lived. She wandered to the main living area and when she looked out the window, Sam's SUV was pulling into the driveway.

Amelia grabbed her bag and locked the door before climbing in next to Sam. While they were still parked, Sam turned to Amelia. "I don't want you to feel pressure to take Faith. I was just so excited when you mentioned a dog, and Faith has been on my mind. It seemed like a perfect solution, but I don't want to overwhelm you or for you to stress about this."

"I appreciate that, Sam. I honestly don't know. I worry I won't do a good job or won't be able to handle it. Part of me would really like the company. I need something in my life right now, and a golden puppy sounds terrific, but I do have a few doubts. I'm in a weird place right now."

"Totally understandable. Let's just go meet her and see what you think. No pressure. You can take your time and think about it."

Amelia sighed. "That sounds great."

As Sam drove, they chatted. "I was glad to see you talking to Noah today. He's normally very quiet. Tends to keep to himself."

With a nod, Amelia said, "Yeah, I think there's much more to him than what we see on the surface. I absolutely love his books, so meeting him was pretty exciting."

Sam turned onto a gravel driveway. "Yeah, he's quiet but deep. I get that same vibe. He's very personable and is a great dad to Goose. I tend to judge people I don't know well by how they treat animals, and he gets an A-plus from me."

"That's good to know. I'm going to walk with them tomorrow morning." Amelia tilted her head at Sam. "Most likely with Faith."

Sam grinned. "That would be awesome, but again, no pressure. Let's see how it goes."

A woman with short, dark hair came from the front of the house and waved.

Sam and Amelia made their way up to the porch, where Sam introduced Amelia to Erica. Erica shook her hand and held it in hers for a few moments. "When Sam called to tell me she had someone looking for a dog, it just made my day. Faith is the sweetest girl."

Sam cleared her throat. "Amelia isn't sure yet but wants to meet her and see if they're a good fit. She might foster her for a time just to make sure, but I told her no pressure today. It's just a time to meet her."

Erica nodded. "I completely understand. I want Faith to go to the right home. She's already traumatized from losing her mom. She's a bit timid since then."

Erica motioned them to follow her indoors. Once inside, she took them to a lovely sunroom off the back porch.

As Amelia stepped into the room, she spotted the beautiful dog sitting on her bed, atop the tile floor. She was that iconic rich, golden color, the same as Goose. She had a sweet face and soulful brown eyes and was sporting a cute pink bandana.

Erica urged Amelia closer to the dog and as soon as Amelia bent her knees to get closer, Faith rose from her bed and put her head on top of Amelia's thigh. Her tail wagged as she stayed there focused only on Amelia.

Amelia petted the top of her warm, soft head. Faith

inched closer to her, still keeping her head on Amelia's thigh. Faith's eyes moved upwards and stared at her potential parent

As Amelia met the dog's eyes, her own filled with tears. Pure love radiated from the sweet dog, and Amelia felt an instant connection to her.

Sam and Erica were both quiet as they stood back and let the two of them get acquainted.

Before long, Amelia was sitting on the floor, and Faith crawled into her lap, nestled against her, with her head atop Amelia's leg. Through tears, Amelia stroked the dog's silky fur, running her hands from her head, all the way down her back.

The dog never flinched and at one point closed her eyes as Amelia rubbed the top of her head.

Amelia turned her head to get a glimpse of Sam and Erica. They were both smiling, and Erica whispered, "I think Faith has found her new person."

As much as Amelia told herself she wouldn't rush into dog ownership, she couldn't resist the warm pile of fur nestled close to her and the warmth that filled her as she rested her hand on Faith and felt the steady beat of heart.

The two of them could heal each other's broken hearts.

CHAPTER EIGHT

An hour later, Sam helped Amelia unload Faith's beds, toys, food, and other supplies. There was already a dog bed in the living area for Suki, but Amelia added one of Faith's and put her second one in the master bedroom.

With Sam's help, they got everything organized and made sure Faith's water bowls were filled, both the one indoors and the one on the patio. Although skittish, Faith plopped onto her bed and watched the two women as they went back and forth, carting in her belongings.

Erica made a point of letting Amelia know Faith had a favorite blanket that came from her time as a puppy and held the scent of her mom and littermates, and it was tucked next to her. Faith was also a huge fan of balls and squeaky toys.

Sam hung out for a bit and had an iced tea while she and Amelia showered Faith with attention. While she was there, she showed Amelia how Faith's harness worked and gave her a few tips.

With a gentle hand, Sam stroked Faith's face and scratched under her chin. "She's a real sweetheart. What's great is she's already trained." She pointed at the bell they tied to the handle of the patio door. "You might have to keep a close eye on her initially since it's a new house, but I have a feeling she'll adapt and have no problem alerting you with her bell when she has to go outside."

Amelia nodded. "Erica said her owner used a crate with her initially, but she was in the habit of sleeping with her owner. I'm not planning to leave her unattended, but I am worried about letting her roam the house if I do have to leave her on her own."

"Yeah," said, Sam. "The best thing to do is plan to stay with her all the time for the first week or two, until she's comfortable in the house and you feel confident she won't get into anything. Most everywhere is very dog friendly and if you get in a pinch, she can always stay with us or Jeff at the hardware store. He usually has Zoe and Bailey with him there. Erica said she adapted to her house without a problem, but she has other dogs, so they sort of train each other."

Amelia nodded. "I want to introduce her to Sunny and Ruby and of course, Goose. She'll meet him tomorrow morning on our walk. Hopefully, if she has some dog friends she gets to see, she'll be happy."

"I think she'll be your best friend before you know it. Dogs are incredible, and they're resilient, especially with a loving owner. We'll have a doggy get-together soon, and she can meet all the dogs." Sam stood and walked toward the door. "Jeff is picking us up pizza for tonight, and I told him to drop one by here on his way home. That will give you an easy dinner and leftovers."

Amelia couldn't hold back the tears that spilled from her eyes. She embraced Sam in a hug. "I'm not sure what I did to deserve all of you, but I'm so thankful. I appreciate you all very much."

Sam smiled and reached for the door handle. "It's wonderful to have friends who are like family. It's meant the world to me, since I don't have a family left. Now, you're part of our family, too." She paused and looked down at Faith. "I think you and Faith were meant to be. Call me if you need anything."

Amelia thanked her again and closed the door behind her. She looked at Faith, and the dog stared back at her.

As Amelia walked back to the oversized leather recliner she preferred, Faith took a few steps and followed her. As soon as Amelia settled into the chair, Faith sat in front of it and gave her a glance of her puppy dog eyes.

They were enough to melt any heart, and Amelia imagined it would go a long way in getting Faith out of any trouble she might find.

Amelia couldn't resist patting her lap, offering Faith a place. As soon as she gave her the okay, Faith climbed up and settled into Faith's lap.

She curled her warm body against Amelia's and tucked her head between her and the thick armrest. Amelia leaned back and sighed, running her hand over Faith's head and down her back. The weight of dog and her warmth breath against Amelia's hand filled her heart.

As Amelia enjoyed the bonding time with her new friend, she imagined Nat smiling down on both of them, and the ache in her heart eased. She bent her head close to Faith's and sniffed in the scent of her. She closed her eyes and inhaled the trace of grass, dirt, and the roses Faith had gotten close to on her way in from the patio.

Within minutes, Faith was asleep, content as she snuggled closer to Amelia. As she watched the dog sleep, taking note of the gorgeous color of her eyelashes, Amelia knew Faith was here to stay. She couldn't imagine letting her go.

The next morning, Amelia's alarm chimed early. She turned it off and glanced over at Faith, who was nestled against a pillow on the opposite side of the bed. Amelia hadn't been able to resist letting her sleep on the bed. After Erica said her owner had allowed it, Amelia thought it only fair she do the same.

She lingered for a few minutes, petting Faith's head and smiling as the dog stretched and yawned. She appeared totally relaxed and satisfied with her new sleeping arrangements.

Amelia climbed out of bed and took Faith out the back door so she could take care of her morning business. After that was done, she hurried inside and checked the time. She didn't want to risk being late to meet Goose and Noah on the trail.

She took a few minutes to brush her hair and loop it into a loose ponytail before donning a pair of exercise pants and a long-sleeve shirt. After adding a baseball hat, she attached Faith's leash, and they headed out the door.

They were right on time but found Noah and Goose already waiting. The moment Goose spotted them, his tail went into a full wag, and Faith was eager to get closer to him, tugging on her leash.

Noah grinned. "It looks like your visit to meet Faith was successful."

Amelia smiled and shrugged. "I found her irresistible."

Goose and Faith were still involved in the obligatory sniffing ritual new dogs always employed. Once they had thoroughly examined each other, Noah led the way, and Amelia followed, positioning Faith next to Goose to see how she did on the walk.

Both dogs were focused on their walk, and Amelia was impressed with how well Faith did. She didn't tug or get distracted, which made it easy to chat with Noah while they made their way around the course.

He pointed at Faith. "She's a good walker. Her owner must have taken her for lots of walks."

Amelia nodded. "I think she did, and she's housetrained and uses a bell to alert me when she needs to go outside. I'd say she had a wonderful owner."

"She's a cutie. She and Goose look like they could be related. Same color and same happy attitude." Noah glanced over at Amelia. "I wish I could be as carefree and happy as they are. No worries. Just live in the moment and squeeze out every bit of joy."

With a heavy sigh, Amelia nodded. "I'm a bit of a worrier by nature, so it's a struggle for me. Now, it's even worse." Her voice cracked and trailed off as she focused on the happy wag of the tails next to her.

As they walked, she noticed Noah leaning a little too far to his right, pushing into Goose. Later, he did the same to his left but caught himself before he tripped off the edge of the trail.

They were almost to the section of the road that would lead them across to the beach. He pointed it out. "We can head down to the water if you're game."

"Sure, that sounds great. I'd love to see how Faith reacts."

When they crossed the road, he led the way down the pathway. Again, she noticed him teeter to the side a couple of times, but Goose seemed to compensate and steady him.

The foursome made their way to the edge of the water, and it was obvious this wasn't Faith's first experience. She showed no fear of the gentle waves and stepped into them as they rolled over the beach.

The beach was quiet, with them being the only ones walking along it. Noah picked up a stick, and Goose focused his eyes on him. With a chuckle, Noah said, "Let's see how they do with a little fetching."

He tossed it into the water, not far from shore. Goose made a beeline for it, and Faith didn't dart after it but followed Goose with a curious look on her face and careful steps.

By the time she reached him, he'd captured the stick and rushed back to Noah to surrender it.

After Noah threw it several more times, Faith caught onto the game. Goose, like a good older brother, let her grab it first several times, and they both pranced together over to Noah.

Amelia stood next to Noah and watched as the dogs dashed into the water with abandon. Soon, he grabbed his arm and handed the stick to her. "I'm worn out. You throw a few for them."

She glanced down at the two eager faces pleading with her to continue the fun. She reared back and tossed the stick into the gentle waves. Both dogs rushed into the water, and Goose let Faith retrieve it.

With a delighted wiggle in her walk, she hurried back to Amelia and let her take it from her. Amelia threw it again and again. The sweet faces the dog gave her made it impossible to quit.

As Amelia watched the two carefree dogs, having such a fun, she couldn't help but smile. They made her laugh as they splashed and played, vying for the prize stick. It felt good to laugh, and she realized how much she needed Faith.

Finally, she'd had enough, and both dogs were soaking wet. As Amelia wrestled with the idea of giving Faith a bath and kicking herself for not thinking to bring a towel, Noah pointed out at the water. "Looks like those clouds the weatherman promised are rolling in. Might get the rain they forecasted."

"We should get going. I need to clean her up."

Noah nodded. "I've got a nice setup at the house with a nice area and a sprayer to rinse off Goose, and I can help you do the same for Faith."

He led the way back to the golf community and to his house, which Amelia remembered seeing from the trail around the golf course. He led them directly to the backyard.

There was an outdoor shower stall, and he guided Goose to it. Noah turned on the water, tested it to make sure it wasn't too warm, and used the special wand he told her was designed for dogs. In no time, Goose was rinsed clean with very little overspray or splashing.

"Wow, I'm going to have to get one of those." Amelia kept hold of Faith's leash until Noah and Goose were out of the way, and Goose flopped down on a clean towel, while Noah used another one to dry him.

Noah pointed at the shower. "Give me a second here to get him semi-dry, and I'll help you with Faith."

After some drying action, Goose sat on his towel and watched Noah guided Faith into the shower stall. He demonstrated the switch on the special wand and ran it over Faith's back.

Amelia kept hold of her leash, not sure how amenable the dog would be to a bath, but she didn't budge and after a couple of swipes with the wand, Noah handed it to Amelia. "You give a go."

It didn't take long for her to finish rinsing Faith. Her feathering was only slight, and her puppy fur was still on the short side. Goose, on the other hand, had very thick fur and long feathers along his belly, legs, and tail.

With all the sand and saltwater rinsed, Amelia pronounced her done and turned off the water before leading her to a clean towel Noah had set out for her.

Amelia got down on the ground and proceeded to dry Faith, who closed her eyes, while Amelia rubbed her fur with the thick towel.

As she was finishing the job, the sky darkened, and the clouds they'd seen earlier were directly overhead. A fat drop of rain fell from the sky, then a few more splattered on the patio.

Noah helped Amelia gather the towels and ushered the dogs through the back door into the house. "I guess the weather guy was right for once."

Once inside, Goose hurried to his big bed in the living area, and Faith followed, where she curled up right beside him. "Aww, look how cute those two are," said Amelia. "They're really hitting off."

"Goose is a happy boy. He's used to spending his time with me and no other dogs. I think he's enjoying this." He pointed toward the kitchen. "How about some coffee or tea? I haven't eaten breakfast yet and was going to have some eggs. Care to join me?"

Amelia glanced out to the patio where the downpour was in full swing. "Looks like we won't be going anytime soon. If you're sure it's no trouble, eggs sound great."

"I'll get started, and I was going to get Goose his breakfast, too. I wonder if Faith could eat a bit of his food."

He pulled out a bag from the pantry, and Amelia stepped into the kitchen. "Oh, that's the same brand she eats. She's on the puppy formula still, but I think one meal would be fine."

Noah nodded. "I always add some eggs to Goose's. I'll do the same for Faith." He went about getting the ingredients together, and Amelia offered to brew tea for them.

It didn't take long to get the dogs' breakfast in their bowls and their eggs on plates. The dogs finished it off in no time and wandered back to the bed they shared.

Noah looked at their plates and grimaced. "I'm sorry, I don't have any bread or toast to offer you. I'm on a strict diet. No sugar and very limited carbs."

"This is perfect. We'd all be better off with less sugar and carbs." She dug into the fluffy eggs, scrambled to perfection, laced with a bit of cheese. "Delicious, I might add."

He shrugged. "I'm not the best cook, but I can do eggs. Sometimes I eat them for all three meals since they're so easy."

She took a sip of tea. "I used to cook quite a bit. Back when I was married, and Natalie was younger. Now, though, I mostly grab something or like you, make something simple."

Her thoughts drifted to her daughter. She'd never be able to cook for her again. She'd been looking forward to spoiling Nat with all her favorite holiday dishes and making some of her favorite treats when she came later in the summer.

A tear slipped down her cheek. She reached for her napkin to dab it away but wasn't quick enough. Noah frowned at her. "What's wrong?"

She finished wiping her eyes and took a deep breath. "I didn't tell you the rest of my story the other day. Why I'm here now."

He pointed at the patio door, where a steady rain streamed from the sky. "I think you're stuck with me for the foreseeable future. I've been told I'm a good listener."

She gave him a weak smile. "I have a hard time talking about it, so fair warning, I'll need a box of tissues."

He rose and retrieved a box from the counter. "All set."

He smiled at her. "Seriously, you don't have to tell me anything, but I'm happy to listen."

She glanced over their empty plates. "On one condition." She held up a finger. "I clean up our dishes, and then I'll share the worst with you."

He smiled at her and said, "Deal."

CHAPTER NINE

O ver another pot of tea, Amelia spilled out the grief that had brought her to the island. Through a few bouts of sobs, she managed to tell him about the accident and the unexpected loss of Nat, along with her ex-husband.

She even told him about finding out Ron still loved her and was sorry he'd insisted on a divorce. She hadn't divulged as much information about her feelings to anyone and, as she spoke, realized it was sometimes easier to tell a stranger difficult things. Noah was also a very good listener.

He never interrupted and let her go at the slow pace she needed. With gentle pats on her hand and kind eyes, he lent his support. The rain continued to fall, and the dogs snoozed through her story, worn out from their escapades on the beach.

As she told him more about her childhood and being adopted, his eyes widened. "I found out I was adopted after my mom died. My parents never told me. I was cleaning out her house and found some paperwork and then looked into it more."

"How long ago was that?"

"Just last year," he said, with a sad look in his eyes.

"Wow, that's a double blow. I'm so sorry, Noah."

He sighed and fiddled with the napkin in front of him. "Thank you. It's been tough. Nothing like losing a child, but one of the roughest times of my life. I thought I was a pretty tough guy, but losing Mom was awful. Now, I have all these questions that nobody can answer."

"About the adoption?"

He raised his brows. "That and other more complicated things." He took a swallow from his cup. "I told you I had a long story." He pointed out the window. "It doesn't look like it's letting up anytime soon. I know telling me about Natalie and Ron was hard for you, and I'm sure you're tired. If you're up for staying, I'll try to keep it as short as possible."

She poured them more tea, and they settled into the couch, closer to the dogs. The summer storm chilled the air, and Amelia was grateful for the warm throw blanket she settled on top of her.

"So, I grew up in Virginia, outside of DC. My dad worked in the government, and I went to Georgetown. I met my now ex-wife in college, and we got married. Too young, I think. We have a son, who's closer to his mother than me. My ex, Tanya, remarried. A lawyer who works for a big lobbying firm in DC. They live in Virginia still. My son is also a lawyer. His stepdad is well connected and helped get him a position."

Noah smiled. "I didn't spend enough time with him when he was young. I let my career dominate, which is the biggest reason Tanya and I divorced. Missing out on Will's life is my biggest regret."

He took a long swallow from his cup. "I got offered a position as an intelligence analyst when I graduated and spent my career in that line of work. It was all-consuming work. I was dispatched to places all over the world. I couldn't discuss my work, couldn't always tell Tanya where I was or when I'd be home. Looking back, I really think the job isn't suited for anyone with a family. It's just too hard."

Amelia caught his sorrowful gaze. "I'm not sure the world is fair when it comes to men and their work. You're raised to be a provider for your family and to take care of them. I know that's how my dad was. It's how Ron was. When that work requires you to be gone or put in tons of hours, it's an impossible situation. An impossible choice."

He chuckled. "Tanya didn't see it that way. In reality, I could have found another job, but I was addicted to the rush of it and really enjoyed the actual analysis and research. Bottom line, I was selfish, while convinced I was providing a good life for Tanya and Will. That's a lesson that comes with the wisdom of age and realizing what you lost along the way."

"You still have time to change things and build on your relationship with your son. It's not too late."

He didn't say anything, but his eyes filled with tears.

Noah blinked away the emotion and went to the kitchen to refill the kettle.

Amelia didn't want to pick at what was an obvious wound. "Your intelligence work sounds exciting and now, I'm understanding why your books are so riveting. You have the first-hand experience in the world of political thrillers."

He grinned as he returned to the couch. "I did enjoy the work, for the most part. The political element was the worst, though. I came to despise politicians and the methods they employed, which often discounted credible intelligence when it didn't match their reelection goals or party talking points. By the time I retired, I was disgusted with it all and ready for a new chapter."

Amelia chuckled. "I see what you did there. Chapter. Author. I get it."

With a slow smile, he continued, "I had been all over the world but was technically living in Arlington. My parents were in McLean, not far away, so I opted to stay there when I retired from the government. After my dad passed away, my mom moved to Oregon, back where she grew up and had old friends and a few distant cousins."

The dogs stirred from their sleeping positions and wandered toward the patio door. Noah stood. "I'll let them out. We'll just need to dry them off before they come back in."

After their quick foray outside, Amelia took over the towel duty and made sure Faith was dry, giving special attention to her paws. She did the same with Goose, who was happy to let her massage him with the towels and rolled onto his back to give her maximum access.

Once the dogs were back in the house, Noah took out several toys so they could play and chew while they were stuck in the house. With both of them occupied, he and Amelia returned to their cozy spot on the couch.

Noah frowned. "Let's see, where was I?" Moments later, he said, "Right, so I started writing books, using my experience to craft some plots and characters, and I had a few connections in the publishing world, so it wasn't long before I had an agent and an offer from one of the big publishing houses. I wrote several books before my dad died and then helped Mom move to Oregon, took a little time off, and then came back to Arlington and continued to write.

"After a few months, I realized I only stayed there to be close to my parents and Will. Sadly, I didn't see much of Will.

He had his own life and was making his way in the world. In reality, I had no right to expect him to go out of his way to make room for me. I decided to leave, sold my condo, and moved to a small mountain town in Wyoming."

Amelia nodded. "That's about as far as you can get from the DC area."

"Exactly. I was done with cities, people, traffic, and most of all, lobbyists and politicians who are all about money. I just wanted to enjoy nature, exercise more, and write."

"How long were you there?"

"A couple of years. I churned out more books in that time than I thought possible. It was some of the best writing I did. Then, my mom started to decline. So, I moved to Oregon and lived with her. That's where I am now."

"I'm impressed at your devotion to your parents. That's admirable. I had a strong connection to mine, too. My adoptive parents. I don't remember my birth mother, which is a blessing. I've been so fortunate to find my older sister after all these years. Georgia has been my rock during all of this."

Noah's solemn eyes met hers. "That's part of what's plaguing my thoughts now. I have no idea if I have any siblings and know nothing about my birth parents. I'm a researcher at heart and am pretty good at finding things but have very limited information about the adoption. Part of me thinks it's someone my parents knew. It was a private adoption handled by a lawyer who died, and nobody took over his practice. No records exist."

As he spoke, Goose stopped playing and wandered over to sit next to him, leaning against Noah's leg. As he talked, Noah kept a hand on Goose, petting his head.

Amelia tilted her head. "It sounds like you adored your parents and had a great relationship with them. Do you think they were just trying to protect you by not telling you? Or protect your birth mother?"

He shrugged. "I don't know. I've been asking myself those questions since I found the paperwork in Mom's house. Now, my house." He sighed. "It's become more important to me in the last couple of months. I, uh, hadn't been feeling great and chalked it up to grief and all the work that goes with losing a parent and settling her estate. I finally went to the doctor and although he's not a specialist, he's got me booked in at the Oregon Health & Science University. He, of course, wanted me to get there right away, but I just couldn't do it. I'm set up for more tests in September, but he suspects I have Huntington's."

Amelia gasped. "Oh, Noah. I'm so sorry. I can understand why you'd want to know more about your family history."

He nodded. "Anyway, that's why I'm here. Please don't say anything about it to anyone. I decided I had to escape it all. I need to finish the books I have under contract. I was way too distracted at my mom's house and then when I got the news from the doctor, my world imploded. My first inclination was to run away. I remembered Mom mentioning these islands and that she'd visited them with her parents and how beautiful they were."

She pretended not to notice the glint of tears in his eyes. He swallowed hard as he whispered, "If Mom were here, it might be easier. She was someone who had a way of making whatever was wrong better."

Amelia reached her hand across the couch and gripped his. "I know that feeling of wanting your mom more than anything. I can understand wanting to escape, and I won't say a word."

She shrugged. "I mean I escape here, too. I think it's our

natural defense. Our bodies and minds can only handle so much. I'm sorry you're going through all of this."

As he scratched under Goose's chin, Faith abandoned the chew toy she was working over and scooted up to the couch between Amelia and Goose. Amelia couldn't resist her soulful eyes and reached out to pet her.

With each stroke, she felt her anxiety and worries ease and noticed Noah was doing the same with Goose. Sam was right. She and Faith needed each other. As she sank her fingers into Faith's soft fur, Amelia thought she was the one who was rescued, not the dog.

As the afternoon waned on, they continued to visit, with Amelia doing the supporting this time. Noah talked more about his mother and how he wished she would have told him about the adoption. His mood lightened when he shared cherished childhood memories of spending time with his mom, who was an artist, in her studio.

Noah glanced down at the dogs, who'd given up on adventure and became bored with their humans talking all afternoon, napping next to the couch. "I'm not much of an artist, like she was, but I do think watching her inspired me to write books. She always talked about doing what brought her joy. She was also a very happy and optimistic person. After leaving the government, I was looking for joy."

Some of the sadness left his eyes as he told her about the excitement that never got old when he published a new book. "Writing has been my escape for many years. This is the first time in a long time that I've felt stressed about a deadline. I don't know what the future holds, so I want to get these next two books done before I go back in September."

Amelia popped an eyebrow. "Wow, that's ambitious. I can't imagine writing three books over the summer. You must be a very fast writer."

"To be fair, the first one was done. I just had to wrap up the final edits. The other two are outlined, and I have a good start on the second one. I typically churn out a book in a month, but right now, it's hard to get motivated. I've been spending far too much time online, researching Huntington's. I need to get one of those parental control software packages that would keep me from going online while I'm writing. Sometimes, I do need to pop over and research something though."

He glanced at his watch. "Enough of my problems. It's time for dinner. I've got a standing order down at the club. I can add something on for you, if you and Faith would like to stay for dinner?"

Amelia glanced down at her sleeping puppy. "I hate to overstay my welcome. We've been here all day."

Noah smiled. "And it's been one of my best days. As much as I've resisted sharing, I think talking to you has done me a world of good. Thank you for being kind enough to listen."

Amelia picked an entrée from the menu Noah pulled from a kitchen drawer and offered to feed the dogs while he drove down to the clubhouse to pick up their order. As she set the table, she realized she'd also had a good day. Outside of sharing about Natalie with Noah, she hadn't been focused on her loss throughout the day.

It was an odd feeling, but she remembered what Kate told her and embraced the moments that weren't filled with grief and anxiety. Stretching out those moments and hours into longer periods was her only chance of surviving this.

Like Faith, Amelia had a feeling Noah appeared at the right moment in her life.

CHAPTER TEN

Over the next week, Amelia and Faith got in the habit of walking with Jess or Izzy in the morning and then trekking into town to Sam's coffee shop around noon, when Noah would be winding down his writing session.

Along with an afternoon visit and sometimes lunch together, they took an evening walk with the dogs down to the beach. She looked forward to it each day.

Each morning, Mel sent her an email with a recap from the prior day and passed along any messages from customers or vendors. Things were running smoothly under her care, and Amelia looked forward to the snapshot updates from her store. She just couldn't bear the thought of going back yet.

In her spare time, Amelia scoured online sources for information about Huntington's. She didn't know much about it and, after researching, had a sinking feeling. No wonder Noah was worried about his future. There was no cure, and the disease was fatal.

From what Noah described, he was in the early stages but still, the outlook was bleak. His first symptoms centered around depression and memory lapses, which he'd written off to his mother's death. Then, he'd started stumbling and dropping things. He tripped often and sometimes fell, like he'd mentioned when Goose introduced them.

Noah admitted the reason he was on such a strict diet was in hopes of helping keep the disease at bay. He'd read dozens of articles and studies and was open to alternative therapies that might buy him more good days.

As Amelia looked across the table at Noah, her heart broke. He was such a talented man. A kind man. One that didn't deserve to suffer such a ravaging disease. Amelia hoped he could find a doctor to help him.

As they wrapped up their lunch at Soup D'Jour, Amelia promised to see Noah and Goose for a walk later in the evening, and she and Faith headed back to Sam's.

She waited for a lull in the line and caught Sam's eye. "I need to talk to you, privately."

Sam nodded and came around the counter, letting the young woman who was helping a customer know she was taking a quick break. She reached out for Amelia's arm. "Let's walk down by the harbor. I have a favorite bench."

They made their way through the tourists, and Sam pointed at the bench that was set in the shade of a large tree in the park and hidden from view by a high mound of grass. She gestured to the empty seats. "Only locals know it's here, and it's got a wonderful view."

Faith settled into the cool grass at their feet. Sam reached down and petted her head. "She's such a love. I'm so glad you have her."

Amelia smiled. "Me, too. She really does make each day better for me."

"So, what's up?"

"Well, I don't want to divulge much, but I've been spending quite a bit of time with Noah."

Sam wiggled her brows. "Yes, I've noticed. I think that's wonderful."

The color rose in Amelia's cheeks. "While we've been chatting, I learned something, and I'd really like to get him connected with your friend Max. I think he could help Noah with some medical advice. I don't want to suggest it outright but was hoping they might meet, at a dinner or something at your place, and I could guide the conversation."

Sam nodded. "Consider it done. I'll invite Max and Linda, plus Kate and Spence. We can keep it a small group so it's not overwhelming for Noah or the dogs. We can make sure Noah and Max have some time alone to chat."

Amelia breathed a sigh of relief. "Thank you, Sam. That sounds perfect. What can I bring?"

"Whatever you like. Jeff will grill the meat, so some sort of side dish works. I'll make a few things and will do dessert. Linda is swamped, so I won't ask her to make anything, but Kate will make something, I'm sure. We'll have plenty."

They stood and made their way back toward Sam's shop. As Sam walked, she laughed. "We didn't say a day. How about Saturday? That will give you two days to talk Noah into coming, and I'll prod him when he comes in tomorrow morning."

"Sound great. I appreciate your help so much."

"Happy to do it. We need to get the dogs acquainted, so it's a great excuse." She left Amelia with a warm hug and hurried up the steps to the deck to clear a few tables on her way back to the counter.

Next, Amelia made a quick stop at Cooper Hardware, where Jeff was always willing to watch over Faith while she ran to the market. She found him in his office in the back with both Zoe and Bailey, who were in full wag mode when they saw Faith.

She dashed down the street, picked up a few things, and put them in the SUV before collecting Faith, who she found stretched out between her two friends on their oversized cot.

After thanking Jeff, she and Faith hurried down the sidewalk. Pleased with herself and the success of her covert mission and happy her shopping was done, Amelia guided Faith back to her SUV, which was parked close to Kate's store. As she walked by the window, Kate tapped on it and motioned her inside.

Amelia pointed at Faith, and Kate smiled and nodded.

Moments later, Amelia guided the dog through the door, and Kate came from where she was adjusting a display in the far window. "Our dog Roxie is in the shop all the time, so I can definitely allow this sweet girl a visit. How are you two doing?" She bent down and petted Faith.

Amelia smiled at her new furry companion. "We're doing well. She's an excellent roommate."

Kate put her cell phone on the counter next to the register. "Sam just called and said we're having dinner at her place Saturday, and you're bringing Noah. She had to explain he's the guy I've said hello to a few times in her coffee shop. He's always on his laptop and has that gorgeous golden retriever. I'm excited to meet him."

"He's very interesting, and I was over the moon to meet the author behind the books I love reading. I'm hoping I can convince him to visit my bookstore. Goose is his dog, and he actually introduced us one morning when I was out walking. He's renting a place for the summer near Georgia's house."

"That's wonderful that you connected with him. Spence and I will be there for sure. We never say no to an invite to Sam's. We'll bring Roxie so she can meet your sweet girl."

"She'll love that. She's quite smitten with Goose. It's been nice to have another dog for socialization." She petted Faith's head. "We need to get going; I've got groceries in the car."

The bell above the door tinkled, and a throng of people fresh from the ferry came through the door.

Kate raised her brows. "I best get back to work, too. We'll see you Saturday for sure."

Amelia guided Faith around the largest of the crowd and out the door. They made their way to the SUV and headed back to the golf community.

After she unloaded her shopping, Amelia took an iced tea with a splash of lemonade out to the patio and settled onto a lounge chair with a book. Faith sprawled across the cot next to her.

Before long, both of them slept in the shade.

An hour later, Faith's tongue licking her fingers startled Amelia from her nap. It took her a moment to get her bearings. She'd been dreaming of Natalie. At least it had been a happy dream with snippets of their lives when Natalie was in grade school, but when she woke, the weight of her loss was heavy.

Tears leaked from her eyes and within seconds Faith, crawled up beside her and snuggled close to her shoulder, licking at her cheeks. She couldn't help but smile at the pure love Faith's warm little body provided.

She nestled closer to the dog and rested for a few more minutes. It was wonderful to have a friend like Faith and since her arrival, Amelia had more opportunities to smile and never felt alone.

Despite the nap, Amelia was tired and didn't feel like

putting in much effort for dinner. She opted for leftover taco salad from yesterday and fed Faith her dinner before she sat down at the table.

As she ate, her phone chimed with a text message. She smiled as she reached for the phone. Over the last weeks, she and Georgia had developed a habit of texting each evening and sometimes each morning. Georgia shared updates on Dale, who was improving each day and doing well and always asked Amelia to tell her the best thing that happened that day.

Amelia shared lots of photos of Faith and even a few of Goose and Noah. She told Georgia about her new friend from down the street and how they'd been chatting and spending time together. When she felt low, she often scrolled those text exchanges and was reminded of all the happy moments she'd experienced each day. It helped keep her grief in perspective and boosted her spirits when they fell.

Georgia's text included a funny photo of Suki, taking up the whole of Dale's lap while he was taking a nap in his chair, his clunky walking boot in full view.

As she ate the rest of her salad, Amelia typed in a reply and let Georgia know they were getting ready for their evening walk with Noah and Goose and that Sam invited them to her house for dinner on Saturday night.

Georgia asked her to pass on their greetings and reported that she and Dale were making the trip to Lavender Valley in a few days and would be staying there all of July for the festival, as planned. She was anxious to see her sisters and take part in the festival. She'd been passing her time sewing items to sell at their shop on the farm.

They signed off with virtual hugs and a promise to text tomorrow.

Amelia set the phone down and sighed. It wasn't the same

as having her sister with her, but it was better than nothing. Texting let them both reply when they could rather than a prearranged time for a call or video chat. Georgia did promise a video from the farm so Amelia could see the lavender in all its glory.

Faith rested, as was her habit after eating, while Amelia tidied the kitchen. The minute she reached for her walking shoes, Faith bolted from her spot and joined her at the door, ready for their ritual.

Amelia attached the leash to Faith's collar, which now had a shiny new tag with Amelia's cell phone number on it. She also attached the brand-new GPS tracker she found online. One night last week, after tossing and turning, her thoughts turned negative. She was filled with worry at the thought of Faith running off and being unable to find her. The peace of mind Amelia had when she pulled up the app on her phone and could see Faith's location was worth the price.

It was difficult to shake the fear of loss. Faith provided such comfort and companionship but since her arrival, Amelia struggled with the suffocating worry, especially in the dark of night.

Although Faith was still a pup and had no training, she was a natural therapy dog. Whenever Amelia's emotions got the best of her, Faith would rest her snout on her arm or any bit of skin she could access. Her simple touch often brought Amelia back to the present and was enough to keep the most negative of her thoughts at bay.

The grief came in waves. It was unpredictable, and the smallest thing could set it off. She'd walked by the bakery when she was in town last week and burst into tears when the scent of peanut butter cookies wafted from the door. They were Nat's favorite and just smelling them was enough to elicit sobs.

Each day was a roller coaster of emotions. At times, she didn't think of Nat and enjoyed whatever she was doing. When she was busy or focused on Faith, things were better. Other times, like with the cookies, she crumpled in despair.

She set out the door with Faith, determined to focus on the progress she'd made since her arrival on the island and push the struggles from her mind. When they arrived, Noah and Goose were waiting for them, ready to cross the road to the beach.

She raised a hand to greet them. "How are you two this evening?"

Noah smiled. "Not bad at all. I made lots of progress on the book today, so I'm feeling accomplished." He glanced down at Goose. "Goose took a long nap this afternoon, so he's aching for a walk."

As they made their way to the beach, they chatted, and Amelia told him about running errands after she left him in town. "I ran into Kate and Sam and got my shopping done. Sam invited us to dinner at her house on Saturday. Kate, who has the antiques store, and Linda, who has the florist shop, along with their significant others, will be there. They all have dogs and are bringing them, too. I hope you and Goose will come."

Noah was quiet as they walked along the shoreline, leashes tethered in his hands, so as not to let the dogs run and get soaked.

Amelia didn't say anything else. She feared she might have overstepped, and Noah might not be ready for a crowd.

He stopped walking and rested his eyes on hers. "I don't think I've been invited to dinner in years. I'm a bit of a loner if you haven't noticed. When you're working, your friends come from that social circle. Not that I had much time for socializing, but after I retired, my circle shrank."

The dogs urged them forward, and they strolled along the packed, wet sand. "Frankly, I'm almost a hermit. My social skills are rusty at best. Are you sure you want me to come?"

Amelia grinned at him. "You're one of the most interesting people I've ever met. I think you're selling yourself short. You'll love all of them. They've been so kind and accepting of me. You already said you know Sam and Jeff from all the time you spend at the coffee shop. I'm sure you've seen the others in there."

He chuckled. "When I'm in the writing zone, I honestly don't notice much."

He paused and added, "I'd love to come. Thanks for inviting me. And, Goose, of course." He reached down and patted the dog's side.

"You'll love Sam's place. It's got a jaw-dropping view and a gorgeous deck."

They walked a few more feet, and she asked, "How was your day outside of getting lots of words on the page?"

"Better," he said. "Much better than I've been in a long time. I think talking to you and sharing helped. Thank you for listening."

"I could say the same. I guess we're living proof in that old adage of a burden shared is a burden halved, right?"

He chuckled. "I think it's more about not feeling alone. Goose is an incredible friend and listener, but I realized how much an actual conversation helps."

"It's definitely easier to travel through the dark valleys with someone by your side." Amelia reached out for his hand and squeezed it.

CHAPTER ELEVEN

A melia blamed her tears on the red onions she chopped, but in reality, she knew it was the memories dredged up by making the potato salad with a lemon and mustard vinaigrette that had been one of Ron's favorites. It was the perfect potluck dish since it could sit out without the fear of going bad.

She finished tossing the potatoes and added a bit of fresh parsley to the bowl before covering it and sticking it in the fridge. A shiver of unease ran through her. She was both excited and nervous about the dinner at Sam's.

It almost felt like a date, not that she had any recent memory of one. She hadn't dated anyone since the divorce, and the ripple of excitement was quelled by the guilt that followed. She and Georgia had a long visit earlier, an actual call instead of a text, and Georgia's advice about finding joy in her life rang true.

Losing Nat didn't mean Amelia had to quit living. It was important that she seek out happiness and hold onto it with all her might. That's what Georgia told her, and Amelia was determined to heed her big sister's counsel. Georgia encouraged her to turn to her faith and trust that there was a plan for her.

As Amelia got dressed for the party, her thoughts turned to Kate. She was a guidepost. She'd lost her daughter and didn't wear her grief on her sleeve. She embraced life, had a successful business, a man she loved and who loved her, and a wonderful group of friends. She kept living, even though she admitted to Amelia, she didn't always feel like it. Spence had been the one to help her through the darkness, along with her son who still needed her.

As she added earrings and a necklace to a soft-blue blouse and cardigan she paired with white jeans, she glanced down at Faith, who was always by her side. Faith had given her a purpose and a reason to get up each morning. She was the best friend she'd ever had.

She opted to forego the ponytail that had been her permanent hairstyle since her arrival on the island and curled her hair into loose waves that framed her face. With a quick swipe of lip color, she and Faith loaded her SUV.

When they pulled in front of Noah's place, he and Goose were waiting on the porch. Noah toted a bag and loaded Goose into the backseat with Faith. Noah climbed into the passenger seat and set the bag on the floor. "I'm not drinking alcohol these days but bought some wine. I hate to come emptyhanded."

"I've got a huge salad in the cooler in the back. Don't let me forget to grab it when we get there."

She started to pull away, but the dogs and their wagging tails blocked the view in her mirror. Noah turned in his seat and with a quick gesture, Goose sat down, and Faith followed.

It didn't take long until Amelia took the turn off the road

and into Sam's driveway. When the house finally came into view, she glanced over at Noah, awaiting his reaction. She was rewarded with a gasp as he uttered, "Wowza."

"Exactly what I thought when I saw it. It's beyond gorgeous. Wait until you see the rest of it."

She parked and opted to take charge of the food and wine and left the leash wrangling to Noah. Jeff answered the front door and welcomed them in with a warm smile and a hug for Amelia.

He looked down at the dogs. "I've got our two outside, and they're itching to see their friend Faith, and I think Zoe has met Goose at Sam's shop." He laid a hand on Noah's shoulder. "So glad you could join us, Noah. I know we've said hello a few times at Sam's when I've stopped by for a drink, but it will be great to get to know you better."

Jeff led them through the house, with its dramatic high ceilings and pointed at the kitchen. "Sam's in there. I'll take Noah and the dogs outside so they can run free and play."

Amelia rounded the corner and found Sam busy at the kitchen counter. "Hey, Amelia," she said, looking up from the cutting board where she was slicing fruit. "Welcome. I'm about done with this, then we can sit outside and visit."

Amelia held up the bag. "Noah brought some wine to share, and I have a big potato salad."

"Oh, yum. I think there's room in the fridge for that. Just muscle it in there if you have to."

Amelia rearranged a few things and made it fit. She was about to take some things out to the table when Max and Linda came in from the deck. The mouth-watering scent of meat cooking on the grill drifted through the open door. Max carried a huge charcuterie board. "Shall I put this on the table outside?"

Sam eyed it. "Wow, that looks terrific. Look how fancy. I

guess all those years of surgery paid off in your ability to carve meats and cheese that look like art."

He smirked and rolled his eyes. "I like making them. It's my new hobby."

Linda put her arm around his shoulders. "Max has become our full-time chef this summer. I've been quite impressed."

He tilted his head toward hers. "My lovely wife works way too hard, so I told her I'd be in charge of meals."

Sam turned toward Amelia. "You both remember Amelia, I'm sure. She brought Noah. He's staying down the street from her for the summer. He's a bestselling author. He's outside with Jeff and the dogs."

Max's eyes widened. "Oh, that will be fun. Let me get this situated outside, and I'll get Lucy from the car and find him."

Amelia offered to walk with him and when they reached the driveway, she took a deep breath. "Max, I have a bit of an ulterior motive in asking Noah to join us tonight."

Max wiggled his brows. "Do tell."

"He has no idea I'm telling you this and wouldn't be happy with me, but I was hoping you might help him with some medical advice. He lives in Oregon and saw a doctor there before he arrived. The doctor, who is a family physician, is pretty sure he has Huntington's but wants him to see a specialist. Noah is struggling with the diagnosis and other things, but he has an appointment in September. I think the news was overwhelming on top of losing his mom, and he escaped here for the summer. He's got a heavy workload on top of it."

Max frowned. "That's a tough diagnosis. I'm not very experienced in that arena. My wheelhouse is the heart, but as it happens, I have a good friend who's a renowned neurologist. She classically trained, but a few years ago retired from her practice and is now using more alternative and holistic therapies to treat patients. She lives in Florida now. I'm happy to connect Noah with her."

Amelia's nerves eased. "That would be wonderful. The only caveat is he can't know I spoke with you. I'm hoping he might divulge his issue, and you could make a suggestion. I'm going to try to encourage him. He needs some help and guidance. I don't think he can wait until September."

Max nodded. "I've been trying to get Jan to visit the islands." He raised his brows and stepped over to open the door for Lucy, who was hanging her head out the window, anxious to join the others.

The Labrador looked at him for a cue and when he clapped his hands and pointed to the yard, she took off like a rocket. He chuckled. "This is her home away from home."

They wandered back toward the house at a slow pace. "I'll reach out to her and see if I can convince her to come over the summer. She'd been promising, so I'll press her. That would make it very convenient for Noah to speak with her and at least get her opinion."

Amelia lowered her voice. "That would be nothing short of a miracle. I just don't want to upset him."

Max pulled out his cell phone and nodded. "Leave it with me. I'm going to text her right now and see if I can get her to commit. If I know she's coming, I can bring it up in casual conversation, which will give Noah the perfect opening."

She admired his thinking. "I trust you and can see why Sam adores you." Amelia hurried off to the backyard with a quick wave and found Noah and Jeff playing ball with all the dogs.

Within a few minutes, another golden, who Jeff introduced as Roxie, came from the deck. Roxie joined in the fun and after she sniffed at Faith, the six dogs tumbled and played in the enclosed area.

Noah stood next to Amelia and bent closer to her. "They're going to sleep good tonight."

"Oh, yeah. I was a little worried with Faith being so young, but she's having the time of her life."

Jeff refilled the large trough in the corner with fresh water and encouraged Noah and Amelia to join him on the deck. "They're safe in there, and I'll check on them often. Since Roxie is here, I know Kate and Spence arrived. I need to check on the grill."

Amelia introduced Noah to Kate and Spence and then joined the others around the table, where everyone nibbled on Max's creation. Sam poured iced teas for anyone who wanted them, and Max handled the wine, which Kate and Linda happily accepted.

As Amelia popped a cube of cheese in her mouth, she noticed Noah, staring out at the water. "Some view, huh?"

"You weren't kidding. This is quite the place. Ever since Mom died, I've been trying to decide where to go. I'm okay at her place, but sometimes it's hard to be there with all of her things, memories. You know. I wouldn't mind living here." He sighed and added, "All of that is secondary until I figure out this diagnosis and what it means. I'm stuck until I know more."

"I know exactly what you mean about memories. That's why I left everything behind in Seattle. Ron offered to give me the house, but I couldn't stay there, staring at everything we had. Everything we lost."

Noah reached for her hand and held it in his.

It had been a long time since a man had held her hand. She liked the feel of it. The warmth. The soft texture of his skin against hers.

Jeff announced dinner was ready, interrupting the moment. Noah offered to check on Goose and Faith before they took their seats around the dinner table.

As Amelia watched him disappear from the deck stairs, her heart swelled. He was a good man, and it had been a good day.

CHAPTER TWELVE

I t was dark and late by the time they gathered the dogs and loaded them into Amelia's SUV. Noah drove, since Amelia indulged in a couple glasses of wine after dinner.

As he made his way down the driveway, he turned to her. "They really are a great group. Thanks for inviting me."

"I had a good time, too. I'm glad you came."

"I don't want to get my hopes up but did you hear Max telling Linda he finally heard from a friend of his about a visit, and she was coming in a few weeks? Turns out his friend is a neurologist, but she's retired from her practice. Now, she treats patients using both traditional and alternative medicine. A more holistic approach, he called it."

"Really? That's incredible. You should ask him about meeting with her."

"I know. Max and I were chatting while Spence and Jeff were playing with the dogs. You were in the house helping with the dishes. I told him about my doctor suspecting I have Huntington's and my appointment in September. He offered to connect me with his friend Jan. He thought she'd be willing to video chat and meet with me here on the island."

"That's fabulous news." She noticed the upbeat tone of his voice. With the cover of the night around them, she smiled, happy that her plan worked.

"I don't want to set myself up for disappointment, but the idea of working with someone who has experience and comes recommended, plus is well versed in alternative treatments, is much better than an appointment with a specialist I know nothing about. Max is so easy to talk to, and he helped ease my fears."

"It's easy to see why he had such a successful career, and he still helps out at the local hospital. He's one of those old-school doctors, who take their time and really care."

Noah nodded. "He also made me promise to join him and Spence for a golf game next week. I think Jeff's going to join them, too. Max told me there's more to life than work."

"He is right about that. I hope you go with them. I'm happy to watch Goose whenever you need it."

"I haven't golfed in years, but I think I might take him up on it. It felt good to be part of a group of such nice people. Like I said, I've lived the life of a hermit, so peopling is not my forté."

"They make it easy. Georgia told me how wonderful they all are, and she was spot on. In fact, she said she met several of the ladies when they came for a visit to the lavender farm that she and her foster sisters brought back to life. It's in Oregon, near Medford in Lavender Valley."

"I'm sure my mom knew about it. She was a flower aficionado. She lived close to a tulip farm, and she loved to make the trip to Salem for the peony garden and the iris festival, along with the dahlias in Canby. She loved flowers and painted many."

"Listening to Georgia talk about the lavender farm and the festival makes me want to go. I've never explored much of Oregon."

"It's a beautiful state. I especially like the coast." He laughed. "That's why I'm drawn to the island. Something about water."

"Sam and Jeff have the ideal location. I think I could have fallen asleep curled up next to their fire pit tonight. Love that sound of the sea, especially at night."

"It is relaxing. Can you hear it from your house in Driftwood Bay?"

She shook her head. "No, not really. I'm not close enough to the water, but a friend has a place near it and has invited me more than once. She restored her family's old guest cottages on the property, and there's a trail leading from her place right down to the water."

"Sounds perfect." He took the turn to the golf community.

He parked the SUV in Georgia's driveway. "We'll see you two to the door, and we can walk home."

She gritted her teeth. "Oh, I hate that you have to walk in the dark. I should have passed on the wine tonight."

"Don't give it a thought. The streets are lit, and it's not far. We'll be just fine."

He and Goose walked them to the front door. "Thanks again for the invite. We had a great time." He glanced down at Goose. "Let's go, boy."

Amelia and Faith stood at the door and watched them until the man, who she was getting more attached to with each passing day, and his faithful friend disappeared around the curve in the street.

———

On Monday morning, Amelia and Faith met up with Izzy and Jess, along with Sunny and Ruby, for a walk. As they walked, Jess mentioned that she and Dean were flying out on Wednesday. She was going to stay for a month, with Dean staying only a week, since he had work obligations. She was looking forward to spending time with her son, who recently reconnected with her, and she was over the moon to see her new grandson.

As she spoke, she glanced down at Ruby. "I hate leaving my poor girl behind, but I know she'll have a great time with Sunny. She won't even know I'm gone."

"Aww, I'm sure she'll miss you," said Izzy. "We'll take good care of her."

Amelia nodded. "On the days Izzy works, I told her I can watch them, and that will give Faith the opportunity for some play dates."

Jess smiled at her. "That will be great. Faith is such a sweet pup." She paused and added, "I have one more favor to ask. I thought since you're a bookshop owner, you might be willing to watch over my Free Little Library downtown. I just check on it a couple times a week to make sure it's in order. If you need books to add to it, I've got a bunch in my garage, and I'll give you the code to get in."

"Oh, I would be happy to do that. I love that you have one."

Izzy raised her brows at Jess. "Told you she'd be all over that."

Jess chuckled. "Bookworms have to stick together, right?"

Izzy stopped walking and turned to Amelia. "That reminds me, I was in a meeting last week and found out the local food pantry needs volunteers. After we talked about how helping others is often a wonderful way to heal grief, I thought of you."

"That sounds like a good possibility. I'll definitely check it out. Thanks, Izzy."

"I'll email you the contact person."

The three of them kept walking, with the dogs sniffing at the bushes and flowers along the pathway.

Izzy remarked that Jeff and Sam were hosting their big Fourth of July celebration this weekend. "You and Noah have to come. It's always a wonderful time. We're celebrating Sam's birthday, too."

Amelia nodded. "I got her text last night. Noah is holed up in his writing cave, but he's going to try to make it provided he makes good progress on his book. I'm on Goose duty this week. I told Noah I'd let him hang out with Faith for a few hours each day. We can get in some exercise while Noah works. I'm hoping if he has all that time to dedicate to work, he can squeeze in that golf game with Colin, Max, and Jeff on Friday morning."

Izzy laughed. "I think Colin is planning to abduct him if he doesn't show up."

They completed the loop, and Jess left them with a hug and promised to call to check in on Ruby while she was away.

Amelia waved to both of them as she wandered down the street toward Georgia's house. "I think it's time for breakfast," she said to Faith.

Faith's ears pricked, and she looked up at Amelia, clearly in agreement.

After she fed Faith and fixed herself some toast and tea, Amelia changed her sheets and tackled the pile of laundry she'd let get too high. While it was washing, she dusted and cleaned the floors.

With the house looking much better, she poured herself a glass of iced tea and checked her phone.

Izzy's text was waiting with the name and number of the food bank manager, Tessa, who was anxious to hear from her. She chuckled as she read the text and understood why Kate and Sam touted Izzy's abilities. Without being pushy, she managed to organize a meeting and guide Amelia to something she'd only mentioned in passing, but Izzy thought it was important.

She transferred the laundry to the dryer and took a notepad from the drawer in the kitchen before calling Tessa.

The woman had a pleasant and young voice. She was happy to hear from Izzy's friend and invited her to come to the food bank on Tuesday. She was in dire need of help on Tuesdays and Saturdays, with delivering food to homebound residents.

Tessa sighed as she spoke, "If you can handle driving and delivering, which involves toting some boxes of food from your car, that would be wonderful. We can always use help at the center, sorting and organizing, plus filling orders, but right now, my main need is someone to deliver twice a week."

"I can do that. My only concern is I have a new-to-me golden retriever. Is it okay if she rides with me?"

"Oh, of course. In fact, many of our seniors are dog lovers. We just ask that you don't bring the dog into a home without checking with the owner first. You're in and out quickly, so your dog won't be sitting in the car long if she has to wait. Sometimes our participants get chatty, so you'll need to use your own judgment on that front."

"Sounds good. I can do that. I'll see you tomorrow."

"That's wonderful, Amelia. I've been praying for a miracle, and I think you're it. I'll have a list and a map ready for you and can give you a quick training."

"I'll be there. Looking forward to meeting you."

With a sense of triumph, Amelia disconnected. She looked at the calendar she'd picked up from Kate's shop. It was one of Dean's with gorgeous photos of the island. She wrote in the food bank on each of the Tuesday and Saturday squares and added a note to check Jess' little library on those same days. Since she'd be in town anyway, it made sense.

She checked her email and read through the information Mel provided. The vendors needed her order for the holidays, and Mel had worked up a draft order of titles and a few gift items for her approval.

Mel also scanned all the invoices and bills that needed to be paid, and Amelia spent a few hours reviewing them and paying them online. She used a payroll company to handle paying Mel, and they'd also sent a recap for her review and approval.

By late afternoon, with all her chores done around the house, and all the paperwork caught up from the bookstore, Amelia closed her laptop and collected the leash from the hook by the door.

In a flash, Faith vacated her lounging position and sat at her feet, ready for adventure.

They made the short trek to Noah's and circled to the back of his house. She opened the patio door, and Goose ran to greet them. With his leash attached, they headed for a long walk and left Noah to his keyboard in his upstairs office.

She took the dogs to the beach and, not in the mood to deal with rinsing them both, kept a tight hold on their leash and didn't throw sticks. She suspected Goose would come when she called him, but she didn't want to take a chance.

The part of the beach beyond the private section was also busier than usual. The upcoming Fourth of July holiday brought in even more visitors, and they were out exploring.

It was time for dinner by the time they reached Noah's.

She measured out his food and added the blueberries and veggies he liked to the top of the kibble, while Faith watched and drooled.

While he ate, she filled up his water bowl and then texted Noah to let him know they'd walked, and he'd had his dinner. She wouldn't put it past Goose to pretend he hadn't eaten and get a second dinner.

She also let him know they'd be home if he felt like walking later.

Before they said goodbye, she wiped up the puddle of drool Faith made and ruffled Goose's ears.

As they left, she looked back and saw his sweet face staring at them. He looked a little sad. Like her. She missed chatting with Noah but understood that he needed to focus all his energy on his work right now. He was determined to finish his books before Max's doctor friend arrived in late July.

When they walked through the back door at Georgia's house, Faith made a beeline for her food bowl and looked surprised to find it empty. With a chuckle, Amelia remedied that, and the dog dug into her dinner with gusto.

Amelia was tired and opted to reheat some leftover soup for her dinner. After that, she and Faith snuggled on the couch and tuned into a series she'd starting watching last week.

Georgia subscribed to a couple of British streaming channels, and Amelia was addicted to the detective series based on Ann Cleeves' books. With one hand on Faith, she settled in for an evening in the Shetland Islands of Scotland. She took it as a good sign that she could finally concentrate and enjoy an entire episode. She would make it through this after all.

After two episodes, she turned off the television, let Faith outside once more, and then the two of them padded to the bedroom.

As she was crawling into bed, her phone chimed. She reached for it and smiled. A text from Noah lit up on her screen.

Thanks for looking after Goose. Just finished up for tonight. I'll try to make a walk work tomorrow evening. Thanks for understanding. Sweet dreams to you and Faith. She noticed the little heart and dog emoji he added.

She typed back and wished him a good night, let him know the dogs had a good time, and added her own fun sticker of two dogs on a bench with a little heart between them.

After she pressed send, she worried that he might take the sticker the wrong way. She couldn't deny that she cared for him but also wasn't ready for a serious relationship. In his current state, she didn't want to create any pressure for him.

She debated trying to send another text to clarify things and decided it wasn't worth it. Her eyes were heavy, and she wasn't at her best when she was tired. She'd explain things in person if it came up.

After pulling the covers up to her chin, she reached over and rested her hand on Faith. She was already asleep, not a care in the world. The steady beat of her heart under Amelia's hand was a comfort.

CHAPTER THIRTEEN

Tuesday morning, Amelia woke early, excited to get to the food bank. She was on her own walking today, so she made a point of stopping at Noah's and picked up Goose. She'd be tied up most of the day and didn't want him to miss out on some fun and exercise.

The patio door was unlocked, as she and Noah prearranged. He told her when he was working like he was now, he often stayed up late and slept in, but sometimes, he worked early in the morning. He didn't have a predictable schedule and most of the time didn't even remember to shower or eat until the situation was dire.

They had promised to text each other with regard to Goose's meal status. As much as he would enjoy double-dipping, they didn't want him to overeat.

After a brisk walk around the golf course, with both dogs happy and prancing together as they stepped along the trail, Amelia dropped Goose at home, fixed his breakfast, and texted Noah to let him know he had eaten.

She was due at the food bank at ten o'clock for her

training session. After a shower and breakfast, plus a quick stop at Sam's place for a coffee, she and her faithful friend pulled into the parking lot with five minutes to spare. She found a spot close to the building under the shade of a large tree.

Amelia took hold of Faith's leash, and they walked toward the open garage door. The food bank was housed in a building that looked more like a house than a commercial enterprise. It was situated in a quiet neighborhood near a church.

A young woman with short, dark hair stood in the garage where several boxes were staged. She wore shorts and a t-shirt, with a bright green apron over the top of it. "You must be Amelia," she said, smiling. "I'm Tessa."

Amelia extended her hand. "Great to meet you." Faith wiggled with excitement. "And this is Faith."

"Aww, she's a sweetheart." Tessa reached out to pet her. "You can have her out here in the loading bay, but we can't have any animals in the other part of the building where the food is kept."

Amelia nodded. "Understood."

Tessa grabbed a clipboard and another bright green apron from the table along the side of the room. "You can slip this apron on to protect your clothes, and it helps our participants recognize you're with the food bank."

After she helped Amelia tie the strings, Tessa reviewed the delivery sheet with her, pointing out the address of each recipient and the corresponding box labeled with the order number and the name of the client. The sheet also included the phone number of the recipient.

"You can just have them initial here when you deliver. If by chance they aren't home, you can leave it at the door and just note that you did that and the time."

Tessa ran her finger down the list. "Most of these are close to town, but there are a couple who are further out." She took a highlighter from her apron pocket and drew a line through two names and addresses. Then, she gave Amelia an idea of how to get to them; one was on the road near Lime Kiln State Park, and the other was near the Island Winery.

Amelia assured her that she'd have no trouble and was used to using her phone for directions.

Tessa nodded. "Wonderful. You'll have the same route on Saturday, unless we pick up any new participants between now and then. When you're done, just return the clipboard with the sheet and if by some chance I'm not here, there's a drop box by the front door, and you can leave it there."

They exchanged cell phone numbers, and Tessa told her to call if she had any problems or questions along the way. After they loaded the back of Amelia's SUV, Tessa sent her off with a warm hug and her thanks for coming to her rescue.

Amelia tapped in the highlighted addresses on her phone and opted to get them delivered first and then make her way back to town and deal with all the closer ones.

It took about twenty minutes to reach the first address, where she made a successful delivery to a charming elderly couple, who asked if they could pet Faith when they saw her stick her head out the window.

After she soaked up all the attention she could, Amelia wished them a good rest of the day and took off for the address near the winery.

She hadn't explored much of the island yet, so it was fun to see new parts of it. She passed the turn for the winery and moved it to the top of her list to visit on her next outing.

Blake and Ellie were always working but had invited her to come out more than once.

She slowed to look for the turn for her next delivery. She spotted the mailbox and drove down the driveway.

When she parked, Amelia noticed a tall, older woman trimming roses along the front walkway of a gorgeous two-story farmhouse. She retrieved her box and hollered out a hello, hoping not to startle her.

At the sound of Amelia's loud greeting, her shoulders jumped, and she turned around. Within seconds, a smile replaced the startled look on her face.

"Hello, dear. Sorry, I didn't hear you. I'm not wearing my hearing aids. Blasted things don't work anyway."

Amelia was surprised at the woman's deep voice. "No problem, Mrs. Taylor. Can I take this in the house for you?"

"Oh, that would be wonderful. You're new, I think. I recognize the apron but not you."

"Yes, ma'am. Today's my first day. I'm Amelia." She moved her hand from the side of the box and extended it.

"Pleased to meet you, Amelia. You can call me Doris." She pointed at the front door. "Just take it through there, and the kitchen is down the hall, first opening on the left."

Amelia climbed the steps to the porch and followed her directions, emerging from the house within a minute. "I left it on your counter, Doris. Hope you have a great day. I'll see you next time."

"I'll make us a fresh pitcher of tea; maybe you can visit for a few minutes."

Amelia pointed at her SUV. "I've got my dog with me, so I can't stay too long."

"Oh, she's welcome. I used to have dogs, but at my age, it's too much now."

"She's my best friend, but they are work." Amelia waved and continued down the pathway. "I'll see you soon, Doris."

She headed back to town and realized it had taken her an hour to do those two deliveries. Tessa stressed it wasn't a speed contest and to go at her own pace, but that seemed like a long time. On the other hand, if she stayed to visit and have tea with her clients, it would take even longer.

Once behind the wheel, she took a few minutes to plot the remaining addresses and come up with a route that would be the most efficient.

On the way back to town, Faith put her snout out the partially open window in the backseat and sniffed at the air. She was having a grand adventure, and her wagging tail brought a smile to Amelia when she glanced in the rear-view mirror.

The next four stops were quick, with each of the recipients reserved and quiet, uttering a reserved thank you, but not inviting a conversation.

On her next stop, she pulled in front of a duplex, where two children were playing in the front yard. A woman in her thirties answered the door and accepted the box from Amelia. Her appearance was harried, and she was dressed with a black apron tied around her waist, like a server.

She sighed and took the box from Amelia. "I thought you were the babysitter. She's late again." As she turned to deposit the box of food, she kept talking. "I'm going to be late for work, and I can't be."

Minutes later, she returned to the front stoop. "I need this job." She glanced at the children playing in the yard.

Amelia felt for the woman with the frantic look on her face. She extended her hand. "I'm Amelia. I'm new to this volunteer job, and I know you don't know me, but I can hang out and wait for your sitter." She pointed at her SUV parked at the curb with Faith's sweet face sticking out the window. "I've got a golden retriever who would love a chance to stretch her legs and play. I don't want to pressure you, but if you need a reference, you can call Jeff at Cooper Hardware or Sam at Harbor Coffee & Books. They'll both vouch for me."

The woman, who gave her a weak smile, said, "I know Jeff. His sister Jen does my hair." She paused and added, "I'm Monique, by the way." She pointed at the two children. "That's Cody and Ember."

Amelia smiled. "Nice to meet you, Monique. Jen just did my hair, too. You can ask her about me. I'm trustworthy and happy to help."

"I need to get to my shift at the Front Street Café. My sitter is named Pauline, and she should be here within ten minutes. If you can stay, I'd really appreciate it."

"Not a problem. I'll just get my dog and introduce her to Cody and Ember."

Monique hurried into the house, and, moments later, she returned with her purse. She stared at her phone and smiled at Amelia. "Jen just texted me back and said I could definitely trust you."

She sighed and hurried to explain what was happening to her young children and then dashed past Amelia to the old Toyota parked in the driveway. "You're a lifesaver. Thank you, Amelia." She handed her a sticky note. "This is my cell number. Just call if you need me."

"Happy to help," said Amelia, opening the door and taking hold of Faith's leash. As soon as the dog walked up the sidewalk, the two kids hurried toward her, all smiles and giggles.

The two of them were still enthralled with Faith and giving her pets and attention when a young woman pulled in the driveway, her red hair flying as she rushed from the car. "Sorry, sorry. I'm late. I know."

Amelia looked up from where she was kneeling and met the young woman's eyes. "I'm Amelia. Monique had to get to work or risk being late, so I offered to watch over them until you arrived."

"Oh, thanks for that. I know Monique is tired of me being late. I'm Pauline, by the way."

Amelia stood and shook Pauline's hand. "Well, we need to get moving. I've got more deliveries to make." She said goodbye to the children, who were almost hanging on Faith, begging to play some more.

"We'll be back soon and visit with you," said Amelia. She waved to Pauline, wondering if having a stranger fill in for her would make any impact on her ability to manage her time.

After Faith slurped up some water from the bowl she remembered to pack, they set out for the next house.

She didn't have to babysit any more children, and the vast majority of the new people she met on her route were happy to see her. Many asked her to stay and visit. As she accepted another glass of lemonade from a woman with a beautiful rose garden in her yard, Amelia realized delivering was much more than dropping off a box of food.

Most of the people she met were alone and anxious for a conversation or a kind word. Several were quiet and reserved and didn't invite a chat, but with Amelia being a new face, they might be reluctant until they got to know her.

She made her way to the last delivery and pulled up in front of a white one-story home with blue trim. It was next to a small park, with the senior center just down the street. The large yard was neat as a pin, with gorgeous flowers nestled along the white picket fence surrounding the thick, green grass.

She made her way up the steps, admiring the pots with purple and orange blooms, and noticed a ramp connected to the far end of the small porch that bypassed the steps. She rang the bell and after a few minutes, a man, using a walker, opened the door. The smooth voice of Tony Bennett singing a jazzy tune drifted through the opening. Behind his reading glasses, his bright blue eyes were framed by sprouts of white hair. "Mr. Jenkins, I'm Amelia. I've got your order from the food bank."

He moved out of the way and motioned her inside.

"You've got a beautiful yard. I love all your flowers."

He smiled. "My late wife loved flowers. I'm not able to take care of them, but Linda from the nursery sends her workers over to do my yard now."

"Oh, I know Linda. She's terrific."

As she followed his slow steps, she took note of the black and white photographs covering the walls and nestled in the open bookshelves of the glass-doored bookcase. She also spotted the antique wooden radio standing in the corner, which was the source of Tony Bennett.

The wingback chairs, with their dark-green velvet cushions and curved legs, and the armoire that held the television, caught Amelia's eye. It was like stepping back in time as she made her way through the living room. The leather recliner was the only modern piece of furniture in the room.

Another beautiful wooden piece that looked like an old card catalog found in libraries was nestled in the corner of the dining room.

"You can just leave the box here, dear." He tapped his hand, his knuckles gnarled with arthritis, on the counter.

Amelia did as she was asked, noticing how tall he was, despite the slight hunch of his shoulders. He was on the thin side, and Amelia hoped he got enough to eat. Then, she turned to him. "I'm happy to put your perishables in the fridge."

The quiet man rewarded her with a slow grin. "That's kind of you. Thank you."

She opened the box and retrieved the fruits and vegetables. With that done, she pointed at the box. "I've got my golden retriever in my car, so I don't want to leave her for long. Do you want some help putting the rest of this away? You're my last delivery of the day, so I've got time."

His blue eyes sparkled. "You have a golden retriever?"

"Yes, I just adopted her, but she's still a pup. Her name is Faith."

Tears formed in his eyes. "You're welcome to bring her in. I love them. My last one passed away a few years ago." He shrugged. "At my age, I wasn't sure I could handle another one."

She glanced at his walker. "I'll keep her on her leash. She loves people and will be excited to meet you. It might be best if you sit in your chair, so we don't risk you falling."

He nodded. "I'll get settled." The soft thuds of his walker against the hardwood floor followed his progress toward the living room.

Amelia went to her SUV and gave Faith another drink of water before she took hold of her leash and guided her up the pathway to Mr. Jenkins' house. As they walked, Amelia explained she needed to be calm and gentle with their new friend.

By the time they returned, Mr. Jenkins was in his recliner, and Tony Bennett had been turned off. Faith was in a hurry to meet her new friend, but Amelia kept a firm hold on her and slowed her advance. As she let Faith get close enough for a pet, she gazed at the bookcase along the wall and noticed all the leatherbound books in the shelves.

The marble-topped table next to Mr. Jenkins' chair also held several books. Amelia smiled at her luck of meeting a kindred spirit who obviously cherished books.

He spoke softly to Faith, and a wide smile lifted the edges of his mouth. Faith licked at his hands, and her tail swept in quick arcs. "Easy, Faith. Be easy with Mr. Jenkins."

He looked up at Amelia. "She's beautiful. Please call me Henry."

Henry kept petting Faith, and Amelia ran her hand across the dog's back. "She's also a real sweetheart. I'm so glad I have her. I'm on my own, so it's nice to have the company."

"Yes, I know all about that. My last golden, Daisy, was my best friend, too. Well, they've all been, but she was special."

The more Henry petted Faith, the more talkative he became. He assured Amelia he was fine, and she could unbox things in the kitchen without watching over Faith.

Amelia worried Faith would try to jump on him, but he used hand gestures and could control her without saying a word. She wanted to know more about that but left them to bond while she worked in the kitchen.

It didn't take long to figure out where Henry kept his pantry of food and staples. The space was more modern but still had those vintage touches that blended with the vibe in the other rooms she'd seen. She loved the white cabinets with glass fronts and the bin pulls on all the drawers, not to mention the beautiful white and gray marble counters. The color palette was mostly white with soft blue accents and all stainless-steel appliances.

After she added the canned goods and boxes of pasta to his stock, she noticed the electric tea kettle on the counter and the mug next to it. She plucked the fresh box of tea from the food order and put it next to his mug. She toted the empty box back to the living room, where she found Faith sitting smartly at Henry's feet.

"I can take this back to the center for you, unless you want to keep it." Amelia tapped the cardboard box.

Henry shook his head. "I don't need it. Thank you again, dear. I appreciate the help and you letting me visit your dog."

"Would you like me to brew you some tea before we go?"

Henry sighed. "That would be lovely. It's all on the counter in the kitchen. Earl Grey sounds good to me."

Amelia stashed the empty box outside the front door and went about fixing him a mug of tea. She returned to find Faith sleeping and Henry's eyes almost closed.

When she put the mug on the table, his eyelids fluttered. "Oh, thank you. You've been a huge help, Amelia. I appreciate it."

She took hold of Faith's leash. "You have a good rest of your day, Henry. I'll see you next time."

He started to rise from his chair, and she motioned to him. "Don't get up. Just relax and enjoy your tea."

"Thank you, again. I hope you'll bring Faith back, and maybe you can join me for tea next time."

"I'd love to, Henry. See you soon."

She waved as she shut his door and grabbed the empty box before leading Faith back to the SUV. She was surprised when she looked at the clock in the dash and realized it was after three o'clock.

She hurried back to the food bank building and found it locked up tight. She deposited the clipboard with her completed sheet in the drop box and slid behind the wheel.

As she drove home, she realized how wise Izzy was to connect her with the food bank. She'd had a great day meeting lots of new people and hadn't thought about her own grief once.

Seeing some of the recipients on her route helped her understand just how much she had. For that, she was grateful.

CHAPTER FOURTEEN

The rest of the week, Amelia kept busy with her walks in the morning and picking up Goose to join them. Most days, Izzy, along with Sunny and Ruby, met them, and the four dogs had a grand time.

She missed popping into Sam's shop to visit with Noah each afternoon but respected his need to immerse himself in work. She texted with him, rather than call and interrupt him, but he was always late in replying and sometimes didn't reply at all. It worried her, but she rationalized it as him being too focused on work to interact.

On Friday, she dropped a container of soup and a salad off at his house while she let Goose and Faith play. Later in the afternoon, he called to thank her and say how much he appreciated her thoughtful gesture. He also promised he would be at the Fourth of July celebration.

On Saturday, she and Faith headed to town to load their food bank deliveries, but first, they stopped to check on the Free Little Library. After organizing the titles by grade level, like Jess had shown her, she retrieved a few more books from the box she'd taken from Jess' garage and made sure the shelves were full.

With that done, she made her way over to the food bank. Tessa was busy organizing things but helped her load the deliveries in the back of her SUV.

Amelia noticed the delivery route was the same as Tuesday, which would make things easy. She'd always had a good memory and had no trouble duplicating the route she took before.

This time, she and Faith made time to visit with Doris and linger over a glass of iced tea, while they enjoyed the view of her roses from the porch. Doris even provided a big bowl of cold water for Faith.

As they walked through the house, Amelia noticed the gorgeous baby grand piano. "Your home is so beautiful. You have quite the setting out here. Not to mention that stunning piano," remarked Amelia, admiring the porch.

"Ed and I always loved music, and I love to play. Taught piano for years." The smile faded from Doris' face. "I've lived here my entire adult life. I lost my husband a few years ago, and my son came to visit me this week." Tears formed in her eyes. "He says this is too much for me. He's not wrong on that point. It's a struggle to keep up with everything and paying for help is taking a toll. Not to mention the stairs. I took a fall a few months ago, and it was scary."

"I'm so sorry, Doris. Stairs can be such a struggle."

She sighed. "He wants me to sell and move closer to him. He lives in Michigan." After a sip from her glass, she continued, "It wasn't the best visit. He can be bossy and was in rare form. He doesn't seem to understand how much I love it here. The island is my home and was our home. It's where Ed and I had the happiest of times. I can't bear to leave it."

"I wonder if you could find something smaller, more manageable for you here on the island."

She nodded. "I told him I'd see if I can find something and reach out to a realtor. He wasn't happy, and I know he'll keep pressing me to move." She looked across the grassy pasture. "I see his side, of course. It's not easy for him to get away and make the trip here. We're not the most convenient of places. I just know I wouldn't be happy in Michigan."

"I have a friend with a father in real estate. Jack Martin. I could get his number for you."

She smiled. "I've known Jack and Lulu, along with Nate, for years. You're right to recommend him. He's got an excellent reputation." She gazed across the porch. "The idea of moving is just overwhelming."

"I'm sure Jack has all the connections to make that happen if you want help. I bet your son would pitch in, too."

She chuckled. "If I were going to Michigan, he'd be here in a heartbeat. Not so sure if I find something here, but I can cross that bridge when I get to it." She swallowed the rest of her tea. "It's funny, but I don't feel as old as I am. I mean, I realize it when I try to do too much, but overall, I never remember how old I am until I catch a glimpse in a mirror. Since losing Ed, it's been harder. I miss the company. I miss cooking for him. I miss dancing and listening to music. Old people used to talk about how time went by so quickly. Now, I know what they meant."

Amelia's heart broke for Doris. "I hope you find something that works here. I'm sure your son is worried about you and doesn't want anything to happen to you." She took hold of Faith's leash and stood.

"You're a kind soul, Amelia. Thank you for visiting with me and bringing sweet Faith. I can tell you two are fast friends."

Doris walked them to the door and stood on the porch, waving as they left for town and their next deliveries.

This time, Amelia had three recipients who weren't home, so she left their deliveries and noted it, hoping they weren't gone for the weekend. She made sure to save Henry for the last delivery and stopped by Sam's before heading to his house.

She picked up an iced tea and a lemonade and drove the short distance to the neighborhood bordering the small park. Kids were playing baseball, and their cheerful voices and the thwack of the bat hitting the ball carried in the gentle breeze.

Amelia carried the drinks to the door and rang the bell. Henry must have been watching and opened the door within a few seconds. "Amelia, so good to see you. I hope you brought Faith."

"I sure did." She held up the drink tray. "I also stopped and got a lemonade and iced tea. I wasn't sure which one you'd prefer."

His eyes twinkled. "Oh, I like both. We could combine them and have an Arnold Palmer."

"Wonderful idea. I love those, too." She came through the open door. "I'll put these in the kitchen and then get your food box and Faith and be back in a jiffy."

With all the deliveries they'd made, Faith was getting very good at matching Amelia's pace and didn't tug on her leash while Amelia was toting the box of food. She didn't quite trust her furry friend about jumping, so she opted to set the box by the front door and take Faith inside.

Henry was in his chair, with a broad smile, ready for Faith. Amelia walked her over, reminding her to be gentle and with her little bum wiggling, she stood in front of Henry but didn't jump.

He took the leash and winked at Amelia. "We'll be fine."

She retrieved his box and went about stocking his cupboards and fridge before she found two glasses and mixed their afternoon drink.

After placing Henry's drink on the table next to him, she sat in one of the velvet chairs and soaked in the ambience of the room. "This room is so relaxing, and I love your antique furniture."

He gazed at the bookshelf and the rows of photos. "It's just home to me. Nothing special. My wife, Abigail, was the one with the eye for decorating. Most everything you see are pieces she found or bought." He patted the arm of his chair. "Except this chair."

"I love a good recliner." Amelia took a long swallow from her glass.

"You're welcome to take a tour. I kept most everything she loved, except her old piano. It was just too difficult to transport."

"How long have you lived on the island?"

He gazed out the window. "I came here in 1962."

"Wow, I bet you've seen so many changes."

"Yes and no. In some ways, this little island is much the same. That's what I love about it."

She pointed at a wedding photo. "I love this. I assume that's you and Abigail."

He beamed. "Yes. We were married after the war in 1946. My sweet Abigail promised to wait for me and when I came home, lucky to be alive, the first thing I did was marry her."

Amelia's heart warmed as she listened to him and recognized the deep love he held for her.

"We grew up together in a small town in Missouri. After we were married, we both longed to come out west and set our sights on Seattle. We found a cute little house in Queen Anne and made our life there." He pointed at another photo of him holding a little girl by the hand. "We had our daughter Mary. Mary Faith was her name."

She caught the hitch in his voice. "I'm so sorry, Henry. You lost your daughter?"

He nodded and took a handkerchief from his pocket. "I lost Abigail and Mary the same day. They were killed in an accident in 1962."

Amelia gasped. "I'm so very sorry, Henry."

He blotted his eyes. "It was a long time ago, but it still gets to me."

"I, well, uh, I recently lost my daughter and my ex-husband in an accident."

His eyes widened. "My dear, that's something no parent should ever have to endure." He brought his hand to his chest. "My heart breaks for you and is with you."

Tears clouded Amelia's eyes as she took a sip from her drink to soothe the dryness in her throat.

With a crack in her voice, Amelia asked him more about his early days on the island.

"I was quite heartbroken after losing my girls. They were my world. I lost my only brother in the war we both fought in. My parents were still in Missouri. I was utterly alone."

He paused and gazed at the wedding photo on the shelf. "I was working for a construction firm based in Seattle, and they got a contract to build the marina here. I jumped at the chance to go somewhere new and escape the memories and sadness that hung in the air of our house. So, I took the foreman job and after I was here for the better part of a year, I decided it was home."

He gestured to the armoire and the chairs. "Eventually, I sold our house in the city and built this one. I arranged to have all of Abigail's furnishing shipped here and made sure I designed the house to fit them. The passage of time and being here made that easier. I felt like she and Mary were still part of my life. The things they'd touched and loved let them live on with me."

He shook his head and reached for his glass. "It sounds odd when I say it, but that's how I felt. How I still feel."

Amelia nodded. "Believe me, I understand. My ex and I divorced last year, and we sold our house. The house where I'd always lived and Natalie grew up. I had to leave it, too. I couldn't bear the memories. They were suffocating. I moved to a small town on the coast, Driftwood Bay."

She told him more about opening a bookstore and finding a new life only to have it shattered by her recent loss.

"You've been dealt too many hard blows in a very short time, dear. Time has a way of muffling the pain, but it's been over sixty years and sometimes, it still feels like I just lost them. It took me a long time to be able to even talk about them. I applaud you for doing so. I think it helps."

"It does and so does volunteering. My friend here suggested it might help, and she was right. I feel better doing something that has meaning."

She took another sip from her glass. "Did you work in construction your whole career?"

He nodded. "Yes, I stayed with that firm until they ran out of work on the island and moved to another firm, worked there, and when they were bought out, I stuck with the next one. Built lots of the homes here on the island. I could have worked like that anywhere, but this island helped heal my heart, and I never tired of the stunning views I was treated to each day."

He smiled, and the wrinkles around his eyes deepened. "I'm ninety-seven years old, and I've truly enjoyed my life here. With the exception of a trip home when my father became ill and later passed and few ferry rides to the city, I've lived my life here."

He pointed toward the kitchen. "After my dad died, I built a little guest house out back. I have a big lot here and plenty of room. I convinced my mom to come out and live with me. She loved to play the piano, so I made sure to design it with space for that."

"Oh, that's wonderful. I bet she loved that."

He shook his head, and his already slumped shoulders dipped lower. "She never got to see it. A week before she was due to move, she died."

Tears leaked from Amelia's eyes. "Oh, no. That's horrible. I'm so sorry."

"I think she missed Daddy too much. Her heart was broken, and I've always felt a little guilty that I persuaded her to leave the farm. It was what she'd always known. Always loved. I was worried about her and wanted her close. She could have leased out the acreage, but I didn't want her on her own."

Amelia shook her head and reached for a tissue on the small table next to her chair. "You can't blame yourself. You were just trying to do what you thought best. I'm sure your mother knew that."

He smiled and wiped his eyes with his handkerchief. "Her name was Faith. That's why we named our daughter Mary Faith." He reached out and petted the golden dog, who seemed to know he needed her comfort and leaned against his leg, resting her chin on his knee.

As much as she tried, Amelia couldn't stop the flow of tears down her cheeks. This lovely gentleman had suffered unimaginable losses yet was still standing and going strong at ninety-seven. Without knowing it, Henry was an inspiration.

She and Faith spent the entire afternoon with him. Amelia made them grilled cheese sandwiches while he treated her to some of his favorite records, including more Tony Bennett and several from the Glenn Miller Band.

She toured the rest of his house, and he insisted she take a look at the guest house out back. The backyard was even more beautiful and bigger than the front. Roses and all sorts of colorful flowers were tucked into planters around the main grassy area. A curved sidewalk led the way to the guest house, where a bench decorated with colorful pillows sat under the small porch. Hanging baskets of colorful flowers hung along the porch and entryway.

It was painted to match the main house and, like it, was filled with beautiful wood baseboards and crown moulding. It had a small kitchenette, plus a large open living area with another smaller room off it, and a nice-sized bedroom.

Amelia touched the thick moulding around the door and could feel the warmth and love Henry had poured into the space. Her heart ached thinking about the pain he suffered when he lost his mom. The last piece of his family.

She couldn't resist walking across the grass to examine the beautiful plants that made the yard so attractive. The heady scent of roses wafted in the breeze, and Amelia finally tore herself away from admiring the gorgeous pinks and reds in full bloom.

She made her way back inside and found Faith sleeping at Henry's feet. He looked tired, too. It was getting close to the dinner hour.

Henry refused her offer to make him something for dinner but thanked her for making lunch. "Thank you more for spending your afternoon listening to my old stories. It's been lovely to spend it with you, dear." He glanced down at Faith's eyes locked on his. "And with your sweet girl."

"We'll be back on Tuesday. It's the Fourth of July, but we're still delivering. I'll be earlier than usual. Are you going to watch the fireworks or do anything for the holiday?"

He waved his hand. "The senior center is having a picnic and music. I might wander over, but I'm not sure."

"Oh, that sounds fun. I hope you decide to go."

He insisted on walking them to the door. "I need to stretch my legs. Too much sitting today."

As Amelia turned to go, he patted her arm. "I enjoyed our visit, Amelia. I hope you and Faith will come again."

She couldn't resist putting an arm around his shoulder and hugging him. The faint scent of peppermint and spice reminded her of her own grandfather. She closed her eyes and squeezed him tight.

CHAPTER FIFTEEN

On Monday morning, Amelia woke to find Georgia had texted photos from the first weekend of the festival and after Amelia and Faith returned home from their walk, her phone chimed with a video call.

Amelia grinned when she saw it was Georgia. She connected the call and waved at her sister. "This is the best surprise ever."

They had a long visit, shared several cups of tea together over their virtual connection, and Georgia regaled her with accounts of their booming business.

Once again, she'd made pajamas for the goats, which were a huge hit, along with all her beautiful table linens that sold like hotcakes. Georgia lit up when she talked about sharing meals with her sisters and how wonderful it was to spend time with them on the lavender farm.

Amelia smiled. "Sounds like you're having loads of fun. I'm so glad. How's Dale doing?"

Georgia chuckled. "He's enjoying being doted upon by all my lovely sisters. He also insists on helping as much as he can. He does well in the morning, but by the afternoon, he's tuckered out."

After a sip from her cup, Georgia asked, "Enough about me. How are you getting on? I bet Faith is keeping you company."

With a glance toward her best friend, Amelia nodded. "She's the best. I'm so glad I didn't think much and just went with my heart."

"Sometimes, that's the very best thing to do. Speaking of dogs, Suki is having the time of her life here playing with all the dogs and checking on the guests in the shelter. I'm so glad Dale was up to the trip, and we came. When the festival is over, we plan to spend a week or two at the house and then head over to the island. We'll keep you posted on our plans but should be there before September."

"I miss you two, but I've been pretty proud of myself at keeping busy." Amelia expressed how much she loved all of Georgia's friends and how kind they were, inviting her to meals and checking on her. She told Georgia about her new volunteer work and meeting so many nice people, including Henry.

"I knew those ladies would take excellent care of you. I've never had a circle of friends like all of them and miss them. But I love my sisters and seeing all the visitors who come to the farm for the festival. It makes the days go by quickly. I'm so glad Izzy connected you with the food bank. That sounds like a wonderful activity for you. That's something Dale and I could do, too."

Amelia told her about meeting Henry and all he had endured, blinking back tears as she imparted his story. After almost two hours, they finally disconnected and promised to chat again soon.

Georgia always lifted Amelia's spirits, and she had a

spring in her step when she set out for a quick trip to the market. When she and Faith returned, Amelia put together a cranberry cashew salad with pear and apple that was always a hit at gatherings for tomorrow's festivities.

She overestimated and made too much to fit in the pretty serving bowl she found in Georgia's cupboards. After she made the poppyseed dressing, which she planned to take and dress at the celebration tomorrow, she decided to cut up the rotisserie chicken she bought and add it to the excess salad for dinner. It was way too much for one plate, and she added the extra to a container and set out with Faith to deliver it to Noah.

As they left via the back door, Faith's tail wagged in quick arcs. Moments later, Noah and Goose appeared.

He raised his hand in a greeting, and Amelia was surprised when her heart beat a little faster at the sight of him. "Hey, you two. We were just heading to your house to drop off some salad for your dinner." She held up the plastic container.

Goose practically dragged Noah to her back patio, where he and Faith greeted each other with licks to their faces. Noah chuckled. "I sent off my manuscript to my editor, so I thought we'd celebrate with a walk."

"Wonderful," said Amelia. "Join us for dinner." She eyed his frame. He looked even thinner than he had a few days ago.

Noah and Goose followed behind Amelia, and she welcomed them in through the back door. "Ignore the mess but come in and make yourself at home."

She led them into the kitchen with the adjoining dining area. "We can eat in here or on the patio."

Noah looked at the two dogs. "Patio sounds great."

He watched over the dogs while she got their salads and

iced tea on the table. He took his first bite and raised his brows. "That is really good. Thank you again for taking care of me."

She noticed how thin he looked. "I'd say from the looks of you, you haven't been eating enough."

He shrugged. "I tend to forget when I'm writing." He speared another bite of salad. "I also think it's part of the disease. I looked online and found out way more than I wanted to know."

The defeat in his voice made Amelia reach for his arm. "Max's friend will be here soon, and I bet she'll be able to explain things and offer much better advice than Google."

He nodded. "You're right, of course, but it's hard not to get consumed with information."

Amelia opted to change the topic and told him about her experience volunteering and meeting Henry. "His house is filled with vintage things and really is stunning, in a unique way."

She refilled their iced teas and added, "I'm going to see him tomorrow morning and do my best to convince him to go to the senior center for their celebration. He lives just down the street from it. He's such a lovely man."

He grinned at her. "You're a kind person, Amelia. He's very lucky you found him. Much like me. I'm lucky you found me, too."

She blushed and took a long swallow from her glass. "I'm looking forward to the party tomorrow for Sam's birthday at the winery and the fireworks. Jeff said they usually go to his family's resort to watch them, but he's having everyone at their house, since it's a similar view. That way, any of the dogs that might have a fear of fireworks can be in the house."

He nodded. "That's a good idea. Goose isn't a huge fan of the noise."

She patted the top of Faith's head. "We'll have to see how she reacts. I hope Sam is surprised at the shindig Jeff planned at the winery. He told me she's expecting a cookout but has no idea what he put together. She's such a sweetheart and deserves all the love."

"I agree with that. She and Jeff both work hard and do so much to support the community. Not to mention how kind they are to strangers who are here for the summer. She welcomed me from the very first day and let me bring Goose as long as I stayed in the bookstore area."

"They definitely make you feel at home. I'm glad Georgia convinced me to come. Sam and all the others have been just what I needed as I figure things out."

After dinner, they took the dogs for a walk down to the beach. Noah volunteered to rinse and dry them and let them frolic along the shore to their hearts' content.

Amelia used the old beach towel she brought and sat on it, watching Noah and the two dogs, while she enjoyed the comforting rhythm of the waves curling onto the shore.

It made her think of the trip they took when Natalie was little. Ron had a friend at work who had a place in Seabrook. It was idyllic. They had a gorgeous view of the water and a beautiful section of the beach to stroll.

Natalie had loved building sandcastles and playing in the water. Even Ron relaxed and disconnected from work for the week they were there. They had his undivided attention, which was rare. The expectations were high at the firm, and he was in line for a partnership position, so he worked hard, which Amelia always understood.

As much as so many women longed for a high-powered career or enjoyed working, she was happy at home. She loved being a wife to Ron and a mother to Natalie. She was always involved in her school and volunteered for any committee or chaperoning duties that came along.

She gazed out at the water and could almost see Natalie, in her tiny pink bathing suit, darting to the edge of the water and filling her little pail with wet sand.

Regrets plagued her thoughts, and grief made her clutch her chest. If only she would have cherished all those times more. She had no idea how quickly time would pass and her little girl would grow up and leave the nest.

That had been such a difficult time for her and Ron. It didn't help with him losing his mother and then her mother declining. It was too much change in too short of a time. Her world had unraveled, thread by thread.

Now, it was completely gone. There were no more threads to hang onto or try to tie together. All that was left were sweet memories interspersed with the bitterness of regrets.

When she refocused on the present, she noticed Goose and Faith sitting and staring at her. She couldn't help but smile at their gentle faces. As she wiped the tears she didn't remember shedding from her cheeks, Noah walked up to her and put his hand on her shoulder.

"Are you okay?" he asked. His voice filled with concern. "I've been calling out to you."

She blinked several times and looked up at him. "Sorry, I was lost in the past."

"I was going to see if you felt like going into town and getting some ice cream. I'm steering clear of sugar but can make an exception to celebrate finishing up that book. I have one more to do, but with it done, I'm feeling better about it."

Amelia smiled and took the hand he offered her, shaking the sand that worked its way into her shorts and bottom of her white shirt. Noah picked up the towel and shook it clean.

"I'll give them a quick rinse at the house, and then we can go downtown." He called Goose, and they both came running to meet them.

He and Amelia attached their leashes and climbed up the pathway to the road. It didn't take long to get to his patio and rinse both dogs.

With their fur clean and semi-dry, they loaded them into Noah's car and made the trip to Shaw's on Front Street. They ended up parking behind the hardware store where Jeff told them they were always welcome despite his signs that warned parking was for customers only.

They each took a dog and wandered down the street to the ice cream shop. It was packed, and they waited in line, people watching between letting customers pet the dogs.

Soon, they reached the front of the line and walked away with hefty cones. They both opted for the strawberry shortcake and when Amelia took her first bite, she knew she'd be back for more.

They wandered down to the bench Sam had shown her and sat where they had a view of the harbor. The dogs sat in front of them, staring at their ice cream. Amelia giggled as she licked her cone. "Gosh, they make you feel guilty, don't they?"

Noah laughed. "They've perfected the puppy eyes."

As they chatted, she offered to pick up Noah after she finished her food bank deliveries tomorrow. "There's more room in my SUV for the dogs, and Ellie and Blake said to be sure to bring them out to the winery. They've got lots of space for them to play."

"I guess they're technically closed tomorrow, so Jeff said we'll have the whole place to ourselves."

Amelia arched her brows. "I've been wanting to see it, so that will be nice to enjoy it when they aren't so busy."

Noah nodded. "I've only driven by."

"Same. I have to take the road for one of the food bank clients."

"I'm looking forward to it. I need the distraction." Noah sighed and continued to focus on the water. "I think that's part of what had me holed up writing. It's an escape from reality, and I have no time to think. I'm immersed in the story, and that's where I live."

Amelia rushed to lick the ice cream that melted down the side of her cone. "I get that. I think being here on the island is like that for me. It's an escape that lets me dip my toe into reality when I feel like I can handle it, but otherwise it insulates me from it."

"It's a definite escape," he said, taking the last bite of his cone. "Without work, my mind wanders. I find myself longing for the past and regretting so many things. I thought I'd have more time." He shrugged. "Now, I'm not sure I have much of a future, and it's hard to grapple with the things I missed. Well, it's really about my son. I was selfish and now, it's too late."

His voice cracked as he said the last part, and Amelia reached for his hand. She couldn't think of anything to say that would help, so she intertwined her fingers in his and squeezed.

Sadly, there were no words that could take away the pain and agony of loss. Since losing Natalie, she'd come to appreciate those around her who were content to listen without the need to comfort her with words. All she could do was remind him he wasn't alone and that she understood, with the touch of her hand.

He squeezed her hand in return, and they sat with the dogs at their feet and watched the last light of the sky disappear into the ocean.

CHAPTER SIXTEEN

O n Tuesday morning, Amelia and Faith were up early and at the food bank before eight o'clock. Tessa was on hand to help load her SUV, and they set off for their deliveries. When they arrived at Doris' house, Amelia smiled at the patriotic decorations hanging on the railing of her porch and the flag waving in the breeze.

The sound of "Yankee Doodle" being played on Doris' piano drifted from the open screen door. Amelia unloaded her box and carried it up the steps. She paused as Doris shifted into "America the Beautiful" and returned to the SUV to get Faith.

Amelia didn't want to interrupt her playing and waited until Doris finished her song to rap on the door. Minutes later, Doris arrived at the door decked out in red, white, and blue.

"Good morning, Amelia. I'm so sorry. I hope you weren't waiting long. I was practicing for the event today at the senior center."

"We were just waiting until you finished and enjoying the music. You play beautifully."

Doris beamed at the compliment. "Thank you, dear. Music is like therapy for me."

She opened the door wide, so Amelia could tote the box inside while hanging onto Faith's leash.

After she set it on the counter, Amelia turned to Doris. "I'm so glad you're going to the picnic. I recently met a man, Henry Jenkins, and I'm trying to persuade him to go today. He lives down the street from the senior center."

Doris tilted her head. "That name rings a bell. Ed was a plumber so he knew everyone, which is why the name seems familiar. I think I know Henry. I haven't seen him for a long time but tell him to please come. I just recently started playing the piano for them on occasion, and today promises to be one of their best events. Everyone is very nice and friendly there."

Amelia smiled. "Look out for him if you see him. He's a lovely gentleman."

"I will." Doris walked them back to the door. "You two have a Happy Fourth." She waved from the porch. "See you next week."

Amelia loaded Faith, and they set off for the deliveries in town. With it being earlier in the day, she found her clients at home, but she didn't stay long to visit, since she was in a hurry to finish up and get to Sam's party. She also wanted to save her extra time for her last stop at Henry's.

At the stop before Henry's, she rang the bell and didn't get an answer. There was a small car parked in the carport attached to the house. She pressed the bell again and waited, but nobody came.

She checked the delivery list to make sure there wasn't a note on it regarding Mrs. Braxton. Amelia glanced at the carport again and set the box down at the front door. She took a few steps toward the large window to the left of the door and cupped her hands to peer inside.

The curtains were drawn, but she could see through a tiny slit where they met in the middle. As she scanned the room, she stopped moving and gasped. "Oh, no." Mrs. Braxton was lying on the floor.

Amelia rushed back to the door and tried it, but it was locked. She pulled her cell phone from her pocket and dialed 911. Within minutes, the ambulance and police arrived.

They breached the door, and the paramedics hurried to help her.

A police officer stayed with Amelia and asked several questions about when she arrived and what she knew. After several minutes, one of the paramedics came to the door and shook his head. "She's been gone for hours."

Amelia lurched with a sob. She didn't know Mrs. Braxton well but couldn't stop the flood of emotions. The officer put a hand on Amelia's shoulder. "Are you all right? Is there someone I can call for you?"

She nodded and asked that he let Tessa know as he guided her to the SUV where Faith was whining. Amelia reached through the open window and ran her hand over her loyal friend. The officer wrapped a blanket around Amelia's shoulders and gave her a cold bottle of water. He also filled Faith's bowl for her.

"Just sit down and rest for a few minutes. Breathe in and out, slowly."

While Amelia was sipping water and petting Faith, Tessa arrived. She hurried to Amelia's SUV and crouched down in front of her. "Oh, Amelia. I'm so sorry this happened. Are you okay?"

"Just shaken. I feel so bad for Mrs. Braxton. I wish I had gotten here in time to help her."

Tessa shook her head. "The officer told me they thought she passed away very early this morning or late last night. There was nothing you could have done."

Amelia pointed at the box of food the officer had moved from the door. "That's her box."

Tess nodded. "I'll take care of it, and I can finish up your deliveries today. I can have someone drive you home, too."

With a quick shake of her head, Amelia said, "No, I'll be fine. I like to visit Henry, and he's my last one. He loves seeing Faith."

"Only if you're positive you're okay to drive." Tessa narrowed her eyes to assess her.

"Really, I'm fine. I was just shaken initially. I'm good to drive a few blocks to Henry's."

Tessa's forehead creased. "I'll follow you, just to make sure." She held up a finger. "No arguments."

The officer stepped over to check on Amelia, and she signed her statement as to what she witnessed before sliding behind the wheel of her SUV.

She pulled away as the mortuary van was arriving, and a fresh tear slid down her cheek. Her heart ached for Mrs. Braxton's family.

With Tessa following, she made her way to Henry's neighborhood and pulled to the curb in front of his house. Tessa waved and shouted out to call her if she decided she needed a ride home after her last delivery before she drove down the street.

Amelia unloaded Henry's box and carried it up to his front door before she attached Faith's leash. By the time she returned with Faith, Henry was at the door, his hands on his walker, waiting for them.

He smiled at them. "I'm so glad you're here. I was getting worried."

Faith knew the routine and set out for her spot next to Henry's chair, where she sat and waited. Amelia turned from her and said, "We ran into a delay. I'll tell you all about it as soon as I get your box."

Henry maneuvered his walker out of the way, and Amelia carried the box to the kitchen. By the time she unloaded it and peeked into the living room, Henry was in his chair with Faith's head resting on his knee.

She grinned and went back to the kitchen to brew some tea. She needed a cup of hot tea and a conversation with Henry more than anything right now.

With shaking hands, she delivered their tea. Henry reached up to put his hand on hers to steady it. "What's happened, dear?"

She took her chair and related the sad events of the morning. Her voice cracked as she finished the story and plucked a few tissues from the box next to her. "I didn't even really know her well. I'm not sure why I'm so emotional."

Faith moved from Henry's side to Amelia's.

Henry finished a sip from his cup. "In my experience, dealing with a death, any death, so soon on the heels of a monumental loss like you've suffered, often triggers a response that's more about the person you just lost, not necessarily the current loss. It might be like your body hasn't yet healed or dealt with your grief, and then the latest experience tips you over and brings it all back. And then some."

His reassuring words were like a balm that soothed her heart and mind.

"In my experience, that heightened response you feel goes away with distance from your loss. It's too fresh right now.

It's like you're walking around on one leg and learning how to make it work. You're weak, but you're getting by. Then, another blow comes and takes a whack at your one leg. It doesn't take much to knock you down, and your mind goes back to how you came to be standing on only one leg to start with. It happened to me after I lost my mom."

She nodded. "I don't like feeling weak and fragile."

"Nobody does, dear. That's what grief does. It makes one vulnerable. It reminds us of how much we have to lose."

Her forehead creased. "How did you overcome all you've been through?"

He sighed. "It wasn't easy. There were some very dark days. Days I wasn't sure I'd survive. I turned to my faith. I credit a pastor here on the island for helping me the most. He's long gone, but I'll always remember him. He reached out a hand when I needed it most. I found wonderful friends and a family at church. I also kept busy. Like you, I tried to help others, which in turn really helped me."

His eyes rested on Faith. "I made sure I always had a dog. Along with having a true friend by my side, I needed a purpose. A reason to come home and a reason to get up each morning."

A tear leaked from Amelia's eye, and she met Faith's. Her furry roommate was all that and more.

He took a swallow of tea and set his mug back on the side table. "You're going to encounter death, like you did this morning. It's just a natural cycle. But you can insulate yourself from things within your control. For instance, I avoided funerals and memorials after I lost my girls. I didn't do so after I lost Mom, and that was the beginning of a slide into a long period of grief. I felt I had to attend a service of one of the ladies from church, and all that original pain and sadness bubbled out of me, only worse. You have to do what you can to protect yourself because like it or not, you are fragile."

Amelia let her eyes close as his soft tone washed over her. She'd never spent much time with her grandparents. Her parents were older when they adopted her, and her grandparents didn't live nearby, so she only had vague memories of visiting them. Henry was what she always imagined a grandpa to be. Wise, kind, gentle, but honest.

As she sat, resting her eyes, she noticed the soft tune of the music coming from the player. It was more of what she knew as Big Band music.

Her eyes flew open, and she remembered one of the things she wanted to discuss with Henry. "Are you going to the picnic at the senior center today?"

He shrugged. "I'm not sure."

"I met a woman on my route, Doris Taylor. Do you know her? She lost her husband Ed several years ago."

He tilted his head. "That sounds familiar." After a moment, his eyes sparkled. "Ed Taylor. He was a plumber. Good man."

"Anyway, Doris is a gifted pianist, and she's playing music at the senior center. She was practicing this morning, and it sounded right up your alley."

His bushy white eyebrows rose. "Hmm, that sounds promising."

She glanced at her watch. "I've got time to stick around and walk over there with you. I could introduce you to her." She paused and added, "I saw they're grilling burgers and hotdogs, and they've got ice cream for dessert."

His eyes widened. "I never pass up ice cream." He chuckled and looked down at his shirt. "Give me time to change, and I'll take you up on walking across the street. The last thing I want to do is fall, so it limits my activities."

"I understand completely. Don't rush. Faith and I are fine waiting. I might take her in the backyard and let her explore a bit."

"Yes, dear. Please do. Make yourself at home."

He positioned the walker in front of his chair and pulled himself up. Once he was standing, he waited a few moments before heading down the hallway. She waited until the soft thump of his walker against the wooden floor subsided before she led Faith to the backyard.

A high wooden fence enclosed the yard and before releasing Faith, Amelia checked that it was secure, and the two gates were locked. Faith ran and sniffed at all the flowers, her tail wagging with excitement.

Amelia's heart swelled to see her furry friend so happy as she loped from plant to plant and rolled on the grass between dashing to investigate another planter.

The sound of the door opening made Amelia look behind her. Henry stood, dressed in jeans and a button-down shirt with the stars of the American flag on one side and the red and white stripes on the other. He even sported a denim baseball hat embroidered with a flag.

She smiled at his casual look. Each time she'd come to visit, he was wearing trousers and a plaid button-down shirt and depending on the temperature, he often wore a cardigan over it. "You have the perfect outfit for today."

Faith was still busy with her sniffari, and Amelia opted to leave her in the yard while she walked Henry down the street. He double-checked his pocket to make sure he had his keys and cell phone before they set out.

They were slow but steady as they traversed the sidewalk and crossed the street at the corner, where the parking lot was already full at the senior center.

As they approached the entrance, Amelia smiled at the

sound of the piano coming from the building. She recognized the songs as those Doris played this morning.

A man and woman sitting behind a table at the entrance welcomed them. They introduced themselves as Tom and Shirley and the woman made Henry a nametag that she stuck to his patriotic shirt.

Amelia started to object to a nametag, but before she could, Shirley slapped one on her shirt too. She pointed at the open area beyond the entrance. "Just sit anywhere you like. Lunch will be served soon."

They thanked the couple, and Amelia stayed by Henry's side as they entered the main room, decorated with flags and banners. The tables held festive centerpieces, and Amelia scanned the room and smiled when she saw Doris at the piano in the corner.

She hoped Doris was sitting at the table near the piano and guided Henry in that direction. Doris finished up her song as Amelia and Henry stepped to the table. Amelia noticed the white sweater Doris had worn this morning on the back of a chair and pointed at the chair next to it. "How about here, Henry?"

He nodded. "Looks good to me." She helped him position the walker next to him within easy reach and caught Doris' eye.

A woman stepped to the microphone stand near the piano and welcomed everyone to the Fourth of July celebration. Doris slid off the piano bench and stepped to the table. "Hi Amelia, it's so nice to see you."

She put a hand on Henry's shoulder. "I want to introduce you to my friend, Henry Jenkins. He lives just down the street."

Doris stepped closer and extended her hand. "Wonderful to see you, Henry. Your name rings a bell. I think my husband Ed may have done work for you. I did all his books, so I know names, and I think we may have met, but it's been a long time."

He shook her hand and smiled. "A pleasure, Doris. When Amelia mentioned you, I told her I remember Ed. He was a fine plumber. A fine man."

With a quick smile, Doris nodded. "Yes, he was. I miss him."

The woman at the microphone urged everyone to take a seat and promised lunch was on the way. After she pointed out Doris and thanked her for her musical accompaniment, a round of applause erupted.

With her cheeks rosy, Doris waved to everyone and slipped into the seat next to Henry.

Amelia bent down between them. "Henry, I'm happy to come back when you're done and get you home. If you give me your cell phone, I'll put my number in it for you."

He handed her the phone. "Thank you, dear. Are you sure it isn't too much trouble? I hate to have you come back."

"It's no trouble at all." She finished tapping keys on the phone and handed it back to him. "All set."

Doris glanced down at Amelia. "I'm happy to make sure Henry gets home. That would save you a trip. I'm on duty at the piano until the dancing is over, though." She paused and added, "But they're serving ice cream after."

Henry grinned. "That's why I'm here."

They all laughed, and Amelia whispered to him, "I don't mind coming back, so if you want to leave early, just call. Or if you need help."

He patted her hand. "I'll be fine, dear. I'll call if I need you, but I think I'm in good hands with Doris."

Amelia chuckled as she left the two of them chatting and eager for their lunch to arrive.

She hurried back to the house where she picked up Faith and made sure the doors were locked behind her.

With a glance at the clock, she sighed. It was later than she intended, but the extra time with Henry had been well spent. She was so happy to see him and Doris hit it off. She couldn't wait to hear what Henry thought of her.

CHAPTER SEVENTEEN

By the time Amelia pulled up to Noah's house, they were due at the winery. He and Goose were waiting at the curb with her salad for the party, and within minutes, they were on their way.

Noah turned to her as she turned onto the highway. "So, your text said it had been an eventful morning. What happened?"

"I was late getting to Henry's because when I went to deliver at the house before his, I found our client dead."

Noah gasped. "Oh, no. That's awful."

As she drove, she explained about Mrs. Braxton and despite not really knowing her, how she broke down and had a difficult time. Then, she told him about spending time with Henry and how he helped her feel better about it. "He decided to go to the senior center picnic, so I couldn't just leave him. I walked him over there and introduced him to Doris."

He chuckled as she slowed for the turn to the winery. "You're quite the matchmaker."

She grinned. "Not really. Just a friend maker. They both need a friend right now."

She followed the signs for the barn and parked around the back of the building like Blake had asked and pulled into a spot next to Kate's car.

She and Noah hurried to get the dogs and her salad unloaded and darted through the open door. Blake and Ellie greeted them and led them to the end of the barn where everyone was gathered, waiting for Sam and Jeff.

Blake pointed at the dogs. "We've got a nice fenced area set up where the dogs can play. It's just off the other end of the barn. I can show you."

Noah offered to take care of getting Goose and Faith settled in with the others and followed Blake.

Ellie added Amelia's salad to the array of food set up buffet style. She pointed at the ice-filled trough. "Help yourself to something to drink. They should be here in about ten minutes."

While she perused the beverages, Izzy and Kate came up beside her. They were both holding wine glasses. Kate slipped an arm around Amelia's shoulder.

Izzy's eyes narrowed as she gazed at Amelia before speaking. "Tessa told me what happened this morning. Are you okay?"

Kate squeezed her shoulder. "You should have called one of us to get you."

Amelia's heart warmed at their sincere concern. "I'm fine now. I would have called if I needed help."

They both raised their brows at her. Amelia chuckled. "Really, I'm fine. I spent a few hours with Henry, my new friend on my route. He's ninety-seven and filled with wisdom."

Noah and Blake joined the three of them. Noah put his hand on Amelia's arm. "Faith is all set and having a ball with Goose and all the other dogs."

Blake nodded at the trough filled with bottled and canned beverages. "Grab something to drink. Of course, we've got wine up at the bar, too. We want everybody to hide in the corner as much as possible until Sam arrives."

Izzy met Amelia's eye. "I think you could use a nice glass of wine after the day you had." She moved in the direction of the bar, next to the stage set up for a band.

Noah nodded. "I'm not drinking, so feel free to indulge. I can drive us home."

Amelia sighed. She didn't need much convincing and took the glass Izzy brought her and followed the others to the corner that was least visible from the doorway.

Within minutes, two car doors slammed, and then Jeff opened the barn door for Sam. He peered inside. "I wonder where Blake is. He said he'd be in the barn."

Sam took a few steps forward and moments later, the chandeliers overhead came to life and provided a warm glow. Together, with the canopy of twinkle lights strung from the beams, the barn was illuminated enough for the group of friends to jump from the dark corner and yell out a surprise greeting.

With a jolt, Sam brought her hands to her mouth. "Oh, my goodness. You guys." She turned to Jeff and reached for his hand. "You got me."

He grinned. "That was the plan. Happy Birthday." He grabbed her around the waist and dipped her, then kissed her.

Everyone cheered and clapped.

Blake and Ellie directed the guests to the buffet table and as everyone made their way, the band played softly.

Noah and Amelia stepped in line behind Kate and Spence. They chatted while they filled their plates with all the wonderful side dishes everyone brought and selections from the platters of food Jeff ordered from Lou's restaurant. His famous crab cakes, lobster macaroni and cheese, ribs, pulled pork sandwiches, and fish tacos were on the menu.

Amelia hadn't eaten all day and was starving. She loaded her plate, and she and Noah sat at the table where they left their drinks. Soon, Kate and Spence joined them. Moments later, Dean and Rebel arrived.

He apologized for being late. He'd arrived in Seattle late last night after his flight from Florida. He joined them with his plate piled high with food and sighed as he slid into a chair. "The ferries are super busy today. I didn't think about that, and we had to wait longer than usual."

Rebel took his cue and rested with his head under Dean's chair.

Kate smiled at Dean. "We're just so glad you're here. How's Jess doing with that new grandson of hers?"

He grinned. "She's over the moon, of course. It's been great for her to be there and enjoy her family. She's sorry to miss the fun here, though."

"I'm sure you'll be busy capturing photos of the fireworks tonight," said Kate.

He nodded. "Yeah, they're always spectacular over the water. I'll be working nonstop these next few weeks until Jess returns. It's the busy season."

Regi and Nate joined them, along with his parents Jack, and Lulu. Jack put a hand on Dean's shoulder. "Good to see you back on the island, Dean. We've got a pile of work waiting for you at the office." He chuckled as he put his plate down at the chair next to Dean's.

Dean grinned. "I was just telling them I'll be working around the clock to catch up for taking time off."

Jack patted Dean's shoulder. "You deserved it, but we're so glad you're back."

Nate introduced his parents to Noah, and Lulu couldn't resist peppering him with questions about being an author.

As they finished the meal, Jeff took the stage and stepped to the microphone. "Thank you all for coming and keeping the surprise for my lovely wife a secret. Thanks to Blake and Ellie for the use of their beautiful barn venue. My favorite band is here and will play for us; I never pass up a chance to listen to them or dance with my sweetheart."

He smiled at Sam. "Blake and Ellie gave us full run of the property, so feel free to stroll the grounds, play with the dogs, and enjoy the outdoor pavilion. We'll open the back doors, and you'll be able to hear the music and dance outdoors, too. Most of all, enjoy yourselves, and remember to wish my girl the happiest of days. You're all invited back to the house to watch the fireworks tonight and join us for birthday desserts."

Jeff turned to the band, who at his cue, played "Happy Birthday," and everyone joined in to sing to Sam. As Jeff stepped from the stage, the band played a country tune, and he and Sam took to the dance floor. Spence and Kate soon joined them, along with Jack and Lulu.

As Amelia was watching them, Max came up behind Noah. "How are you two doing?"

Amelia patted her midsection. "Stuffed, but it's wonderful."

Max laughed. "Yes, we rarely go hungry around here." He bent closer to Noah. "I heard from Jan, and she'd like you to get some specific tests and imaging done before she arrives next month. She wants to have everything she needs to help you when she's here. It would require a trip over to Seattle, but I could arrange everything and go with you. It might mean an overnight, but Sam's got a great friend who lives there, and we can stay with her if need be."

Noah nodded, and Amelia noted the flash of trepidation in his eyes. "Sure, that makes sense. I'd appreciate it if you're sure it's no trouble for you."

Max grinned. "Not at all. I'm happy to do it. Do you have a preference on days that work best for you?"

Noah looked at Amelia. "Could you take care of Goose while I'm away?"

"Of course. No trouble at all. Tuesdays would be the only bad day of the week because of the food bank."

"Right," he said, nodding. "Sounds like any day but Tuesday. I'm open and flexible, so whatever works best for you."

Max stood taller. "Okay, I'll get on the phone tomorrow to see what I can arrange and let you know."

"Thanks, Max. I appreciate all your help." Noah shook his hand, and Max wandered back to his table.

Despite not being a dancer, the band played "Man! I Feel Like a Woman!" and succeeded in getting Amelia to join in the girls line dancing to it, with one of the vocalists leading the dancing.

All the men cheered and whistled as the ladies laughed, and Amelia, despite some missteps and nervousness, enjoyed herself.

After that, the band urged the men to come up and join in for another line dance. This time it was "Boot Scootin' Boogie" and despite his initial reluctance, by the time they finished, Noah was smiling.

Amelia led the way back to their table. "I think I'm going to check on the dogs. Do you feel like a walk? I'd like to see the rest of the property."

Noah nodded. "Sure, I think walking is safer than dancing." He chuckled, and they made their way outside.

Faith was sprawled out with her head against Goose, and the other dogs were also lounging. They were all spent from their hours of romping and playing together. Noah took the two leashes he'd left hanging off the gate and attached them, which made all the other dogs snap to attention, no doubt thinking an adventure was on tap.

He handed Amelia their leashes while he locked the gate behind him. "We'll be right back," he assured the others, who were tilting their heads with their ears pricked.

They wandered along the pathway that led back to the main building and let the dogs run free. Although reluctant to let Faith run, Noah assured her Goose had excellent recall, and Faith followed him around like the proverbial puppy.

They romped in the green pasture that covered the ground, stopping to sniff at weeds and wildflowers, while Noah and Amelia strolled near them. As they walked, Noah released a heavy sigh. "Talking to Max earlier makes my situation seem real. I tend to escape into my manuscripts and drown out the real world."

Before Amelia could respond, he stumbled, and she reached for his arm, which helped to steady him before he fell. He shook his head with disgust. "Another reminder of the reality of my situation. Huntington's is primarily a movement disorder. That's what made me see the doctor initially. Way too many tumbles, stumbles, and falls."

She kept hold of his upper arm as they continued to walk along the path. "I don't have much to offer. I do think your plan to meet with Max's doctor friend sounds like the best option. I can also assure you that whatever the outcome, you're not alone. I understand that fear of facing the unknown by yourself and no matter what, I'll be there for you." She squeezed his arm. "I know everyone else in that barn will be, too."

He whispered, "Thanks, Amelia. That means so much."

She kept her arm linked in his. She would do all she could to support him through what she suspected would be a difficult time. She'd only done a cursory bit of research into the disease and from what she learned, there was little hope for those diagnosed.

Looking into that abyss alone wasn't something he would have to do. She would make sure of it.

CHAPTER EIGHTEEN

In spite of the fun and late evening they had at the winery and the spectacular fireworks at Sam's house, Amelia and Faith were up early. They picked up Goose from Noah's house and met Izzy and Sunny for a walk. Dean had taken over caring for Ruby and was staying at Jess' house with her, so she didn't join them this time.

As the three dogs walked, their tails swishing in unison, the ladies' conversation centered on the surprise party and how much they'd enjoyed themselves at the fireworks party at Sam's. As they set out for their second trip around the loop, Izzy said, "I love that view they have. I've decided having a friend with a house on the water is even better than having one myself." She chuckled. "They, along with Linda and Max, are always so generous when it comes to hosting all of us."

Amelia nodded. "You've all been so wonderful and welcoming to me. I was a bit skeptical when Georgia said she had to leave, and my first instinct was to leave, too. Now, I'm so glad I stayed. It's been the perfect place to spend time and try to heal from the pain of losing Natalie."

"I don't think you'll ever be without that pain. I say that based on watching Kate struggle even after so long. It's no comparison to your grief but dealing with my own daughter Mia and our estrangement, I understand that void in your heart. Being constantly rejected and having no relationship with her, it feels like I don't even have a daughter. I struggled with that for a long time. It's one of the main reasons I moved here."

As they rounded the last corner and approached Izzy's yard, she sighed. "It hurt too much to be close to her. Within her reach. Mia is a master at doing anything in her power to hurt me. Just when I think I can trust her or things are better, she opens another trap door underneath me. In my mind, I think of her as gone. As I said, it's different from what you're dealing with, but I have an inkling of those feelings of coming to terms with the end of something you thought would last forever. I had so many dreams for our relationship, and I finally had to accept the fact that it will never happen. I had to let her go, which broke my heart."

Her voice hitched and betrayed her sadness. Izzy, who was usually so strong and had a solution to every problem, had a vulnerable heart. Her sunglasses hid her eyes, but Amelia suspected they were glinting with tears.

Amelia stopped at the edge of Izzy's yard. "I'm so sorry, Izzy. It's hard to escape the sadness that so often plagues motherhood. I thought if I could just get through the horribleness of an empty nest, everything would be okay. I'd eventually recover from the divorce, and I thought I'd always have my girl, no matter what. Then, in the blink of an eye, she was gone."

A tear slid from under Izzy's glasses. "Being a mom is the hardest job I've ever had. I've never failed at much, but I often feel like an utter failure as Mia's mom. I'd also be lying if I told you it gets easier. There are times it's easier, and then there are days when it's all I think about, and I can't escape the thoughts. I'm always in awe of Kate, because she, like you, has a permanent loss, and yet she thrives and has rebuilt her life. I just know you can't give up. Kate's a good example of that strength mothers have that allows them to carry on in the harshest of realities."

She swiped at the wetness on her cheek. "You remind me of Kate. You have the same inner strength and will. I know it isn't easy, but I know you'll overcome this." She reached out and hugged her. "I hate to leave on such a downer, but I need to get moving. I've got a meeting downtown today."

"I'll see you tomorrow morning. Noah's busy working, so we're on our own."

Izzy waved goodbye as she hurried across to her patio.

As horrible as it was to lose Natalie, Amelia couldn't imagine her being here and not wanting any part of Amelia's life. Her heart hurt for Izzy.

She and Faith dropped Goose at home, gave him breakfast, and left him to rest. The house was still as quiet as it was when she picked Goose up to walk. She suspected Noah worked late into the wee hours.

With Noah intent on getting as much done on his next book as he could manage in the next few weeks, Amelia focused on a new project.

After breakfast, she loaded Faith into her SUV and drove to town. Yesterday, she'd forgotten to check Jess' library, so they stopped there first and restocked it. Then, they dropped by Sam's, picked up some iced drinks, and headed over to Henry's for a surprise visit.

When they pulled to the curb, they saw one of Linda's

nursery trucks parked and a team of workers in Henry's yard. She rang the bell, and Henry's face lit up when he came to the door. "Oh, two of my favorite people."

He opened the door wider, and Amelia guided Faith to the place she liked next to Henry's chair. She put one of the Arnold Palmer's on the table next to it and took a sip from the other one.

Once Henry was settled, she took her seat. "We had to run an errand, and I thought we'd stop by to see how the picnic went yesterday."

"It was surprisingly good. The food was excellent, and the ice cream was even better." He grinned as he sipped from his drink. "Mmm, that's good."

"How did you get on with Doris?"

"Oh, she's lovely. Plays the piano beautifully. I enjoyed listening to her repertoire of patriotic songs. She played on until the end of the event, so I didn't get home until late in the afternoon."

"I'm glad you had a good time."

She took a long sip from her drink and sighed. "I had a thought. I just want you to think about it and see what you think."

"Sure," he said, reaching down to pet Faith's head.

"I'm not sure if Doris told you, but her son wants her to sell her place and move to where he lives. She doesn't want to leave the island, but her place is big, and I think he's right that it's too much for her. She's very spry and seems to handle it, but I think he fears she works too much, and it's two stories, so not ideal for someone her age."

He nodded. "She didn't mention her son and told me she was talking to Jack about selling her place. She didn't seem very eager though."

"Right. I think she has lots of memories there. Practically, she understands her son's concerns, but her heart isn't ready. She doesn't want to leave the island. It's her home."

The wrinkles in Henry's forehead deepened. "I understand that."

She smiled. "I knew you would. Listening to her got me thinking. I wondered if you might consider letting her move into your guest house. I know it's a big ask, but I think it might be a great solution for both of you. She could help around the house with meals, shopping, errands. She loves to garden. Not sure that she could do the mowing, but she has gorgeous flowers she's always tending when we visit. You could look out for each other. You also have the same tastes in music."

His eyes widened. "Wow, that's unexpected. I thought you might be going to ask me to look after Faith." He chuckled. "What does Doris think about this idea?"

With quick shakes of her head, Amelia said, "Oh, I haven't even mentioned it to her. It was just an idea I had the other day, and I wanted to get your take on it first. She may not be interested at all. I just have a feeling her place will sell quickly, and she'll have to come up with a place to live, or her son will insist she move in with him." She sighed. "I know she doesn't want that."

"Let me think about it. I can see the up side, but I'm just so used to being alone, and I'm pretty set in my ways." He paused and added, "She's very nice, and you're right about our shared love for music. She's also an excellent driver. She insisted on driving me home yesterday. She's quite capable."

Amelia suppressed a laugh. "I'm glad to hear it, and I understand you need to think about it, Henry. I appreciate you considering it. If you decide against the idea, no worries. Doris will never know."

"I'll definitely think about it. I admit the idea of a bit of companionship doesn't sound bad." He cleared his throat. "I also wanted to invite you to attend church with me Sunday morning. Are you up for a nine o'clock service?"

She couldn't resist his smile. "I'd love to go. I can pick you up if you like, and you can come to brunch at my house afterward. That's non-negotiable."

His wide smile let her know he was thrilled at the invitation. He chatted more about the little church he attended and how he only wished they had a piano player as talented as Doris.

Amelia sipped her drink and opted to let the idea she posed about Doris percolate with Henry. She didn't want to pressure either of them, but it seemed they could both use each other at this time in their lives, and she hoped her idea would work.

Thursday morning when Amelia returned Goose to Noah's house, she found him in the kitchen at the stovetop amid the inviting aroma of bacon. He greeted her with a warm smile.

He pointed at the pan on the stove. "I was hoping you could stay for breakfast."

Amelia nodded. "Smells delicious. I'd love to."

She fed the dogs while he finished cooking. While the dogs lounged, Amelia and Noah dug into the cheesy goodness of the scramble he made along with strips of bacon. He gestured to her plate. "I apologize for not having toast. I'm still trying to eliminate bread from my diet."

"No need to apologize. This is delicious."

"I wanted to tell you Max arranged my appointments for next week. We go over Wednesday afternoon, and my appointments start early on Thursday morning. He arranged for us to stay with Sam's friend Becky and her husband."

"That's great news."

He shrugged. "I'm trying to have a positive attitude."

"I'm sure it's scary, but you'll have Max with you, and he's such a calm person. The perfect one to have there."

"That's true. I'm beyond grateful to him. I've just been thinking about things."

She sucked in a breath. "I know what too much thinking can do."

He grinned. "Exactly." He took a sip from his water glass. "With this disease hanging over my head, my priorities are realigned. For years now, I've told myself I don't need anything beyond my writing. My life, the one I cobbled together after my divorce, was good enough. I escaped dealing with the loneliness by sitting in front of my computer and writing other people's stories."

Amelia poured herself more tea. "That part sounds fascinating and ideal to me. I just love books, and reading is such a wonderful escape."

"It's much the same with writing. I almost become the character when I'm working on a book, especially a series like I am now."

"That's why your books are such excellent reads."

He smiled at the compliment. "The author in me loves that. I'm more worried about the other part of me. Just Noah. For the first time in a very long time, I meet a wonderful woman, someone I feel a strong connection with, an instant bond, and I have no future to offer her. I can only promise things will get worse." He smirked. "Although words come easily for me on my keyboard, in real life, not so much."

Her pulse quickened at his heartfelt confession. She

reached her hand across the table to his. He squeezed her hand. She smiled at him and sighed. "I have to admit, I feel some of those same things. I've never even thought about another relationship after the divorce. I used my move and bookstore to distract myself from it and the fact that Natalie was out of the house and in college, and like you, immersed myself in that project to distract myself from the loneliness."

She ran her finger across the edge of her napkin. "Then, my reality took a turn for the worst. Despite the connection and enjoying my time with you, I keep pushing those feelings away. I don't trust myself right now. I'm in such a weird place, and you're only here for the summer. I'm only here until I can face going back home. It doesn't exactly spell stability."

He continued to hold her hand. With a slow grin, he said, "I guess we're two of a kind. Lost, uncertain, a bit broken, in my case, very flawed. I love those attributes in my characters, but in real life, not so fun."

"I meant what I said at the winery. You don't have to face anything alone."

"That means so much, Amelia. Having you and Max really helps. I was dreading my appointment in September, and I think this will be better for me to find out now and come up with a plan while I've got people to support me. I'm not great at asking for help and have zero friends in Oregon."

"I think you're in a situation similar to mine. Everything I thought was permanent is gone. I feel untethered. If not for Georgia and the bookstore, I wouldn't have an anchor. It's unnerving to face the future with everything wrong. I can't even think about the future most of the time. We're both in a valley right now. One that requires us to take things one step at a time."

He nodded. "I'm also not good at that. I'm a planner by

nature. I think ahead and normally, I find that comforting. Now, it's downright frightening. I'm waiting for the day to come when I can no longer concentrate to write or when my fingers won't work like they do now. It's bad enough to think about the physical problems, but the psychological ones scare me to death."

"I think you'll have more answers when you can speak with Max's friend. Then, when you know more and are up to it, you've got me and a great group of very caring people here who I know will pitch in and help and do whatever they can."

He reached for his glass. "I don't think I can go back to Oregon. I have nobody to rely on there. I've been wanting to sell Mom's place anyway but wasn't sure where to go. Those ideas went on the backburner the minute the doctor told me what he thought. Now, with a little time, I think I need to plan on moving. It's just a matter of where, and it needs to be somewhere I have access to the medical services I'll need."

"If Max's friend can treat you long distance, which it sounds like she consults with patients all over the country, it might not matter as much."

"True. The other thing weighing on me is my son. I need to tell Will, once I know what's going on. It will be up to him to get tested, of course. I haven't been the best dad, and it kills me to think the one thing I'll give him is this horrible disease." His shoulders slumped. "Then, I need to tell Tanya. She'll be upset if I don't tell her before Will, but he's an adult, and I'm just dreading having that conversation with her at all."

"It might be easier if the doctor explains it to both of them. I'm sure, if she confirms the diagnosis, she would be willing to help you do that."

He brought her hand closer to him and kissed the top of it. "That's what I needed. A voice of reason. That's a great idea. I'm sure they'll both have questions I won't be able to answer."

"Maybe you and the doctor could do a video chat with both of them at the same time?"

"That's a possibility. I just know if I tell Tanya first, she won't give me a chance to tell Will. She'll call him or drive over to his place and get in the middle of it. It's not something I'm looking forward to telling either of them but especially Will. He doesn't deserve this."

She moved her hand from his and patted his arm. "One step at a time. Remember?"

He nodded. "Yeah, it's just hard to do. From what Max said, she'll be here the last week in July, so not much longer to wait. Then, I'll have to tell my agent and editor." He shook his head. "I'm not looking forward to that either."

"It sounds like you're going to fulfill your contract early, so that should help. I'm sure the doctor will give you more insight into how your work might be impacted. Would you be able to survive, financially, if you had to stop writing?"

He frowned and after a few moments, nodded. "Yes, my royalties are substantial. I just don't know how sales would be impacted if I stopped altogether. The publisher pushes my books because I'm producing, but if I have to stop, sales would take a hard hit. I'd still be fine. I've invested my royalties and get retirement from the government. I also don't have any bills."

"That's good news, then. One less thing to worry about, at least in the short-term. Georgia helped me deal with the overwhelming feeling I had by making me focus on the immediate, rather than wandering too far into the future. I'm lucky to have someone I trust managing the bookstore and taking care of things for me."

He leaned back in his chair. "Thanks for listening, Amelia.

I've been struggling with my feelings ever since that first day we met. I know I haven't been the best company lately, especially with trying to cram in all my writing. I'll feel better when I'm done with this last book, and then I won't have anything on my plate author-wise."

"I know you'd rather not deal with all the medical stuff while you're writing, but I do think you'll feel better when you can get answers from Max's friend. I know when I don't have all the information, I can go to the worst-case scenario very quickly. Facts and a plan will help you."

"Not to mention a very wise and beautiful woman who takes care of my sweet dog. I truly appreciate you, Amelia. I so wish things were different."

She smiled at him. "Let's make a pact not to stress about us. You need to focus on your writing and getting through your tests. That's it for right now. Once July ends, and you get answers, we'll know more and can talk again. For now, just know I care about you and will be here, no matter what."

She gathered their plates and silverware, Noah following suit and as soon as he took care of the pans on the stove, he came up behind Amelia and embraced her while she stood at the sink. "Thanks for putting up with me and taking care of Goose. We both appreciate you more than you know." He kissed the top of her head.

She didn't trust her voice and didn't want him to see the tears in her eyes. As much as she cared for Noah, she wasn't sure she could face another loss. She wanted to be brave for him, and she would like nothing better than a future with someone like him. If his diagnosis were right, she wasn't sure her heart could handle the risk.

CHAPTER NINETEEN

Saturday arrived, and Amelia drove to town to make her food bank deliveries. She found Doris working in her yard, her wide brimmed hat atop her head. She waved as soon as Amelia parked and invited her and Faith to join her on the porch for a lemonade break.

Faith rushed to the big bowl of cold water and slurped at it while Amelia took the box into the house. When Amelia returned, she offered to pour from the pitcher, while Doris petted Faith. "I talked to Henry a couple of days ago and was happy to hear he had a great time at the picnic. Thanks for taking him home."

Doris' sky-blue eyes sparkled as she smiled. "He's a delight, and we share a love of music and ice cream." She winked. "It was a good day."

"I don't think he gets out much. His mobility is an issue, and I can tell he's worried about falling."

Doris took a long swallow from her glass. "Yes, I picked up on that. He was very careful when we walked to my car. He's got such a lovely home. He told me he built it."

"I love all the wood trim and with his vintage furnishings, it's quite cozy."

Doris stared at her front yard. "I talked to Jack about listing the house to see what he thought. He gave me a price that's way more than I imagined. The thing is, I'm not really interested in the money, but I know this place is too big for me."

She sighed. "I'm just not sure it makes sense for me to buy something else. I know when I die, my son will just sell it. He has no interest in the island, and Jack suggested I might find a rental or a condo instead of buying a house." She glanced over at the flowers blooming along the walkway. "I'd miss having a bit of yard, though. I love flowers." She shrugged. "I don't know what to do. I've never been great at making decisions. Ed was the boss around here."

Amelia hadn't heard anything more from Henry about her idea but was happy to know Doris hit it off with Henry. It was clear Doris was struggling with everything selling her house would bring. "I was thinking about having a brunch party tomorrow. Henry invited me to church and after, I'm making brunch. Would you be able to join us at my place? Well, my sister's place."

Doris rewarded her with a slow grin. "That sounds lovely. I play the piano at my church, but I could be there by noon."

"Perfect." Amelia gave her the address and made sure Doris had her cell number before she and Faith wandered back to her SUV. "I'll see you tomorrow."

Refreshed from their lemonade and water break, Amelia and Faith set out for town to complete their route.

When they arrived at Henry's, Faith bounded up to the front door, while Amelia toted Henry's box. He was waiting and as soon as he opened the door and stepped to the side, Faith made her way to his chair.

After Amelia unloaded everything in the kitchen, she brewed a pitcher of iced tea and let it cool while she visited with Henry. He made sure to remind her to pick him up no later than eight forty-five in the morning. He didn't want to be late.

She promised to be there early before she wandered back to the kitchen to pour the tea over ice.

After Henry took a sip, he said, "I've been thinking about what you proposed with Doris." He paused for a few moments. "I actually think it's a good idea. I just want to be clear it would be a platonic situation. I'm too old for complicated, and I don't want her son getting the wrong idea."

Amelia suppressed the urge to giggle. He was beyond cute and so serious. "Of course. I never intended it to be anything more than a roommate type of situation. Just friends."

He nodded. "In that case, yes, provided Doris is under the same understanding, and she informs her son."

"Got it," said Amelia, with a serious nod. "She's actually coming to brunch at my place tomorrow after church, too. She doesn't get done until noon but will come out right after. We can have a chat about it and see how she feels. I haven't broached the subject with her at all."

He nodded and sipped his tea. "I'm sure the guest house could use a bit of sprucing. I have a cleaning lady come every couple of weeks for the house but haven't touched the guest house in years."

"I can take care of that for you. No problem."

He chuckled. "I'm beginning to think you're my guardian angel." His eyes went to Faith, resting at his feet. "I should say angels."

Faith raised her head and met his eyes. Her lips lifted into a smile.

He laughed and grinned at the sweet dog.

On Saturday night, after she and Faith got home from spending the rest of the afternoon at Henry's, Amelia put together an egg casserole and a French toast dish that she could bake in the morning. She stayed later than she had planned at Henry's after she volunteered to clean the guest house and get it ready in case Doris wanted to take a look at it tomorrow.

It was dusty and needed a good cleaning. She hauled out Henry's vacuum and between it and several dust cloths, she had it gleaming by the time she left. Her shoulders were even a little sore from all the overhead work of making sure the ceilings and walls were clean and free of cobwebs. She had a busy day and turned in earlier than usual, exhausted.

As she contemplated sleep, with her loyal dog next to her, she realized today was a first. The first day since losing Natalie that she hadn't thought of her until bedtime. It made her both happy and sad.

The week had been busy, and, along with her volunteer work, she received an email from Bob letting her know Ron's life insurance policies had paid out, and he'd had them wire it directly to her account. The amount was substantial and would allow her to pay off the bookstore with plenty left.

It made her feel sick when she thought about it too much. Bob assured her Ron would want her to spend the money and not agonize over it. He'd want her to have a full and happy life. She wished she could trade it all and get Natalie back. And, Ron, too. The money would make her life easier, no doubt, but it meant little compared to her family.

Bob offered to put her in touch with a financial advisor if she wanted to invest any of it and promised to keep in touch. She appreciated his help and kindness. Despite her business degree, she'd never had to deal with financial stuff during her marriage. Buying the house and bookstore in Driftwood Bay was her first solo acquisition. She had enough proceeds from her share of the divorce settlement to buy her small house in Driftwood Bay but had to finance the bookstore. It was a leap of faith but something she had to do for her own sanity.

She expected her love of the store would return when she went home, and the pain of her grief wasn't so fresh and wrapped up in it. It had been something she dreamed of for so long.

She found staying busy and helping others like Doris and Henry fulfilling, and it definitely channeled her energy and gave her a purpose. Along with that, she truly liked visiting with Henry and Doris. She hoped her idea would work, and neither of them would feel any pressure, but instead, they would find friendship and comfort in each other.

A tear slipped onto her pillowcase as she mourned for the daughter she wished she could call. She would get a kick out of Amelia's friend-making scheme. Amelia would give anything to hear her laugh again or see her roll her eyes at her. Natalie was the apple of her grandma's eye and as she closed her eyes, Amelia imagined her beloved daughter and her mother together. It comforted her to think of them happy to have each other, looking down on her.

Sunday morning dawned and when Amelia bounded out of bed an hour before their usual time, Faith opened one eye and then shut it.

She wasn't an early riser and made Amelia laugh at the way she lounged in bed in the mornings.

Amelia threw on her walking clothes, brewed coffee, and got to work cutting up fruit for a salad. Once done with that, she laid out bacon strips on parchment-covered baking sheets, so they'd be ready to pop in the oven after church.

She hauled out Georgia's slow cooker and went about cutting up potatoes, onions, and peppers. She added everything to the pot and set it to cook on low. The recipe she found online this week promised potatoes with crispy outsides and creamy insides for little effort. She was a skeptic but hoped it worked.

With her prep done, she set the table, adding a place setting for Noah who'd promised to come to brunch and meet both of her new friends. He was still absorbed with his writing, but with only the one book left to finish, he was more relaxed and willing to slide in a few outings each week.

When Amelia looked up from doing the dishes, Faith was resting on the floor below the hook for her leash. She was ready for their morning walk.

Amelia still needed to shower and get ready, but a quick glance at the clock reassured her. She had time for one loop, and Faith would be overstimulated today, so she'd need the exercise.

It was a quiet morning with nobody out walking yet. They had the place to themselves and made quick work of the trail around the golf course. As they were nearing home, the whir of a golf cart approaching made Amelia look behind them.

Max was at the wheel, with Dean and Rebel riding with him.

They both hollered out a greeting as they drove by, and Amelia waved and smiled. Noah mentioned Max had invited him to golf next Friday when they got back from Seattle. Sounded like the guys had a golf morning organized, and Dean and Max were getting in some practice.

Once home, with Faith fed her breakfast, Amelia dashed to the shower. She hadn't been to church for a long time and hadn't brought many clothes with her but settled on a cheerful polka-dot sundress with a sweater.

At eight fifteen, Amelia made sure the doors were locked and coaxed Faith to her bed with a cookie. "I'll be right back, Faith. Henry is coming to visit."

At the sound of their new friend's name, Faith's ears perked. "You be a good girl." Amelia hoped she would sleep and not get scared on her own. She hadn't left her alone for more than an hour and didn't want to come home to a mess.

Henry was at the door waiting, wearing a jacket and tie with his usual khaki pants, when she arrived. She helped him maneuver the ramp and loaded his walker into the back of her SUV. He gave her directions to the church, which was off the road that she took to get to the golf community.

The small building was tucked off the road behind a row of trees. It looked more like a house than a church, except for the paved parking lot. As she pulled into a spot near the entrance, she turned to Henry. "Do you drive yourself normally?"

He shook his head. "No, usually the pastor picks me up. I hung up my keys last year."

She retrieved his walker, and they took slow steps toward the entrance. Amelia realized the building was a house with a large room attached to one end. She helped him to the door, where a gentleman opened it for them. "Morning, Henry," he said.

"Morning, Walter. This is my friend Amelia."

The older gentleman, wearing a suit and tie, shook her hand. "Welcome."

Amelia let Henry lead the way, and he chose a chair on the end near the front of the sanctuary, saying hello to a few ladies already seated. It was a small space, with only about twenty chairs set up for the service.

As the pastor took to the pulpit, Amelia noticed there were only about a dozen people in the congregation. Henry leaned over and whispered, "We're an old congregation and have lost so many. There aren't many of us left."

The pastor, a man who looked to be in his late forties, smiled and welcomed everyone. He led them in several hymns, all classic ones Amelia remembered from her youth.

His message was about trials and struggles. He read several passages from Job and highlighted that those who know God, while they grieve, always have hope. They are never alone and can find comfort in prayer and scriptures. He also reminded them of times they would go through darkness, looking for a light, when in fact they might be the light for others.

His words touched Amelia's heart and as the service closed with hymns and a prayer, she dabbed at her eyes. The pastor left them with a verse from Jeremiah that promised a future of hope.

As the small group sang the last chorus of a hymn, the pastor made his way back and stood at the door to greet everyone as they left. His smile widened when Henry and Amelia stepped forward. "So happy to see you this morning, Henry."

"Pastor John, this is my friend Amelia. The one I told you about who has the dog and delivers my food boxes."

The pastor extended his hand. "So happy to meet you, Amelia. Henry is one of the best." He lowered his voice. "He might just be my favorite."

Amelia giggled. "Your secret is safe with me. He's my favorite, too."

Henry chuckled and reached out to pat Amelia's arm. "This one, she's a definite keeper. Pastor John says that only because I'm the oldest original parishioner. I started coming to this church decades ago. They met in the park down by the harbor for years because they didn't have a building. I've outlived everyone else."

Pastor John nodded. "Yes, I'm the newbie of the group. I've only been here for two years."

Henry turned to Amelia. "Our previous pastor passed away. We hit the jackpot with John and his family."

Pastor John smiled at him. "Amy is home today with the kids. They're under the weather."

"Sorry to hear that. I hope they feel better soon." Henry tilted his head toward the parking lot. "Amelia is hosting brunch today, so we better get a move on."

The pastor smiled at them. "Sounds wonderful. I hope you'll join us again, Amelia. Henry speaks very highly of you, which is a huge compliment."

She took hold of Henry's arm. "Thank you. I enjoyed your message and am a huge fan of Henry's."

Pastor John wished them a good day and turned to greet the next parishioner.

As Amelia started the engine, she turned to Henry. "Do you need to stop back at your house for anything, or are you good to head out to my place now?"

"I'm ready. I don't need a thing."

She got back to the main road and made the short trip to the turn at the golf community. She pulled into the driveway of Georgia's house and hurried to the back to get Henry's walker. He admired the neighborhood as they made their way up to the front door.

The moment Amelia opened it, Faith's nose appeared in the crack, and she used it to open the door wider, her tail on the vibrate setting. Amelia went in first, urged Faith to step away, and coaxed her to her cot where she could relax and get out from under Henry's feet.

He smiled as he took in the space. "What a wonderful place you've got."

"I'm just a guest. This is all Georgia's, but I agree. It's perfect." She led him to a recliner, and he settled into the soft leather.

"You relax here, and I'll bring you something to drink. Faith will keep you company."

After Amelia checked the slow cooker and added the egg dish to the oven to bake, she returned with a glass of iced tea for Henry and found him dozing, with Faith resting at his feet.

She smiled and tiptoed away, hoping that with Henry onboard with her roommate idea, they'd be able to convince Doris.

CHAPTER TWENTY

A few minutes after noon, Faith rushed to the front door, her tail wagging. Amelia followed and waved at Doris and Noah, who arrived at the same time. Amelia hurried outside to help Doris, while Noah led Goose into the house.

In a blue dress that matched her eyes, Doris greeted Amelia with a hug. "I've got a dessert in the cooler in the back of the car."

"Oh, you didn't need to bring anything." Amelia opened the back door of Doris' car and took out a glass trifle dish, loaded with gorgeous strawberries nestled between layers of cake and whipped cream. "Oh, my goodness that looks delicious."

Doris followed Amelia to the door. As Amelia reached for the handle, she turned to her guest. "Faith is here, and you noticed Noah with his dog Goose. They're both super friendly and love people, but if they get overwhelming, we can put them outside in the fenced area."

Doris shook her head. "Nonsense. We'll be fine. I love

dogs and wish I had the energy to have another. Visiting with them is the next best thing."

They came through the door and found Goose and Faith on her cot, looking like angels. Noah stood close to them.

Amelia stepped into the living area. "I'm so sorry I didn't introduce you, Noah. I assume you met Henry, and this is my friend Doris."

She stepped toward Noah and extended her hand. "A pleasure to meet you."

Noah shook her hand and smiled. "So nice to meet you, Doris. Amelia is always talking about you." He pointed at Henry. "And this guy, too."

Amelia held up her finger. "I'll be right back."

She dashed into the kitchen, put the trifle in the fridge, checked on the bacon and the French toast casserole, and retrieved two gift bags from the table. She gave Doris and Henry each a bag.

Doris settled into the other recliner and smiled at Amelia. "What's this?"

"Just a little surprise for both of you. I wanted to introduce you to Noah's work."

They both pulled a book from the tissue. "Wow," said Henry. "When Amelia told me you were an author, I wanted to read one of your books."

Doris chuckled. "Me, too. It's so exciting to meet an author in person."

Noah shook his head. "You're both very kind, as is our hostess. If you'd like, I'll sign those for you."

They both nodded with enthusiasm, and Noah borrowed a pen from Amelia and signed them.

Doris clutched it to her chest. "I can't wait to get started."

Amelia pointed at Henry's. "I gave each of you a different book. That way, you can trade when you're done."

The buzzer on the oven sounded, and Amelia raised her brows. "Reading will have to wait. We have eating to do."

Noah helped Henry to the table off the kitchen and once he and Doris were settled, he carried the hot casseroles to the table for Amelia.

As they ate, Henry heaped his praise on Amelia for the delicious food. Doris forked a potato and glanced at Amelia. "I can't believe these were done in a slow cooker. I want that recipe."

Amelia winked. "I'll write it down for you."

"You can just email it if it's easier. I'll give you my address."

Henry shook his head. "I never got the hang of email. I don't even have a computer. I think I missed the technology boat."

Doris chuckled. "You sound like my Ed. He never liked it, either. I liked it for keeping track of our business stuff. It made things easier. I no longer have the need for a big computer, but I have a tablet I use all the time. I read books on it, listen to music, even watch shows."

Henry raised his bushy brows. "I'm too old to worry about it now."

Noah sighed. "I'd be lost without it. If I had to use a typewriter, it would take me a year to write a book. Probably longer. Not to mention the research I have access to, at my fingertips."

Henry nodded. "I can see the benefits. I admit I'm content with the old-fashioned ways. I'm happy reading the newspaper, using the telephone, listening to my radio and records. Although, listening to Doris play the piano is even better."

At that, Doris blushed.

Amelia glanced at the table and their empty plates. "Does anyone need more?"

All three of her guests shook their heads. Henry patted his mid-section. "It was delicious, but I'm stuffed."

With a chuckle, Amelia pointed at the casseroles. "Well, you're all getting doggy bags to take home, then."

Henry wiggled his brows. "I won't refuse that." He turned toward Doris. "And I'll be ready for some of that yummy-looking dessert soon."

Amelia gestured to the patio door. "It's such a lovely day, why don't you all sit on the patio while I make quick work of these dishes."

Noah stood first. "I'll get you two settled outside, and then I'll take the dogs for a quick walk, so they'll be more apt to rest this afternoon."

"Great idea," said Amelia, as she gathered the plates.

As she rinsed the plates and loaded the dishwasher, she rehearsed the conversation she was about to instigate with Doris. As she put the leftovers into containers for everyone to take home, she heard laughter and Noah's voice coming from the patio.

He really had no idea how charming and interesting he was. Despite being one of the bestselling authors in his genre, with his books consistently in the top ten books sold, he was humble and down to earth. She could see herself spending her life with him. As much as she wanted to talk to him about a possible future, his illness held her back.

The last thing he needed was more stress and pressure. From that first day in Sam's shop, that tingle of attraction she felt for him hadn't wavered. At first, she chalked it up to her love of books and authors and her tendency to fangirl over the authors she loved most. As the weeks went by, she realized it was much more.

She pushed those thoughts to the back of her mind. They'd have to wait until the end of the month when the specialist would see him, and they would know more. First, she needed to tackle the Doris and Henry issue.

Noah had taken out iced teas for the pair of them already, but she added two more glasses and the pitcher to a tray and carried it to the patio.

Noah pulled out her chair for her, and she glanced at Henry. He raised his brows, urging her on.

After a long sip from her glass, Amelia turned to Doris, who was petting Goose and Faith, the pair of them more than interested in her and relishing her chin scratches. "Doris, I had an idea I wanted to share and see what you think."

"Of course, dear. What is it?"

Noah urged the dogs back to the cot he'd brought out for them and after a slurp from their water bowl, they settled in the shade.

"First, let me preface it by saying, I'm not trying to butt in, but after you told me about selling your place and wrestling with what to do, I came up with a possible solution."

Doris smiled. "I'm all ears."

"Well, Henry has a lovely guest house he built behind his house. It sits in a gorgeous yard, filled with flowers. He built it for his mom, but sadly, she passed away before she could move out here. It's like new and even has a large room he built for her piano. It's not huge, but it's got a small kitchenette, nice bathroom with a walk-in shower, and an open living space, along with a bedroom. It even has a little porch."

Amelia took a quick breath and continued, "The idea would be you'd have your privacy and live there in exchange for helping Henry with errands, shopping, cooking, and cleaning. Both of you could help each other out. You have so many things in common, I just thought it would be a good fit and give you both some company, when you want it. Just a platonic roommate type of situation." She moved her eyes toward Henry and received an approving look from him.

Tears glistened in Doris' eyes. "That's so sweet of you, Amelia." She moved her eyes across the table to Henry's. "And you, too, of course. I assume you approve."

He nodded. "Yes, ma'am. I had to give it some thought, of course. I've been on my own for sixty years now. I'm set in my ways and wasn't totally sure, but the more I thought about it, and when Amelia told me your situation and that you don't want to leave the island, it made sense. With your love of the piano, I can think of nobody better to bring life to the place."

He held up his hand. "And I want to make sure your son understands the arrangement. I don't want to be in the middle of any family issues."

With a long sigh, Doris reached for her tea and sipped it. "I really appreciate you thinking of me, Amelia. You, too, Henry. Jack is looking at options for me. He showed me some condos, but I didn't like any of them. We're meeting again next week. He thinks my place will sell quickly, so I need to have a plan in place. The whole mess has me wound in knots." She wadded the paper napkin in her hand. "I wish I could just stay where I am, but I know I need to downsize and get rid of the stairs and the huge yard, not to mention the acreage. It makes sense. I'm just having a hard time coming to grips with it."

Her voice caught, and she paused for a few moments. "My son and his wife live above their means, and I think along with wanting me to have a smaller place I can handle and no stairs, he's hoping I move back with them and infuse the proceeds from the sale of my place to help them. They've got a big house on a lake, kids in college, lots of debt."

Tears dotted her rosy cheeks. "That makes him sound horrible, and he isn't, but I think he's looking for an easy answer to his problems, too. I wish he'd just come right out with it and ask me for help, but I'm sure he's embarrassed."

Amelia understood that pain and met Doris' eyes. "I know how hard it is to face something new. Something you didn't want to face. I don't want to pressure you at all. It was just an idea that I thought might benefit both of you."

Doris used the napkin she crumpled to dab at her eyes. "It's a fine idea, Amelia. I never would have thought of something like that on my own. I just need time to think and figure out what I'm going to do. Wherever I go, it will mean selling the bulk of the furniture in my house. There are so many memories there." Tears pooled in her eyes and slipped down her cheeks.

Henry cleared his throat. "I understand what you're feeling, Doris. When I lost my wife and daughter so long ago, it pushed me into a reality I never imagined. One I wasn't sure I'd survive. I had a bit of the opposite problem. I couldn't stay in our house and had the urge to escape. That's what brought me here to this lovely island."

He shared his story of loss and how he rebuilt his life but had a house filled with the furnishing and collectibles that his wife loved. "Even after all these years, they're a comfort to me. I'm sure most people think I live in the past, and to some degree, I do. I love touching the things my wife and daughter held dear, and I cherish those old memories."

Doris sniffed, and Noah retrieved a box of tissues and set them next to her. She looked up at him and smiled. "Thank you, dear."

Amelia's throat was dry, and she took a sip before speaking. "That's how Henry and I bonded so quickly. I just lost my daughter and ex-husband in an accident. That's what brought me here. My sister offered to let me stay and try to heal at her house. Henry has definitely given me hope."

"Oh, my heavens, Amelia. I had no idea you've been going through such a hard time. I can't imagine losing a child. I'm so very sorry. And here you are volunteering to help us old folks. You are such a sweetheart."

She reached for more tissues and after blotting her face dry, she turned her gaze on Henry. "I'm also so sorry for your loss, Henry. You're quite the inspiration to have overcome that to live such a full life."

He chuckled. "Not sure I'd call it full, but I found happiness in my new life. Not traditional happiness like some might view, but I'm happier than I imagined I could be when I found myself alone."

Doris nodded at him. "It's not easy, I know. My son wanted me to move right after Ed passed. I couldn't do it, and he finally quit asking, but since I fell a couple of months ago, he hasn't shut up about it."

Noah drummed his fingers on the table. "Speaking as a son, I imagine yours is also worried about you. When my mom got older, I worried all the time. I lived far away and opted to move in with her, which at the time, she welcomed. It wasn't easy for her, either. That role reversal that seems to happen when the kids become the caregivers is not fun for either party. If you choose to live in the guest house, your son might be relieved knowing someone is nearby, and you'd have help if you needed it."

Doris bit her bottom lip. "I do know he's worried about me. He just doesn't seem to understand my ties here. He doesn't feel drawn to the island like me, so he discounts my feelings when I tell him I just can't leave. And, as I said, I think he's looking for an infusion of cash."

Amelia refilled their glasses. She didn't want to get in the middle of their family issues and focused on Doris and her happiness instead. "You could take a look at the guest house and see what you think. That might give you an idea of what furniture you could keep, if you decide to move."

With a smile, Doris nodded. "I'd like that. I will give it some thought, too. I'm just in a state of flux right now."

"Completely understandable," said Henry. "You just take a look and give it some thought. No need to rush at all."

Amelia glanced over at Noah. "Who's ready for some of Doris' wonderful dessert?"

All three of them raised their hands and with a chuckle, she stood and moved toward the house. "I'll dish it up for us."

Noah stood and offered to help, but Amelia waved him back to the table. "Just relax and enjoy the company."

He grinned. "Impossible not to. They're wonderful."

Amelia pulled the stunning dessert from the fridge and opted for paper bowls from Georgia's cupboard. As she scooped out the trifle, she couldn't help but smile. Today had been a good day, and she had a feeling once Doris saw the guest house and Henry's house, she wouldn't be able to resist the offer.

CHAPTER TWENTY-ONE

As Amelia loaded Faith in the SUV Tuesday morning, her cell phone rang. She smiled when she saw Doris' name on her screen. "Morning, Doris."

"Hi, Amelia. I'm sorry to bother you. I just wanted you to know I have a meeting with Jack this morning, so I won't be home when you come with the delivery. I left the back door unlocked for you. Could you just leave it in the kitchen for me?"

"Of course. Not a problem. I'll see you Saturday, if not before."

"I'm sure I'll see you before then, dear. Be careful on the road and have a good day."

Amelia disconnected and slid behind the wheel. Hearing Doris telling her to be careful reminded her of her mother. Although she set out to help others by volunteering at the food bank, she realized how much having Doris and Henry in her life made it better. They had the same qualities of her parents.

Their quiet wisdom and reassurance provided a stability

Amelia needed now more than ever. They truly cared about her, and she always felt better after spending time with them.

She hadn't talked to Henry since their brunch on Sunday. Since Doris wanted to see the guest house, she offered to drive him home after brunch. Amelia was dying to know how it went.

She hurried through her other deliveries and arrived at Henry's a little earlier than usual. Still, he was waiting and opened the door moments after she rang the bell. Faith made herself at home, waiting by Henry's chair, while Amelia went about her routine.

There was just enough iced tea left in the pitcher for the two of them. After she poured their glasses, she brewed another batch.

She handed Henry his tea and raised her brows, giving him a questioning look.

He frowned as he took the glass and sipped from it.

"So?" Amelia asked, as she sat in her chair.

"I think I missed the question, dear."

"How did it go with Doris on Sunday? Did she like the guest house?"

He nodded. "Oh, yes. She did. Very much so, in fact. She stayed until after the dinner hour. We had some of your leftovers before she went home."

"I talked to her this morning, and she's meeting with Jack. Did you get the feeling she was leaning toward taking the guest house?"

His forehead creased. "She didn't really say. She did seem to think it had plenty of room for her piano and access would be easy to place it with the French doors off the back. She loved the yard and all the flowers."

He paused and took another sip from his glass. "I think she's struggling more with the upheaval in her life. She's comfortable where she is, and the idea of leaving it all behind is troubling. With the move being forced, I think she's weighing her options."

"I got that sense, too. It's a big change for her. Forced change is never fun."

He nodded as he stared at a photo in the bookcase. "We both know that," he whispered.

Wednesday, Noah dropped Goose off on his way to the ferry dock. Along with his treats and food, he came with his bed and a basket of his favorite toys.

As soon as he came through the door, the dog rushed to Faith, and they greeted each other with licks and wags. Noah chuckled. "Obviously, he won't miss me much. He'll be in heaven here with his two favorite girls."

"We'll have lots of fun, so don't worry about him. I'll take good care of sweet Goose. We're going walking with Izzy and Sunny tomorrow. I think Jethro is joining us, too."

"Goose will love that. At this point, anybody is more exciting than me. I haven't been the best dog dad lately."

Amelia wrinkled her nose. "I think Goose understands." As they walked to his car, she reached for his hand. "Try not to stress. Think of it as a mini vacation, with a few tests squeezed in."

He laughed. "I'm just so glad Max is going with me. Doing this alone would be even more stressful."

"You've definitely got the best copilot you could ask for." They stopped when they reached his car. She enveloped him in a tight hug and relished the squeeze of his arms around her. "Try to relax and enjoy yourself a little. Text me when you can, and I'll see you tomorrow night. It will be good to have this behind you."

He sighed and whispered, "Thanks, Amelia. I'll miss you. I'll text you later."

She stood and waved as he drove away from the house. When his car disappeared around the curve, she returned to the house and her two furry charges.

They were playing with some of Goose's toys and romping through the living area.

After a bite of lunch, Amelia turned on her laptop and caught up on emails from Mel at the bookstore and took care of a few business items. The dogs wore themselves out and were stretched across the floor, napping.

Before she knew it, she looked up and realized it was time to feed the dogs their dinner and head over to Izzy's for hers. She'd invited them to join her and Sunny.

After the two scarfed down their meal, Amelia let them rest while she finished up her work and changed into a clean shirt. She opted to walk to Izzy's, which the dogs enjoyed, even though it was too short for their liking.

As they waited at the door, Amelia looked down at the two of them, their eyes filled with excitement. "We'll take a walk after dinner, I promise."

Izzy opened the door, and Sunny bounded past her to welcome her guests. Between the two of them, they herded the dogs inside, and they went running through the entry and past the kitchen.

With a laugh, Izzy urged Amelia to the kitchen. "I only wish I had their energy."

She pointed at the island. "I kept it simple. Taco salad and some chips and salsa."

"Oh, that sounds yummy," said Amelia. "Thanks again for inviting us."

They opted to eat at the granite-topped island, and Izzy poured wine for both of them, in addition to the pitcher of iced water she set next to their place settings. As they ate, Amelia filled Izzy in on Doris and Henry.

After Izzy listened to her explain Doris' predicament, Izzy reached for her wine glass. "Sounds like she needs some help and options figuring out her estate plan if she sells her property, too. Sadly, I think she's onto something with her son needing the cash from the sale of the property, and he doesn't want to wait until she passes."

She shook her head. "Trust me, I've seen it all when it comes to family situations.

I'm happy to do that and help her navigate the options and tax situations and connect her with a good accountant, if she needs it."

As she scooped up more salsa onto a chip, Amelia nodded. "That sounds like a wise idea. I'll mention your offer and let her know."

Izzy stood and retrieved a business card from her handbag. "Here's my contact information. Let her know I can do a free consultation with her and if she decides to have me do any work, I'll discount it, too."

Amelia smiled at her. "I'll do that. I know she'd appreciate the help. I think she'll have plenty of money when her place sells, but she's very careful with her money and lives frugally."

"I just want to make sure she doesn't outlive her money or give her son too much. It sounds like she'd rather not own another house and wants to simplify things."

Izzy gathered their dishes. "Understood. There are a few things she could do, but she would be my top priority as my client. I won't let her son take advantage of her."

As Amelia savored the last of her wine, she smiled. "I have

no doubt about that." Izzy was a formidable attorney, and Amelia would trust her with any situation. In the short time she'd been on the island, it was easy to see how much she was respected, and there were countless stories shared around the table and firepit at Sam's about Izzy's prowess when it came to strategy.

———

Thursday, Amelia couldn't stop thinking about Noah and what he was going through. He'd texted last night to let her know they were settled in at Becky's and how nice she and her husband were. He promised to let her know when they were done and on their way home.

After their morning walk, she did some chores and got the laundry started. With her housework done, she led the dogs to the patio, where they stretched out for a nap. Amelia, armed with some iced tea and a book, joined them in the lounge chair. She managed two chapters before the warmth of the sun lulled her to sleep.

Just before lunch, her phone chimed and woke her. Her faithful friends were still on the patio, sitting in the shade, watching her. She moved the book from where it had fallen across her chest and reached for her cell phone.

Noah reported everything went smoothly, and he and Max were on their way to lunch before they headed to the ferry terminal and planned to arrive at six o'clock.

She tapped in a quick reply to let him know she'd have dinner ready for him.

Hearing from Noah eased some of the worry she carried in her shoulders, and she relaxed as she settled against the cushion of the lounge chair. Now, he'd just have to wait for the results and his meeting with Max's doctor friend.

After some leftover taco salad Izzy sent home with her, Amelia dug through the drawer with local menus to figure out dinner. With Noah watching his diet so carefully, she was reluctant to order a pizza, even though it sounded good.

She finally settled on fish from the clubhouse restaurant. That would be convenient and healthy for Noah. She called and placed an order for dinner.

With Noah on his way home and no longer weighing on her, she scrolled the names on her cell phone until she found Doris. She couldn't wait until Saturday to talk to her about what Izzy said last night.

After a few rings, Doris' deep voice came through the speaker. "Hi, Amelia."

"Hi, Doris. I hope I'm not disturbing you."

"No, dear. Not at all. In fact, I'm relaxing with that copy of Noah's book right now."

"Oh, wonderful. Well, I wanted to pass on some information you might need. I think I've mentioned my friend Izzy, who lives down the road?"

"Yes, yes, you have."

"I was telling her I had a friend who was trying to decide how to navigate selling her property and all the financial decisions that come with that. Anyway, Izzy is well versed in estate planning and tax law, and she said she'd be glad to talk to my friend and offer a free consultation. I'll send you her contact information. I just wanted you to have it in case you need it."

"That's a great idea. I talked to Jack yesterday and despite not having listed the property yet, he said he has a couple of potential clients he knows would jump on it. I still didn't find anything on the market that I like."

She sighed. "Honestly, Henry's home and guest house is the nicest thing I've seen. It's just a lovely setting and although small, the guest quarters has everything I need. Jack even offered Nate to help move my piano and furnishings when the time comes."

"That would be wonderful. I know I could wrangle more help for you, so don't worry about that piece. If you decide to call Izzy, just let her know you're my friend I told her about."

"I think I'll do that. It would ease my mind to fully understand everything. Jack was talking about capital gains taxes, and my head is swimming now. I'm trying to simplify things, not make things worse."

"I'm sure Izzy will have some excellent advice for you."

"I told my son I was meeting with the realtor, and he asked if I looked for an assisted living facility on the island." She chuckled, but the pain came through in her voice. "I don't want anything to do with one of those places. I've warmed to your idea of staying at Henry's. We would be there for each other. That's my version of assisted living."

"I'm a bit biased, but I'd love to see that work for both of you."

"You're a dear, Amelia. I appreciate your help and you looking out for me. I'll see you Saturday."

Amelia disconnected with a smile and a sense of renewed hope.

Her plan might work out.

The minute Amelia grabbed her purse and keys, Goose and Faith hurried to the door, their eyes filled with excitement. She couldn't resist them and loaded them in her SUV for the short ride to the clubhouse to pick up the takeout order.

She left them to wait with the windows down and hurried inside, where her order was waiting. Minutes later, she was back at the house and was about to unbox the meals when the dogs rushed to the front door.

She opened it to find Noah lumbering up the walkway. He smiled at her. "Hey, you're a sight for my tired eyes."

When he reached the threshold, she embraced him. "We're so glad you're back. I just picked up dinner from the clubhouse for us."

Not to be left out of the welcoming hug, Goose and Faith came from around Amelia and surrounded them, their tails beating against the back of their legs. Noah chuckled and reached down to pet Goose. "Aww, I missed you, big guy. Were you a good boy?"

Amelia nodded. "He was excellent. They both were."

Once the dogs had been petted and given belly scratches, they calmed and rested, while Noah and Amelia settled in at the table. While they ate the tasty salmon and roasted veggies, Noah told her about the trip.

"Sam's friend Becky is super nice, and I enjoyed visiting with her and her husband. He's in finance. They're planning a visit this fall to see Sam." He pointed at his plate. "This is really good. Thanks for dinner. I'm beat from the stress of the day."

"I was going for easy, but I'm glad you like it."

He took a few more bites. "It was really nice to get to know Max better. We talked about so many things. He made me realize how important it is to have a support system, whether you're facing an illness or not. He moved here after coming to visit Sam and of course, meeting Linda, but it got me thinking that I have nobody I can rely on, outside of the group of friends I've found here."

She refilled her glass of tea. "Despite being new to Driftwood Bay, I was really lucky to find a wonderful group of friends. People who are willing to pitch in and help. I wouldn't be able to be here today without them. I can't imagine trying to navigate tough things without them."

"Exactly," said Noah. "That's what Max and I discussed in detail. I've decided to sell Mom's house and buy a place here on the island. I'm almost certain Max's friend is going to confirm I have Huntington's. While the island isn't ideal for medical needs, it's where I'm happy and productive. Max assures me he and the others would be on hand to go with me when I have to visit the city for tests. I wouldn't have that kind of help if I stayed at Mom's."

He took a long swallow from his glass and sighed. "Max shared some stories with me. He treated many critically ill people and said the ones who did the best were the ones who chose to view their illness as more of an inconvenience than letting it dominate their lives. They chose to live every moment fully, some with very slim chances of survival, rather than dwell on how much time they had left. It made me think about things differently."

Amelia reached for his hand. "I'm so glad you had that time with him, and I think it's wonderful news you want to live here. It's hard not to be happy in these beautiful surroundings, and I can attest to the support of friends. They're some of the best people I've ever met. Kind, genuine, and caring."

He winked at her. "I'm also hoping you'll be around to visit often, and I'll be able to spend time with you when you're here."

She laughed. "I think that can be arranged."

They finished dinner, and she couldn't resist opening her laptop to search for homes on the island. They sat together on the couch, scrolling the photos while they sipped mugs of tea.

Noah wanted a one-story house or at least one that had

all the essentials on the main floor. He found a few possibilities and planned to visit Jack tomorrow and set things in motion.

Amelia's heart warmed seeing Noah excited and smile on his face. He was determined, which would help him face the unknown.

CHAPTER TWENTY-TWO

After their walk on Saturday morning, when Amelia opened the door to let Goose into his house, she was surprised to find Noah downstairs. He greeted her with a warm smile and the offer of freshly brewed tea.

She took the steaming mug and sat at the dining room table with a view of the backyard and the golf course beyond it. "I'm surprised you're up so early," she said.

"After golfing yesterday morning, I came home and worked. I got tons done and actually went to bed at a semi-normal hour last night."

He set his mug on the table. "I wanted to let you know, after golf, we went to the clubhouse and had a late breakfast. I told the guys about why Max and I went to Seattle and what was going on medically."

His eyes met hers. "I know I asked you to keep it between us, and I just wanted you to know it's no longer a secret. Spending time with Max made me realize I was giving my diagnosis way too much power. Talking about it, sharing it, makes it less frightening. They were all great about it and offered their support and help."

"That's wonderful, Noah. Did you tell them you're looking for a place to buy?"

He nodded. "I did. Jeff gave me a lead on a house that isn't far from his family's resort. It's got a water view but no beach. He said the owners passed away, and their kids were getting it ready to put on the market. I'm going to talk to Jack about it. It sounds like what I'm looking for."

"Oh, that's great news. There's something to be said for a view of the water."

With a grin, Noah nodded. "Yes, I decided I'm going to buy something I truly want. I want that gorgeous view to greet me each morning. I've banked or invested all my advances and royalties, so I have the means to buy something and make it work financially. The old me would have viewed it as frivolous, but the new me wants to make the most of everything."

"I'm so happy you're in a better place, Noah. It's wonderful to see you smiling."

He reached out for her hand. "I'm sorry I was such horrible company this last month. I know you're struggling, too, and I haven't been as helpful as I could be."

Amelia tilted her head and smiled. "I understand, believe me. It's not easy to be happy with fear hanging over you. It's hard to make it through a day when everything around you seems horrible, and you can't control it."

His brows rose. "Especially if you're a natural control freak. Max and I talked at length about Will and after thinking more, I've decided I'm going to invite him here to visit. We can call Tanya and tell her together when he's here, or he can do it. I'll leave it up to him. I don't think it's something I want to share on the phone or a video call. Max gently reminded me how Will deserved to know and make his own decision on getting tested, but it would help to have his doctor friend on hand to explain things."

"Is the test complicated?"

He shook his head. "No, just a blood test, but depending on the results, it can get murky. Specific values can rule Huntington's in or out, but there are some middle values that make it difficult, since they can't say for certain his children will have it. My hope is that he doesn't have it, of course, but I want him to have all the information."

"Had you known you had the gene for it, would you have changed anything in your life?"

Tears glinted in his eyes. "I would have thought twice about having a child. That's part of why I want Will to know everything. I'm so worried about him. There are no easy choices in this mess."

"I would be worried, too. The last thing we ever want is for our children to suffer." Tears leaked from Amelia's eyes.

He plucked a napkin from the holder and handed it to her. "I'm sorry, Amelia. I don't want to burden you with this sadness."

"For what it's worth, I think you're doing the right thing."

He shrugged. "Sometimes I think so and then other times, I doubt myself. Max agrees that I have the disease, based on what I told him about my symptoms, and I think he downplays his expertise, but he watched the scans from the technician's booth. He pointed out that there won't be a way to keep this from Will, so it's best that I tell him while I'm healthy and let him make his own decision on testing. Will's very close to his mom, and I suspect he might want to talk it over with her before he decides, but I like the idea of him being here when Jan is so he can ask her any questions he has."

"That's very wise. I hope he'll come."

"Me, too. I sent him an email early this morning. Didn't tell him why, of course, but I included some great photos of the island and told him I'm on a golf course. I'll call him tonight if I haven't heard. It's not much notice, so I want to make the arrangements as soon as possible."

Amelia glanced at her watch. "I hate to leave, but I need to get to the food bank. Keep me posted on what Will says."

"I will. I'm going to get to work and try to concentrate on my book."

He walked her and Faith to the edge of the patio and waved as they hurried home.

Amelia was late when she arrived at Doris' on Saturday. Doris didn't seem to notice and welcomed her and Faith to the porch, where a fresh pitcher of lemonade awaited them. "I've got news I think you'll like," said Doris, who offered her one of the cookies she had on a plate.

"Oh, that sounds promising."

Doris' eyes sparkled with enthusiasm, and the recent angst that weighed on her was gone. "I talked to Izzy and Jack and have a plan." She went on to tell her that Izzy came up with a solution to shield Doris from the taxes on the influx of cash from the sale of her property. Izzy took the bull by the horns and contacted Doris' son, Larry.

After a sip of lemonade, Doris continued, "Turns out my suspicions were correct. He and his wife are in a financial mess. Izzy suggested I reinvest my proceeds that aren't exempt from taxes and buy their home. I can carry the papers on it, and they can pay me a payment each month, instead of the bank. The monthly amount will be far lower than what they're paying now and allow them to stay in their home. I'll have a comfortable monthly income and have decided to take the guest house at Henry's."

Her smile made Amelia so happy. "That is wonderful news."

Doris chuckled. "Turns out Larry isn't near as worried about where I live now that his financial problem is solved. He's going to end up with all my money when I'm gone anyway, but at least this way, I get what I need and can stay here on the island. Izzy's doing my estate plan for me, too, so everything will be handled if something happens to me. I'll still have a large amount of money in an account to take care of me, if I have to go into some sort of facility, which makes me feel better."

"I'm so glad she could help you and even more so that you're so happy and can stay on the island."

"Me, too. Izzy even drove me over to Henry's, and she came up with an agreement so we're both clear on the terms. He was so sweet and worried about me if something were to happen to him. He has no family and thought it best that I be allowed to stay on the property as long as I lived, then everything would go to the charities he specified."

Tears formed in Amelia's eyes. "He's such a kind man." She didn't want to think about anything happening to him.

"He is, indeed. Izzy is a godsend. I'm not sure how she could figure it all out, and she made it seem easy. Larry is happy, I'm happy, and Henry is happy. I never thought that would be possible."

"So, now you just have to get your place sold, right?"

Her eyes went wide. "Well, Jack called a client he knew was in the market for property like mine. I won't even need to list it and go through that hassle of showing it. He's moving from outside of Seattle and wants to have a small farm and grow vegetables and flowers. It's ideal for that. He didn't bat an eye at the price. It seemed so high to me, but Jack said it's what the market is right now."

"Wow, you have been busy."

"I'm relieved. I know this place is too much for me. I'm just so happy I don't have to leave everything I know. It will be an adjustment moving into such a small house, but I can make it work."

"If you need help packing or having a yard sale, please call me. I'm sure we could get a group together and make quick work of it."

Doris reached out her hand, covered with age spots, and placed it atop Amelia's. "I promise to do that. For now, Jack is organizing Nate to move the things I want to keep over to Henry's. I can get situated there and stay there whenever I'm ready. Then, I can tackle emptying the house and the outbuildings. The buyer isn't in a rush, so I can take my time. I'm sure I'll need help at some point and can't tell you how thankful I am for your offer."

After Amelia finished her lemonade, she made Doris promise to let her know when her things would be delivered to Henry's, so she could come over and help them get organized.

She left with a wave and set out for the rest of her deliveries, anxious to get to Henry's. As luck would have it, all of her clients were home and in a chatty mood. When she finally pulled in front of Henry's house, she was almost two hours late.

He had the door open before she unloaded his box. "I was

getting worried about you two." He smiled as Faith walked through the door and to her spot next to his recliner.

"Oh, we stopped and visited with Doris, then because I was running late, all my clients were talkative today. It's all good, though. Doris told me the awesome news."

Henry's eye's widened, and he grinned. "Yes, your friend Izzy helped seal the deal. She's quite the lawyer. Doris was so relieved."

"I'm so happy for both of you. I feel so much better about both of you having someone around, and you'll be able to have meals together. I'm sure she'll play that beautiful piano for you."

He nodded and smiled as she brought him a glass of iced tea. "I'm looking forward to that. That dessert she made at your brunch was out of this world. I have a feeling I'm going to gain weight with her around the house."

She glanced at him. "I think you could stand to put on a few pounds."

He chuckled. "Maybe just a couple, but I don't want to get carried away."

Amelia sat in her chair and smiled as Henry bent and petted the top of Faith's head. "How's the sweetest girl I know today? You're such a good girl, too."

The dog leaned her head closer to him, her eyes closed, as she delighted in the attention.

"When I visited with Doris earlier, I told her to call me when she knew when her things would be delivered here. I'm happy to help get her situated and don't want either of you overdoing it."

"I'll remind her if she forgets," he said with a laugh. "She's got lots of energy, but she's fifteen years younger. That makes a difference."

"I think you're both amazing. I find you quite the

inspiration, Henry. I don't know too many ninety-seven-year-olds who are as capable and live on their own. You're my hero."

He chuckled and reached for his tea. "Well, I used to be much more independent, and I miss going out whenever I want. These days, I get most things delivered. A nice young man at the market brings my groceries, and the pharmacy delivers, too. If I get a hankering for something from one of the restaurants, they usually deliver for me, and my neighbors are wonderful about helping. It's part of what I love about this place. It's like being part of a big family."

"It's interesting you say that. I was visiting with Noah this morning. He's dealing with a very serious medical diagnosis and has decided to sell his mom's place in Oregon where he's been living and buy a place here. He loves the friends he's made this summer and says the water view inspires his writing."

"I'm sorry to hear he's having a medical issue but very glad to know he's going to make the island his home. There's something special about this place. I know it saved me. Once Doris is settled, and Noah finds a permanent place, I'm sure she would be up for having Noah and Goose over for dinner."

"Aww, I know he would enjoy that. He had fun at our brunch." She paused and took a sip of tea. "I'm going to miss all of you so much when I go home. I told Georgia I'm going to become a nuisance and come over every chance I get."

"Something tells me she'd be all too glad to have you full-time. You're a true gem, my dear. I certainly hope you don't stay away too long. You've got lots of people who care about you here and will miss you terribly."

Fresh tears stung her eyes, and she willed herself to smile

and push thoughts of leaving to the back of her mind. "I've been trying so hard not to think ahead too much, and I'm going to focus on today and how much I enjoy visiting with you and when Doris moves in, I imagine I'll be here even longer."

She glanced at her watch. "It's getting close to the dinner hour. Do you want me to make you something?"

"I'm just having some soup tonight, so no need to worry. My neighbor brought me a big lunch."

Amelia took her empty glass into the kitchen where she washed it and put it back in the cupboard. After refilling Henry's tea, she put her hand on his shoulder. "We better get home. I'll see you Tuesday, but if you need anything, you have my number."

He patted her hand with his. "Yes, dear. I'll call if I need you. Thank you... for everything."

She winked at him and after Faith stuck around for a few more pets from Henry, they carted the empty box to her SUV and headed home.

On the way through town, she noticed an empty parking spot near the park and stopped. While she walked and let Faith sniff at the new smells, she called Big Tony's and put in an order for a pizza.

She was starving and thinking about leaving everyone on the island made her crave the comfort of warm dough, cheese, and the pepperoni she usually avoided. By the time they'd circled the park, it was time to get the pizza.

They made their way down the sidewalk to Big Tony's, where one of the waitstaff took pity on her with Faith and brought the warm box out to her. The aroma of the pizza made her stomach growl all the way to the SUV.

She hurried home and dished up Faith's dinner before

pouring a glass of wine and taking the box out to the patio. She took the first bite of her slice and shut her eyes. It was so good.

The day was one filled with good news, but also the heaviness of what was to come.

CHAPTER TWENTY-THREE

O n Sunday, Faith and Amelia overslept. As soon as she woke and saw the time, she hurried to get her phone to let Henry know she'd be late picking him up. She took Faith outside for her morning ritual and fed her breakfast before she rushed to the shower.

With no time to wash her hair, she did her best to put it up in a messy bun. Emphasis on messy. Thank goodness that was all the rage right now.

She threw on some clean clothes and promised Faith she'd be back soon, leaving her with a tiny cookie treat as she hurried outside.

Henry was on the porch waiting when she pulled in front of his house. As she rounded the front of her SUV, she hollered out. "I'm so sorry I'm late."

"Don't worry," said Henry, as he and his walker started down the ramp. "We have time."

Amelia helped him into the passenger seat and hurried through town. She lucked out, finding a parking spot close to the door, and helped Henry navigate to his favorite row. She sighed as she sat next to him and checked her watch. Two minutes to spare.

Pastor John stepped to the podium and welcomed everyone. The service was similar to last week's, with hymns, prayers, and a message. The congregation hadn't grown this week, either. The same smiling faces from last Sunday greeted Amelia.

As the pastor spoke, her mind wandered. Last night hadn't been one of her best. She blamed the pizza.

It reminded her of the pizza she and Natalie shared when she'd visited for Mother's Day. Pizza was her daughter's favorite food, and last night's meal prompted too many bittersweet memories.

To make matters worse, she worried about Noah and his future. Their future. With her plans to leave in September, she felt a sense of urgency. She couldn't deny her feelings for him and was sure he felt that same way, but their lives were beyond complicated.

As much as she longed for someone to share her life with, she wasn't sure she was strong enough to withstand the struggles he would face and they would need to face together. Anxiety kept her up until the wee hours and why she found herself tired and sitting in church with her skirt on backwards. She'd been in such a rush, she hadn't noticed until she reached for her pocket and realized it was on her backside.

She doubted anyone would notice, since it was one of those pull-on gauzy skirts. At least she hoped they wouldn't. She thought about quickly rotating the waist but decided it would only draw more attention to it. She found it on the clearance rack at a cute little boutique downtown last week and couldn't resist the pretty blue color.

Before she knew it, everyone was standing to sing the closing hymn, and she hadn't heard a word of the sermon.

After the last prayer, they made their way to the door and chatted with Pastor John for a few moments. As Amelia helped Henry into the passenger seat, he leaned over and said, "Young lady, I'd love to treat you to an early lunch. Are you up for a stop on the way home?"

His formal invitation melted her heart. "That sounds perfect. I skipped breakfast."

"Your choice. Pick anywhere you like."

"Hmm. How about you give me a couple of choices you like."

"I've never had a bad meal at Front Street Café or Dottie's."

She grinned. "I like the way you think." She slowed as she entered town and drove down Front Street. The café looked packed with people waiting outside for a table, but Dottie's was promising. She even spied a parking space right in front of the deli.

Amelia helped Henry to a table and went to the counter to order their lunch. They both ordered the beef dip with Dottie's famous potato salad. Henry insisted on paying and gave Amelia some cash.

While they waited, the two of them gazed out the window at the picture-perfect day. Amelia would never tire of the view of the harbor, with the sun glinting off the blue waters. It didn't take long for Misty, the young woman behind the counter, to deliver their trays.

Henry's eyes went wide. "Wow, I hope I can get a doggy bag. That's enough to feed me for several meals."

Misty smiled at him. "I'll bring you a box, Henry. Nice to see you."

He thanked her and dug into the thick sandwich, dipping it in the hot au jus.

While they ate, Henry reminisced about when he first came to the island. "I loved to come down to the harbor. Even though I worked at the marina all day, I usually came down here in the evenings, just to watch the water and relax. There was a little restaurant where I ate most all my meals. It was on the corner, across from Sam's coffee shop."

Amelia loved listening to his memories. At a lull in the conversation, she asked, "So, you never met another woman you wanted to marry?"

He continued to gaze out the window. "I had a hard time with that. I grieved Abigail and Mary for a very long time. Still do if I'm honest. I worked until I was exhausted, slept, and got up to do it all over again. That was my life for over a decade. Work was my escape. My crutch."

He took a long swallow from his glass of lemonade. "I never met another woman like Abigail." He smiled. "She was my one true love. Eventually, I found that pastor I mentioned and surfaced from my grief. I still wasn't really ready to share my life with anyone and realized I was lonely and destined to spend the rest of my days alone. Years before, I'd had a few women express interest in me, but by the time I was ready to entertain that idea, I was too old."

The sadness in his voice made Amelia's heart break.

He turned to face her, with watery eyes. He reached across the table and rested his hand on her arm. "Don't be like me, Amelia. I can see how much you and Noah mean to each other. Looking back, I should have been willing to take a risk instead of using my grief and work to hide from a chance at a life. A different life, of course, but a life. I was too busy mourning what I'd lost and missed what I could have had."

Amelia sighed. "Noah and I both have feelings for each other. His illness is serious, and the future outlook isn't great. He's meeting with a doctor friend of Max's at the end of the month and will know more. I really like him and feel a strong connection to him. I'm just not sure I can risk more heartbreak."

He smiled at her. "Oh, my dear. I know exactly what you mean, but I have to tell you, when it comes to love, there's always a risk of heartbreak. Tomorrow isn't promised to any of us. You and I both know this all too well. There are no guarantees in life. I understand your hesitation, but if you find someone who makes you happy, I think you need to grab on with both hands. Sure, you might find someone down the road who doesn't have a health issue, but the future isn't promised to him, either. If I've learned anything in my long time on this planet, none of us have as much time as we think or need. Don't squander it and give up happiness, or even a chance at it, out of fear."

After a sip from his drink, he continued, "It's like what you did for Faith. Logically, you know you'll have to face the day when you have to let her go. Years down the road, you'll have one of your saddest days, but you took that leap of faith, because you loved her, and she needed you in her life. You needed each other. It wouldn't make sense to give up the years of happiness you'll have together because you fear that loss. As horrible as it is, the joy you'll bring to each other will make it worthwhile."

Misty returned to their table with takeout boxes for their leftovers. She smiled at Henry and said, "I slipped one of those chocolate chip cookies you like into your box, too."

"Aww, you're a sweet one, Misty. Thank you."

Amelia led the way to her SUV and helped him get

situated. As she drove the few blocks to his house, she thought about his advice.

When she pulled in front of his house, she started to open her door, and Henry reached out to her. "I hope I didn't upset you. You're so quiet."

She shook her head. "Of course not. What you said meant a lot." She patted his arm to reassure him. "It's making me think. That's a good thing."

Once he was settled in his chair with a cup of tea, Amelia promised to see him Tuesday and hurried back to the house. She didn't intend to leave Faith for so long and was filled with guilt.

When she got home, she rushed inside and panicked when she didn't see Faith. She darted down the hall and burst out laughing. Faith was sprawled on her back in Amelia's bed, her paws in the air, snoozing.

As soon as Amelia said her name, Faith snapped her head toward her and turned over, yawning. She sat on the edge of the bed, and Faith scooted over close to her. "You're such a good girl," she said, stroking the top of her head. "I'll get changed, and we can go for a walk."

Faith's ears perked, and she jumped off the bed.

As soon as Amelia put on her walking shoes, they were out the door and detoured to Noah's house to pick up Goose. As soon as he saw them, he wiggled with delight and waited for Amelia to attach his leash.

They set out for the loop around the golf course. As they walked, Amelia thought more about what Henry said to her at lunch. Fear was indeed a powerful emotion, one that could inform decisions based upon it and not always in a good way. Henry, in his wisdom, distilled it down for her. It didn't make sense to discard Noah and a chance at happiness because of what could happen.

She gazed at the dog who had filled her heart with joy and purpose. As Henry had reminded her, she couldn't imagine not having Faith in her life. The sweet dog had arrived when she needed her most. It was the same with Noah.

Carts and golfers were scattered all over the course, taking advantage of the weekend and the gorgeous day. It was warmer than their usual early morning time, prompting Amelia to seek out the convenient benches situated along the trail, more than once.

Goose and Faith availed themselves of the water bowl and then rested in the shade next to the bench. She tried to imagine her life without Noah. Could she really just leave and go back to Driftwood Bay and support him by text and calls? He'd have their friends to help him, but what she felt for Noah was more than friendship.

When Ron left her, Amelia assumed she was too old to ever find another love in her life. Along with her devastation at her life taking such a drastic turn, she assumed something was wrong with her. His rejection had done a number on her self-confidence.

Those feelings of inadequacy stuck with her until the day Ron's brother divulged the fact that Ron admitted he made a mistake and even hoped to get back with her. If only he hadn't been so quick to throw their life together away, everything would be different. She might still have her family.

Now, she'd never know.

The what-if game made her tired, and the anguish crept over her.

As she fought back tears, someone shouted her name. She looked up and saw a cart approaching. Jeff, Max, Nate, and

Spence were in it. All of them waved at her and shouted out a greeting.

She returned the wave and chuckled. "Hey, guys. How's it going?"

Jeff stepped from the back of the cart. "Living our dream life. How about you?"

"Oh, just taking the dogs for a walk. I went to church with Henry this morning and was late, so we missed our usual outing."

He stepped over to pet them, their tails swishing in soft arcs. "Speaking of Henry. Doris stopped by the other day and asked if I had any ideas for a ramp he could use out his back door. There's just that one step, but she's worried about him using the walker safely."

Amelia nodded. "That's a good idea."

"I found one we had stuck in the back storage. I was going to stop by and install it for him but didn't want to overstep."

"That would be fantastic. I'll call him to let him know, and I'll meet you over there."

"It won't take but a few minutes. I can grab it later this afternoon if that works for you. How about five o'clock?"

"That works. Just give me a call, and I'll head into town when you do."

He gestured back at the cart. "Nate said he's lined up to move Doris into the guest house this coming weekend. We've got a crew ready to help, so it won't take long."

"Even better news. I'll make sure I'm at Henry's to help Doris get situated. She and Henry are both excited about it."

He grinned. "They're both such wonderful people." He glanced back at the cart. "I better get moving. Have a great day, Amelia."

"Thanks, Jeff." She waved at the others, and they sped off

to their next hole as she picked up the two leashes. The three set off to finish their exercise.

She left Goose with a pet and a promise to see him soon and strolled back to her house. As she and Faith were walking away, Noah shouted her name from the front door.

At the sound, Amelia turned, and Noah hurried toward her. "Hey, sorry. I just hung up from talking to Will. He's coming. I just gave him my credit card number so he can book a flight. He'll be here at the end of the month. He can only swing a long weekend, but at least he'll be here when Jan is here and can help explain things."

She hugged him. "That's great news. I'm so glad he agreed to visit." His smile, wider than she'd seen since meeting him, spoke volumes.

"I feel better just knowing he'll be here. It's been a long time and while I hate the reason for the visit, it's long overdue."

He reached for her hand and held it in a tight grip. "Thank you for putting up with me and all of this. I'm lucky to have you in my life." He glanced down at Goose who was leaning against him, next to Faith. "Correction, we're lucky to have you. I hope to make this up to you one day soon."

She shook her head. "I'm just glad to see you smiling, Noah. I know the pressure you're under is extreme. I'm looking forward to meeting Will. We'll have to plan something so he can meet all our friends."

"That would be awesome, especially with me planning to stay here on the island. I'd like him to know everyone and hope he's enticed to come again."

She squeezed his hand. "Me, too, Noah. More than anything."

He shuffled his feet. "Speaking of living here, Jack's working with the owners of the house Jeff mentioned.

Sounds like they'll be ready for me to take a look at it later this week. Would you come with me?"

Her brows arched above her sunglasses. "Yes, I'd love to come. Count me in."

With a sigh, he let go of her hand. "I better get back to work. I'll let you know what day on the house."

"Sounds good. The only thing on my calendar is helping Doris with packing and next weekend, Nate's moving her stuff, so I want to be around to help."

"I'll keep that in mind when I talk to Jack and make it work around your schedule." He glanced down at the dogs. "Come on, Goose. Say goodbye to the ladies."

She laughed as he led the golden to the house. "We better get a move on, Faith. We've got to run back to Henry's."

Her ears lifted, as did her eyebrows, at the mention of Henry. Her tail wagged as they hurried down the sidewalk. Amelia felt the same way about the gentle man who, in a very short time, had a profound impact on her.

CHAPTER TWENTY-FOUR

F riday arrived, and Amelia woke late, sore, and exhausted. After a week of cleaning and packing boxes at Doris', she was ready for a day off. Noah was due to pick her up at ten o'clock to visit the house he was thinking about buying.

Despite feeling tired, she took Faith for her morning walk. She couldn't resist her happy face and always enjoyed the time to think or visit with Izzy when she was able to meet them. Today, Izzy had another early meeting, so they were on their own.

The work party was organized to start early tomorrow, to help Doris move into the guest house. Amelia arranged to do her food bank deliveries early in the morning, so she could be on hand to help Doris organize her new place.

Despite both of their initial objections, yesterday, Amelia finally managed to get both Henry and Doris to commit to coming to Sam's house for a celebration on Sunday. Sam and Linda had kicked around different ideas, including having the get-together at Henry's, but thought it best to use Sam's larger deck. That would permit Henry and Doris to leave when they were ready, rather than getting overtired with everyone at their place.

Linda, who was swamped with weddings all summer, had to work Sunday morning but had the rest of the day free, so they were set for an afternoon party. Amelia marveled at how hard Linda worked, with barely a day off during her busy season. She wished she had more time to spend getting to know her.

Georgia was already making Christmas plans to host Amelia on the island, so hopefully, Linda would be less busy, especially after Christmas. As much as she hated the idea of leaving everyone, the idea of Christmas with Georgia and Dale, plus all her other newfound friends, gave her something to look forward to and eased the sadness.

Along with celebrating Doris and Henry, Jess was due back home Saturday, and they were incorporating her homecoming into the celebration. It would be a packed weekend.

When they arrived home, Amelia bent to remove Faith's leash and winced. She'd pulled something in her shoulder yesterday, and it was still irritated. She fed Faith breakfast and then opted for a hot shower.

With her shoulder feeling a bit better, she got dressed and made herself some oatmeal before sitting down to tackle her emails. According to the reports from Mel, things were running smoothly, and business was brisk.

She logged into her bank and checked her accounts. She hadn't pulled the trigger on paying off the store yet. Izzy's mention of a good tax accountant made sense, and she remembered Noah mentioning Sam's friend in Seattle and her husband being a financial advisor. She needed to talk to someone before she made such a big decision. She might have a degree, but she needed the help of someone who had practiced in the arena and could give her the best advice.

As she closed the lid on her laptop, Faith rushed to the door. Moments later, Noah knocked on the door, and Amelia welcomed him in, along with Goose. They decided the two furry friends could spend a few hours together at her house while they checked out Noah's prospective home.

Faith had proven herself trustworthy over the last weeks, and the two of them could entertain each other. Amelia bent down and held Goose's face in her hands. "How are you this morning, you handsome boy?"

His long tongue swiped her cheek and made her laugh.

She made sure they each had a cookie and locked the door behind them. Noah held the door for her and then drove toward Smuggler's Cove. He took the driveway that led to the house and when he made the last slight turn, Amelia pointed at the vibrant blue water visible between the tall trees that surrounded the house. Noah grinned and parked behind Jack's car.

Amelia noticed the entry had a few steps, which might need to be addressed in the future, if Noah encountered any mobility issues. The covered porch ran the length of the house, so there was plenty of room to construct a ramp, like Henry had done. Jack met them on the porch and pointed out the beautiful stonework under their feet. "This stone continues and wraps around the house with a huge patio in the back, and it offers a view you're going to love."

As he opened the door, he pointed out the stucco and wood exterior and metal roof, which he touted made the house maintenance-free. Amelia and Noah followed him through the door, and her eyes widened at the finishes, including the heavy wooden beams that ran across the ceilings.

A stone fireplace, wood-cased windows, and built-in bookcases and window seats gave the living space a homey feel. The cushions on the window seats were a bit lumpy and worn, but that was an easy fix.

Jack pointed at the wooden staircase. "I know you wanted a single story, but the only things upstairs are a bonus room and a bedroom. You could easily live here without ever climbing a stair."

Noah nodded. "I like all the wood trim in here. It almost gives it a cabin vibe, despite all the modern touches."

Jack stepped through the living space and led them past a dining room, with a beautiful built-in hutch, to the kitchen, where gray and white granite counters graced the wooden cabinets. A huge island counter dominated the space, and white subway tiles decorated the backsplash behind the fancy cooktop. "As you know, the house is over forty years old but was remodeled and updated about ten years ago, so it's got every bell and whistle you'll need."

The enormous kitchen, boasting a butler's pantry and outfitted with stainless-steel appliances and two sinks, even had room for a small breakfast table tucked under a huge window with an awesome view of the water. Light from the numerous windows filled the house and offered spectacular views of the Haro Strait and the Olympic Peninsula. Like Sam's house, this one was poised to offer some spectacular sunsets.

Jack continued across the wooden floor and led them to the master suite. It had a large walk-in shower and a soaking tub, which looked a little dangerous to Amelia with its slick tile surround and steps up to it.

There were two other bedrooms on the main level and two more bathrooms, plus a half-bathroom near the study, off the main living area. Jack pointed out that every room in the house had a door that led to the wrap-around stone patio that encircled the house.

Jack gestured upstairs. "We can take a quick look and then venture outside, where I would be spending all my time if I lived here."

He led the way up the stairs to a large room he explained had been used as a family room. A guest bedroom and bathroom made up the rest of the space.

As they descended the stairs, Jack pointed at the leather furniture in the living room. "The owner is willing to leave the furniture you see here. They've taken everything they want and rather than going to the trouble of removing it or selling it, they said you can have it, and that includes the outdoor furniture you'll see soon."

Noah detoured to the study and as he gazed around the space, Amelia took his hand. "Can you see yourself writing here." She pointed at the view of the water from the window.

He smiled and chuckled. "Yes, as a matter of fact, I can. This is what I was thinking when I gave living here some serious thought."

They rejoined Jack, who was waiting on the stone patio off the dining room, Noah's eyes widened. "Wow. Like you said, the view is a stunner."

Jack pointed out the connection on the side of the house for a gas grill. There was also a firepit, a small wooden table and chairs, along with a couple of cushioned loungers and several Adirondak chairs scattered across the space. The table and chairs were weathered and needed refinishing. The view, on the other hand, needed nothing.

Amelia followed Noah to the wide rock wall that ran along the perimeter of the patio. They sat next to each other and stared at the blue water. A sense of calm and peace washed over Amelia as she focused on the bay.

Noah reached for her hand and kissed the tops of her knuckles. "I think this is it. I definitely took the long way, but I think I'm finally home. This is where I want to live out the rest of my days. However many or few that might be."

"The house is gorgeous, and the view is breathtaking."

He smiled and pointed toward the water. "Can you imagine sitting here to watch the sunsets? If I can make all this happen before you leave, I'd love to have you come and watch the first one with me."

Her heart fluttered, and she leaned her head on his shoulder. "I'd love that."

He rested his head on top of hers. "You also have to promise you'll come to visit. As you've just seen, I have plenty of room."

She swallowed the lump in her throat and whispered. "I promise."

———

When Jack suggested he might want to look at other properties, Noah was resolute that he didn't need to look any further. He'd found his home, and he was in a hurry to get the ball rolling. Noah dropped her at home while he went to Jack's office to deal with the paperwork to buy the house.

She watched over the dogs, with all three of them taking a nap, before Noah returned in the late afternoon. When he stepped inside, Goose rushed to him, tail wagging.

"Thanks for taking care of Goose." She offered him a seat and a glass of iced tea. He sighed and took a seat on the couch.

"How'd it go with Jack?" She handed him his glass and sat next to him. Within a few seconds, Goose and Faith climbed onto the couch and snuggled between the two of them, in a furry pile.

He glanced at the two of them and grinned. "Good. We submitted an offer, and then he contacted a colleague of his in Salem to discuss listing Mom's house. She'll start the process and send me the paperwork to sign. I'll just need to go back and empty it if it sells quickly."

"Don't try to do all that yourself. You can hire some help."

He nodded. "Yeah, the realtor has some people she works with and recommended them. I want to take my mom's dining room set and put it in my new place. There are a few other things I want to move, too. Her paintings, of course, and all my personal belongings. Most everything else I can sell or donate."

After a few swallows from his glass, he continued, "I'd been resisting the idea of selling her house, but now that I've found such a wonderful place that I love, it feels right. Mom knew she was on her way out, and I remember her telling me she wanted me to be happy and find a place I could call home. She knew I only moved there to help her and didn't want me to feel obligated to stay."

"I'm sure she'd be happy to see the house you found here."

"She would have loved it. It makes me sad that we didn't venture up here and visit this area when she was alive. She talked about coming to these islands long ago, I think when she was in her twenties. She and her parents came here and then over to Victoria on a trip and raved about how beautiful it was."

Amelia rubbed her arms. "That made me shiver. Something tells me your mom is smiling down on you right now and knows all about your new house. I felt that same way when I opened my bookstore. I knew my mom would be so happy for me."

"Speaking of your bookstore, I want to do a signing for you there. We need to make that happen this fall. Maybe when the new book comes out."

"That would be fantastic. I really want to do more author events, and you would be the biggest thing to hit Driftwood Bay in a very long time."

He laughed. "I'm not sure about that. It's been years since I did a signing. I'll talk to my agent and publisher and get it worked out. They'll think I've fallen and hit my head since they're always trying to get me to do signings."

"They probably won't be too excited with my little store in Driftwood Bay, but maybe they'll help promote it and get more people to come."

"I don't care who comes, as long as you're there."

Her pulse quickened as her heart thudded in her chest. He leaned closer to her, across the dogs, and brushed his lips over hers.

She closed her eyes, breathing in the scent of lemons and fresh-cut grass along his neck. She wanted this moment to last forever.

CHAPTER TWENTY-FIVE

Wednesday, Amelia woke with an anxious knot in her stomach. Today was the day Max and his doctor friend, Jan, were meeting with Noah. They were meeting at Max's office at the hospital, where he worked a few hours each week.

Amelia was ready early, waiting for Noah, who was dropping Goose at her place. She was scrolling her email on her laptop when they arrived.

Despite the brave smile, she could tell Noah was nervous. Last night, they took a walk, and he admitted as much. He ushered Goose through the door and sighed, standing as if he didn't want to leave.

"I'll just plan on keeping Goose all day, so don't worry about hurrying back to get him. I'm going to make salmon for dinner, so plan to eat here tonight."

The edges of his mouth lifted ever so slightly. "That's very sweet of you. I can't guarantee I'll be up for it, but I'll try." He sighed. "I've been waiting for this day and now that's it's here, I'm more scared than ever. It's going to get very real quickly."

She put both of her hands over his that were clasped together in front of him. "Try to remember to seek out everything you can do about what you're facing. I know it's not easy, and it's beyond worrisome, but from what you said, Jan gives people hope. She gives people tools to help. That's what you need and remember, you won't be alone. You've got a huge support group right here."

Instead of saying anything, he moved his hands and engulfed her in a tight hug. With a quick nod, he was out the door.

She noticed the slump of his shoulders as he trudged to his car. Her heart broke for him, and she prayed Jan would be able to give him some hope for the future.

To keep busy, she took the dogs for a long walk and then chatted with Mel about the possibility of a book signing with Noah and his new release out in November, just in time for holiday sales.

They batted around ideas and when she disconnected, for the first time since losing Natalie, Amelia was excited about her store again.

In a few days, August would be upon her. She only had a month left on the island, and a big part of her couldn't bear the thought of leaving. She craved the comfort of brownies or cookies, but with Noah coming for dinner, she didn't want to tempt him.

As her thoughts drifted to Noah, she wondered what his son was like. He was due to arrive on Friday, and his coming, coupled with the consultation with Jan, would be stressful.

She'd mentioned having Noah and Will for dinner while he was on the island, but Noah didn't commit one way or the other. It would be challenging enough for Noah to explain his medical condition. He didn't need the extra pressure of springing a new lady friend on him. If that's even what she was.

It was all so confusing and awkward.

As she contemplated her relationship status with Noah and what it meant if he wasn't willing to tell his son about her, her phone chimed.

She smiled and answered, "Hey, Sam."

"Hi, Amelia. Jeff and I were talking about Noah's son visiting. We want to host a get-together at the house so he can meet everyone, but we don't want to overstep. We know his visit might be difficult."

"I was just thinking about the same thing. I suggested I cook dinner for them, and Noah didn't seem excited about that. I do think a group event would be something Noah would be open to."

"What day does Will leave?"

"Tuesday morning."

"Let's plan for Sunday, then. Talk to Noah and let me know if he'd prefer a different day. I'll put a bug in Max's ear, too. He'll be spending more time with the two of them than anyone."

"That sounds great. Let me know what I can do to help."

"We've got things covered but feel free to bring an appetizer or dessert. Also, be sure to ask Henry and Doris to join us. They had such fun when they came before, and we'd love to see them again."

Amelia smiled. "I'll be sure to do that. Thanks, Sam."

She disconnected with a sense of peace. A group gathering would solve her worries about Will's visit and keep the pressure off Noah. With his tenuous relationship with his son, the two of them needed to figure things out before they announced anything to Will.

Filled with worry about Noah, Amelia couldn't quiet her mind. She opted for another walk with the dogs and when she returned, she made a cheesy potato dish she loved to pair with their salmon.

It was after five o'clock when Noah arrived at her door. Despite the long day, he greeted her with a smile and a quick kiss on her cheek. Goose and Faith stood next to them, with Goose focused on his master as he wagged his tail.

Noah rewarded him with a head scratch and lots of strokes to his back. "How's my boy? Were you good for Amelia?"

"He was excellent, as was Faith. They played and napped, and we took two walks." She raised her brows at him. "How about you?"

He sighed. "I'm on overload, but Dr. Jan, who prefers that to Dr. Myers, is wonderful. I never doubted Max, but she is top shelf."

Amelia reached for his hand. "Come on in. You can tell me about it while I finish our dinner."

He sat at the island and took a long swallow of iced tea, while Amelia went about finishing the salmon.

"As we suspected, she confirmed I do have Huntington's. She went through all my tests with me and explained the various blood tests she ran and of course, showed me the imaging. She also assessed my movements and motor skills."

He reached down to pet both dogs, who were sitting next to him. "She was impressed that my doctor, who is just a small-town physician, pinpointed the problem. She tells me I'm at a very early stage. The worst part of the day was when she explained how the disease normally progresses. It's brutal."

He recounted the stages and the increasingly awful symptoms related to being unable to swallow and eat properly, depression and mood swings, increased mobility and movement issues, and ultimately assisted living, where most patients die.

He let out a long breath. "Here's the good news, though. Dr. Jan works with other doctors, who use nutrition and supplements to keep patients at the lowest stage of the disease as possible. She's had good results and has a plan for me to follow."

His eyes glinted with tears. "She gave me some hope. She told me I was on the right track with eliminating sugar, but she also wants me to eliminate more things. It's going to be a real lifestyle adjustment."

She plated their food and carried it to the table. He grabbed the pitcher of iced tea and joined her. "That looks delicious. Thanks for cooking."

Amelia took the chair he pulled out for her and looked at his plate. "You're already so thin. I hope you don't lose any more weight by eliminating more things."

He shrugged. "The good news is, she wants me to eat more fats. The good fats she called them."

As they ate, he related how Dr. Jan explained inflammation is a huge factor in the disease, and eating an anti-inflammatory diet makes a huge difference. He rattled off several supplements he had to buy. "The other thing I have to change is my crazy sleep schedule. She wants me to work at increasing my exercise, just walking, but on a regular basis and getting good sleep. No more working late into the wee hours. She told me the optimum sleep time for most people, when the brain cleanses and heals is from about ten o'clock to two in the morning."

"That's interesting. I wonder how long it will take you to change your sleep pattern. I know that can be difficult."

He nodded. "Yeah, I need to tackle that right away. I'm horrible about that and always have been." He pointed at the salmon. "This is delicious, and Dr. Jan approved. She wants me to eat more cold-water fish."

Amelia grinned at him. "Well, your move to the island is perfect timing."

"Dr. Jan was happy to know that, too. She said with me living here and Max willing to help, she can treat me via telemedicine without a problem. Mostly, I'll need to get specific blood tests and brain scans on a regular basis."

"That's great news. Going back and forth to Florida would be almost impossible."

"She offered to connect me with someone in Seattle or Portland, but I really liked her, and I trust Max, so I was happy she was willing to do the video calls with me. She wants to try to keep me off the mainstream pharmaceuticals as long as possible and get my body working at its optimum level to keep me healthy."

She put her hand on his arm. "It sounds like she gave you some great strategies."

He put down his fork. "I never imagined having to face something like this, but she did make me feel better. Less afraid. Less alone. She made everything sound possible instead of bleak and insurmountable. It'll be work, for sure, but I think I'll feel better knowing I'm doing all I can."

"Is she willing to help you explain things to Will?"

His smile faded, and she wanted to claw back the words. "Yes, she said it's up to me, but she thinks he needs to know before he gets married and decides to have children. I'm trying to decide the best approach. I was hoping he might be able to have the blood test on Friday and get the lab results back by Monday, but Dr. Jan says it takes longer than that. The quickest is a week or ten days."

"Oh, that's not ideal."

"I'm not sure I want to bombard Will with all of this the moment he arrives." Noah sighed and shook his head.

He took a few sips from his glass. "I want him to be able to enjoy our time together and not spend the whole time with the disease hanging over our heads."

Amelia's forehead creased. "That's a good point. I don't know that there's a good answer. Maybe waiting until Monday is better. You could talk early in the day, get the test if he wants it, and I'm sure Dr. Jan would be willing to call him to go over the results or send them to his doctor in Virginia. Once she explains things to him, he might need time to consider everything anyway."

He nodded. "Right. I honestly don't know what to do. I think I'll have to play it by ear and see how he seems. I told him I had something important to tell him, so he knows something is up."

"Maybe you can show him the house and keep it light and happy with your move here, then feel your way." She gasped. "Oh, I almost forgot, Sam called and wants to have you bring Will to her place to meet everyone on Sunday if that works. She's flexible, so if Saturday or Monday is better, I can let her know."

"Oh, that's sweet of her and Jeff. They're a class act. I'd like Will to meet everyone, so that sounds good. I just don't know about timing."

"Well, Max and Jan will be there Sunday. It might be nice for him to meet them in that context before you break the news."

"True. At least he'll be here relatively early on Friday. He's on a nonstop that will get him to Seattle around nine-thirty, and I booked him a charter that will fly him right to the harbor. So, he'll be here before noon. I didn't want him to have to deal with renting a car and driving up to Anacortes for the ferry." After a moment, he added, "Especially not on the return journey. He's bound to be upset, and I don't want him behind the wheel."

"That's smart, and he doesn't have much time here, so it makes sense to make the most of it."

She reached for her tea. "Friday, you could have lunch, show him the new house, and take him around the island."

His eyes went wide. "In all the drama of today, I forgot to tell you... Jack called. He said the owners accepted the offer, and we'll close in about three weeks. He got permission to give me the key so I can show it to Will."

"That's fabulous news." She started to take another bite and paused. "Maybe you could take him golfing with the guys on Friday or Saturday?"

"Yeah, I thought about that. I should book a time. That would give us something to do Saturday. He'll be tired from all the travel on Friday."

"So, we've got Friday covered with lunch and the house. Saturday is golf. Sunday is the party at Sam's. I think it makes more and more sense to tell him about your diagnosis late Sunday or Monday. He might not be ready to get the test right now. That way he could talk to his mom about it when he gets home."

"You're right. I think I just needed a voice of reason. Someone a little removed from all my feelings."

"For the guy who likes to plan, at least you have one."

He chuckled. "It reminds me of work years ago, and we'd say it looks good on paper. We stopped saying that after so many times the plan didn't go as written. I do like having one in mind, though."

They finished dinner, and she urged him to relax with the dogs while she tucked the leftovers in the fridge and tidied the kitchen. When she joined him in the living area, his tired eyes met hers, and she noticed he was struggling to stay awake.

"After the day you've had, it might be a good night to start your new sleep schedule."

He chuckled and stood. "I think you're right. I was going home to order all the supplements from Dr. Jan's list, but I'm exhausted."

She plucked a container from the fridge and walked him and Goose to the door. "That's understandable. It's been an emotionally draining day." She handed him the container. "Take this for tomorrow so you don't have to think about meal prep."

He hugged her close. "I'm not sure what I did to deserve you, but I'm so glad you're here."

She waved at both of them as they walked toward his car. "I'll see you tomorrow."

After she locked the door and doused the lights, she took her own advice and padded to the bedroom. As soon as she rested her head on the pillow, tears spilled from her eyes.

The emotions she'd been holding in throughout the day and mixture of worry, fear, and something that felt like love for Noah, tumbled out in her fresh tears. Faith inched closer to her and rested her head against Amelia's.

She reached out a hand to her sweet girl and shut her eyes.

CHAPTER TWENTY-SIX

F riday, after a walk with Izzy, Jess, and their dogs, Amelia concentrated on cleaning the house. In case Noah brought Will over, she wanted it to look its best.

By the time her laundry was done, and she was happy with the gleaming floors and clutter-free tables and counters, she was starving and opted to dash into town for lunch.

She had to park behind the hardware store, since the street was packed. When she and Faith walked by Sam's coffee shop, Sam hollered out a greeting from the deck. She pointed at the table she just cleaned and waved Amelia over.

"We've been swamped but come sit and enjoy the day. I'll make you something to drink."

Amelia couldn't resist the inviting view under the red umbrella. "I was just going to grab some lunch."

Sam wiggled her brows. "What if I told you I just picked up a sandwich from Dottie's, and I'm happy to share it. Jeff ate early, so there's no way I can eat the whole thing by myself. If you're game, I'll join you out here. I need a break."

"Wow, only if you're sure. I don't want to take your lunch from you."

With a flit of her hand, Sam waved away her concern. "I'd love to share it, and I need a lunch buddy. I'll be back in a jiffy."

While they waited, Faith wandered to the large bowl Sam always kept filled with water and took a few slurps. Amelia sat back in her chair and relaxed as she watched the bustle of tourists make their way down the sidewalk, many fresh from the ferry, toting their luggage.

A few minutes later, Sam returned with a tray and delivered raspberry lemonades for each of them, along with the sandwich, and a plate of warm brownies. Amelia's eyes went wide. "Oh, my. This all looks delicious."

Sam sat in her chair and let out a long sigh. "Fridays are always so busy." She pointed at Amelia's plate. "Dig in. I'm starving."

"Me, too. I've been cleaning the house all morning."

They chatted between bites. Sam reached for another napkin. "Did you get a chance to ask Noah about Sunday?"

"Yes, I'm so sorry. I forgot to get back to you. He likes that idea and was so touched you thought of doing it. He's pretty nervous about Will's visit."

"I can imagine," said Sam, picking up her sandwich.

"At least Noah is feeling better after meeting with Max's doctor friend. She gave him more hope than he anticipated."

"That's excellent news. We've all decided not to bring it up or say anything about it unless Noah does. We understand how hard this all is for him and now especially with Will visiting."

As they nibbled on their brownies, Faith's tail thumped against the legs of Amelia's chair, and her eyes focused on the sidewalk in front of the deck. When Amelia followed her gaze, she spotted Noah, walking with a tall young man, who looked exactly like him.

Before she could restrain Faith, the dog darted to the edge of the deck and captured Noah's attention. He smiled and bent to pet her. He glanced up and saw Amelia and Sam and motioned his son to follow him.

Faith led them to the table, and Noah put his hand on his son's shoulder. "Will, this is my friend Amelia, who is visiting the island and staying at her sister's just down from my rental." He turned toward Sam and said, "And this is Sam, who owns this fine establishment."

He smiled and extended his hand to both of them. "Pleasure to meet you both."

Noah reached over to Faith. "And this sweet girl is Faith. She and Goose are great friends."

Will knelt close to Faith and petted her, smiling and talking to her.

Amelia was struck by the uncanny resemblance he had to his father. She gestured to the empty chairs. "You're welcome to join us."

Sam gathered their empty plates, leaving the brownies. "I've got to get back to work, but I can bring you something to drink if you'd like?"

Noah glanced at Will. He nodded and took a chair. "Sounds good to me."

She suggested raspberry lemonade, and Will nodded. "Perfect."

Noah took a chair and said, "I'll do an unsweetened iced tea, Sam."

She took her tray and promised to return in a few minutes.

Noah pointed toward the sidewalk. "We just came from lunch at Lou's."

Amelia raised her brows. "Oh, that's a good choice. His crabcakes are so good."

Will smiled. "Yeah, we usually make the short drive to Maryland for this place that is famous for theirs, but these were every bit as good."

Amelia moved the plate of brownies closer to Will. "Help yourself. Sam makes epic brownies."

He grinned and reached for one, sliding his sunglasses on top of his head, revealing the same gray eyes of his father. He took a bite and nodded. "Really good."

Sam appeared with their drinks and a refill for Amelia. "I'd love to stay and visit, but customers are stacked up in there. We'll see you this weekend, though."

As she left, Noah turned to Will. "She and her husband Jeff, who owns the hardware store I showed you, invited us to a party at their place on Sunday."

Will finished his brownie and washed it down with a gulp of his lemonade. "Sounds good to me."

Noah turned his attention to Amelia. "I'm going to run Will out to the new house and show him around this afternoon. Thought we'd relax the rest of the day, but if you're up for a walk in the evening, we could swing by and get you two?"

"We'll be home, so that works for us. Faith would love to see Goose."

Will offered the last brownie to his dad, but Noah shook his head. "I'm cutting out sweets; you go ahead."

Amelia noticed the hint of worry in Noah's eyes. No doubt he dreaded having to reveal why and hoped Will wouldn't have to worry about changing his life and diet to thwart a disease he may have inherited.

She reached for Faith's leash. "I think you're going to love your dad's new house, Will. It's got a terrific view.

We're going to head home but hope to see you later tonight."

She stood, and Noah and Will each started to stand. She put up her hand. "Just stay where you are and enjoy yourselves. It was great to meet you, Will. Your dad has really been looking forward to your visit."

"Nice to meet you as well, Amelia. I'm sure we'll see you later."

They both waved as she and Faith made their way off the deck and toward the hardware store.

She loaded Faith in the backseat and wound her way through the traffic of downtown, opting to take a side street to get back to the road for home. Once she and Faith got home, she settled into the corner of the couch and turned on the television.

As she distracted herself with another episode of the mystery series she enjoyed, the busy morning caught up with her, and her eyes grew heavy. She and Faith didn't make it even halfway through it before she fell asleep.

After a restful nap, Amelia ate some leftovers for dinner and scrolled recipes, looking for something good to take to Sam's gathering on Sunday. She found a burrata salad made with heirloom tomatoes and peaches. With the farmer's market tomorrow morning, she hoped to find the fresh produce she needed and scribbled down a list of things to buy.

As she washed her dishes, Faith rushed to the door and spun in circles.

Amelia dried her hands and hurried to the door where Noah and Goose waited. Will, who had changed into shorts, stood next to them. "Come in. I just need to get my walking shoes, and we'll be ready to go."

As she slipped into her shoes, Noah attached Faith's leash and handed it to her after she locked the door. Noah pointed in the direction of the pathway that led to the trail around the golf course. "I thought we could make a loop and then head over to the beach."

"Perfect, lead the way."

Will walked beside Noah, with Goose between them. As they followed the curve of the path, Noah pointed at the green closest to them. "We'll be out there tomorrow morning."

Will nodded. "Looks like a nice course."

Noah grinned. "It's great, and you're going to like the group of guys joining us tomorrow. Colin, he's the manager here, hooked us up and is treating us to breakfast at the clubhouse after."

"Wow, you've got some great friends, Dad."

"I do indeed. That's one of the reasons I'm so glad I'll be living here."

While they were stopped to gaze at the view, Amelia turned to Will. "What did you think of your dad's new place?"

"It's terrific. Like you said, that view is something else. It's a really nice property, and it's quiet so Dad can work."

While they walked, Noah mentioned Will's job and encouraged him to tell Amelia about it.

In an excited tone, he told her about working at the law firm and how much he liked it. He put in long hours but was trying to prove himself to the partners, since his goal was to become one. "My stepdad helped get me a position there when I was still in law school, so I'm on a fast track."

"Sounds like you're a hard worker. I think you come by

that naturally." She chuckled and followed Noah as he continued on the path.

"Yeah, Dad is definitely a workaholic, so I probably inherited that trait."

Noah turned back to them. "I told Will I'll be slowing down, and I hope he can schedule some more trips out here to visit."

"I've never been to the West Coast, only to Oregon for Grandma's funeral, and it's really beautiful. I'd like to come again when I have more time. Dad will have plenty of room, that's for sure."

"I know he'd love to have you."

They finished the loop, and Noah led them to the road and the sandy trail that took them to the beach. Noah and Amelia hung back and grinned as Will took in the view.

"Wow," he said, turning toward them. "This is so cool."

As they neared the shoreline, he slipped out of his shoes and socks and left them on a piece of driftwood while he made his way to the edge of the water. He braved the cold water and walked into the ocean.

When he turned to face them, his smile melted Amelia's heart. He looked like a little boy. She stepped closer to Noah and leaned her arm into his. He looked down at her and grinned.

They walked the dogs closer to the water but didn't let them run into it. The two dogs watched Will, their feet lifting, itching to join him, but it was too late for baths tonight.

Instead, Amelia and Noah strolled along the edge of the water, letting the dogs get their feet wet but nothing more. It was a gorgeous evening, with the sun just above the horizon, sending vibrant orange swathes across the sky.

Will continued to splash in the water and while Noah watched him, his smile never faded.

The sunset, the water, Will's laughter, and Noah's easy smile filled Amelia with joy.

In a word, it was perfection.

As it got darker, the three of them and the dogs climbed the trail up to the road and made their way back to the neighborhood. Noah dropped Will and Goose at the house, so Will could rinse the dog off and insisted on walking Amelia to her door.

She wished Will good night and tried to dissuade Noah, but he took her hand and held it as they made their way along the sidewalk.

"It looks like you had a good day with Will."

He nodded. "It was the best. He's matured since we last saw each other, and we had a great day. He loved the house and was excited about it." He paused and added, "In some ways, that makes all this worse."

His voice cracked, and she squeezed his hand.

They arrived at her door, and he led Faith inside and unclipped her leash. She hurried to her water bowl, and he met Amelia's eyes. "I was worried to tell Will that I'd found someone I care for, but after we chatted with you at Sam's, he brought it up. He remarked how nice you were, not to mention beautiful, and asked if we were a couple."

Her pulse pounded. "What did you say?"

"I asked how he'd feel about that, and he said I deserved to be happy." Tears filled his eyes. "He's right. If you'll have me, I'd love to be able to tell him, yes, we are a couple. Like I told you before,

I felt a connection to you from the first day, but with everything going on, I was afraid to even think about a serious relationship. I have no idea how things will progress or how we'll make long distance work, but more than anything, I want you in my life. You've made me feel something I haven't in a long time. Happy."

He put his fingers to her lips. "Don't say anything yet. I just want you to know. We can talk after I face Will and what I have to tell him."

Before she could say anything, he kissed her and left.

As she watched him hurry down her walkway, she stood, stunned.

CHAPTER TWENTY-SEVEN

A melia was up early on Saturday and dashed to the farmer's market with her list. She was able to find the heirloom tomatoes she wanted, along with some peaches and fresh herbs for her salad. She picked up some other fruit and veggies while she was there, snagged a few other things from the market, and even stopped by Sam's shop for a chai tea latte on her way home.

There was no time for a walk with Faith, but she was excited to load up into the SUV for their Saturday delivery adventure. When they arrived at Henry's house on Saturday, Doris greeted her at the door and welcomed Faith, while Amelia toted their box to the kitchen.

Music drifted from the player, and Henry was in his chair, smiling. Doris followed Amelia to the kitchen and helped her unload the groceries. "I hope you can stay for lunch today. I've made egg salad sandwiches and some lovely fruit I picked up this morning at the market."

She jumped at the opportunity to spend more time with two of her favorite people. As she finished her work in the kitchen, she noticed the little touches around the house, like freshly cut flowers on the table and in the living room next to Henry's chair. They both looked happy and content, which made Amelia's heart happy.

She helped Doris set up their lunch in the backyard at a beautiful outdoor table under a turquoise umbrella. Henry used the new ramp Jeff installed without any issues, and Faith settled in at his feet while they enjoyed lunch.

Henry caught Amelia's eye from across the table. "You mentioned Noah was expecting his son this week. Have you met him?"

"Oh, yes. I almost forgot. Sam is having a little shindig at her house tomorrow. She wanted me to be sure to invite both of you. You can show up anytime after noon. It's just a casual cookout. If you need a ride, we can arrange that, too."

Henry raised his bushy brows. "She's got a lovely place. What do you say, Doris? Are you up for another outing?"

She laughed. "Of course. That was a wonderful time there. What shall we bring?"

Amelia shook her head. "Nothing is necessary. Sam told me if I insisted, I could bring a side dish or dessert but don't feel like you must."

Doris rose from her chair. "Speaking of dessert, I forgot the cookies."

She hurried to the house and returned with a plate of snickerdoodles. Amelia took one bite and was instantly transported to her childhood. Her mom made the best snickerdoodles, and they were often her after-school snack. Doris' rivaled her mother's.

Amelia finished off her cookie and gestured at Henry. "Back to Noah's son. Yes, I met Will. He looks exactly like Noah. Tall, handsome, the whole package. You'll meet him tomorrow. Sam is doing the party to let Will meet all of Noah's friends."

"I look forward to it," said Henry, reaching for a cookie. He winked at Amelia. "I told you if Doris moved in, I would gain weight."

Doris beamed and laughed. "I'll make something to bring, and I can drive us out there, no problem."

"If you change your mind, just call me." Amelia stared at the cookies but resisted the urge for another. "Last night, Noah told me he cared for me and wants to know what I think about being a couple. Seems Will prompted that by asking if we were one."

Doris and Henry looked at each other and nodded. "It's about time," he said.

Amelia's lips curved into a smile. "I have feelings for him, no doubt. It's just complicated."

Doris patted her hand. "Because of his illness, dear?"

Henry took a swallow from his glass. "Noah stopped by the other day and spent an hour here with us while he was waiting for Will's seaplane to arrive. He told us all about the diagnosis and Max's doctor friend."

"It's heartbreaking," said Doris. "He's quite concerned about his son inheriting it."

Amelia nodded. "He's going to tell him Monday, with the doctor's help."

When Noah was here with us Friday morning, he was looking for advice," said Henry.

Doris refilled her glass and Amelia's. He said talking to us reminded him of talking to his parents, and he needed our wisdom."

Henry winked at Amelia. "I gave him the same advice I gave you. It's worth the risk. Illness or no illness. If you love each other, it doesn't matter. You'll find a way to deal with whatever comes your way. Believe me, it's much easier to deal with things when you have a true partner. As much as I built my life while being alone, it's difficult. I wasted many good years floundering in my own grief."

Doris nodded. "We encouraged him to tell you how he felt. We all have a limited amount of time and if anything, I think knowing about an illness makes it even more important to take a leap of faith, especially when it comes to love."

Amelia sighed. "I'm torn. I have a business I can't abandon, but I love it here and can see myself being happy with Noah. His illness gives me pause but like you said, Henry, we both know tomorrow isn't promised to any of us. I guess I'm not sure if I can handle what will come."

Doris shook her head. "My dear, you're stronger than you realize. Look what you've handled thus far. I think you're equipped for anything that comes your way."

Henry nodded. "And you and Noah have a great group of friends and lots of support here. You're not alone."

Doris pushed the plate of cookies closer to Amelia. "The easiest way to answer the question is to ask yourself if you can imagine your life without Noah? Would you be happy?"

They made it sound so simple.

Amelia reached for a cookie and let the sweetness comfort her.

When they got home, Amelia took Faith for a well-deserved walk around the golf course and when Faith finished her dinner, they snuggled together on the couch. Amelia skipped dinner, still full from all the cookies she'd scarfed down at lunch. She tuned the television to a movie she'd seen before, one of those comforting small-town stories she loved. With the drone of it in the background, she scribbled on her notepad.

In reality, like Henry and Doris had reminded her, Driftwood Bay was only a few hours away from the island. It wasn't that long of a distance when it came to relationships.

She couldn't imagine leaving and not being a part of Noah's life. That was the easy part of the answer. She wondered how it might work if she spent part of her time on the island with him and the other in Driftwood Bay. Would he consider spending time with her there? At some point, it might become too difficult for him to travel, but at the moment, that might work.

As she added notes, she circled the word marriage. She wasn't sure she wanted to marry again. She also didn't want to complicate things with Will. She remembered Georgia talking about Izzy helping Dale construct his estate plan and the reason he bought Georgia this house. He wanted her to have something that was hers and hers alone.

Things got tricky for second marriages when kids were involved. She had no clue about Noah's financial status, other than the fact that he could afford the new house without a problem. He mentioned saving his advances and royalties, so he clearly wasn't a wanton spender.

They needed to have a serious conversation if they were even contemplating a future together. What did that look like to Noah?

Amelia woke rested on Sunday. The early night last night had proven to be what she needed. All the emotions surrounding Noah's meeting with Dr. Jan and then Will had taken a toll. Her constant thoughts contemplating a future with Noah only added to her tired state. All of it, no matter how exhausting, was a welcome respite from thinking about Nat. With her mind busy, her grief wasn't near as heavy.

She let Henry know she wouldn't be at church today, and he surprised her by saying he was going to visit Doris' church, where she played the piano. The thought brought a smile to her lips.

Instead of rushing to get ready, she and Faith set out on a walk and took their time, relishing the almost cloudless sky and the gentle breeze from the water that made walking almost effortless.

When she walked by Izzy's house, she made a mental note to probe her for advice on how she and Noah might approach their future together and if it came to it, how a marriage would impact each of them. His medical condition would definitely need to be considered.

The world had changed so much from when she was young and contemplating marriage. She never imagined she would ever consider living with a man. It made her think of Kate and Spence, who seemed to make that work marvelously. She never asked but wondered why they never married. They were perfect for each other.

At this stage in her life, she didn't need complications. Her feelings for Noah were real, but she wasn't about to jump into marriage. She was too old to care what people thought and with what Noah was dealing with, she liked the idea of a trial period for both of them.

He didn't need any extra stress, and the idea of taking things slow appealed to Amelia. She was in a weird place, emotionally. She was stronger than when she'd arrived on the island, but a sense of apprehension came over when she thought about returning to Driftwood Bay and the bookstore. It might be too real.

As her feelings vacillated from eagerness to trepidation when it came to a serious commitment to Noah, she kept walking. Faith finally tugged her toward the water bowl by the bench, and they took a break. She'd lost track of how many times they made the loop but checked her watch and surmised they were on their fourth pass.

After their rest, she led Faith back to the house. While the dog stretched out on her cot and napped, Amelia took a shower and then got busy making the salad. After she had the tomatoes and fruit sliced, she added the ball of burrata and tucked in a few basil leaves before drizzling it all with the lemon and garlic-infused olive oil dressing.

It smelled divine, and she couldn't resist sampling a bite. She closed her eyes as she let the flavors meld in her mouth. It was fabulous.

She tucked it in the fridge while she changed. She chose denim capris just in case she had the opportunity to dip her toes in the water and added a crisp, white, sleeveless blouse. She made sure she packed her sunhat and an oversized white shirt to wear in case it cooled off later in the day.

As she and Faith drove past the turn for Noah's new house, a lump formed in her throat. After today, Will's world would change forever. She hated that his innocence would be lost, and he'd have to face the reality of his dad's illness and fear that the same might be in store for him.

Tears stung her eyes as she thought of Will and his smile at the beach and the joy in Noah's eyes when he looked at his son. She vowed to be there for both of them, no matter what.

CHAPTER TWENTY-EIGHT

J eff met her in the driveway and took hold of Faith, leading her to the backyard, where she could play with Bailey, Zoe, and Lucy, who belonged to Linda and Max. The others hadn't arrived yet.

Sam took the salad from her, and her eyes went wide. "Oh, my, that looks out of this world. I bet I could eat this entire platter."

Amelia lowered her voice. "I did a sneak taste test, and it's beyond yummy."

Sam stuck it in the fridge and gestured toward the deck. "Come on out and meet Jan, Max's friend."

Amelia followed Sam and hugged Linda hello before slipping into the chair next to her. As they visited with Linda, describing the wedding flowers she worked on for an event at Blake and Ellie's, Max and a woman with shoulder-length red hair came up the stairs to the deck.

He caught Amelia's eye and smiled. "I was just telling Jan I was anxious for her to meet you."

Amelia rose and walked closed to them, extending her

hand. "So nice to meet you, Dr. Jan. I've heard such wonderful things about you from Noah and Max."

The woman, with pretty green eyes and freckles across her nose and cheeks, smiled at her. "Lovely to meet you too, Amelia. Just call me Jan. I have my patients call me Dr. Jan because they seem to like using the doctor prefix, but I'm really just Jan."

Jeff fetched iced teas, wine, and lemonades and then took a seat next to Sam. Jan was in the midst of telling Amelia about living in Florida, in a little town called Dragonfly Cove, when Spence and Kate arrived. Spence led their dog Roxie to join the others. As soon as they sat with drinks, Doris and Henry came from the house, followed by Noah and Will, who were watching out for Henry as he made his way to a chair.

Jeff delivered more beverages and introduced Jan and Noah to all the newcomers. Soon, Nate and Regi joined them, along with Izzy and Colin and even more dogs. Blake and Ellie were working until later in the evening.

Dean and Jess arrived with Rebel and Ruby, and Jeff took Ruby to play with the others, while Spence took over the beverage service. Rebel, being the loyal service dog he was, stuck close to Dean and settled at his feet.

Nate and Jeff manned the grill, while the others visited and snacked on appetizers. Each time Amelia glanced over at Will, she found him smiling and engaged in a conversation. Dean sat closest to him, telling him about Rebel and how he acquired a service dog after leaving the military.

Spence entertained everyone with stories from his time serving as a detective with the Seattle Police, and a few of his stories made Will's eyes widen.

Even with what was to come tomorrow and the conversation Noah had to have, it was a perfect afternoon and evening. Henry and Doris left before it got dark, and Ellie and Blake showed up late, but there was plenty of good food left for them.

As the sun set, Jeff lit the firepit down by the beach, and Noah reached for Amelia's hand. "How about a walk on the beach?"

She nodded and let him lead the way. They walked along the edge of the water, content to say nothing and listen to the gentle crash of the waves as they collided with the shore.

Noah stopped and stared at the horizon. The purple and pink sky was breathtaking. He turned to Amelia. "I hate to ruin this perfect day, but I have a favor to ask of you."

"Sure." She nodded. "Anything."

"I asked Max and Dr. Jan to meet me at the new house tomorrow. I want to tell Will there, and I'm hoping you'll be there, too."

"Of course," she said in a steadier voice than she felt. "I'll be there."

He explained he wanted to tell him in the morning, so he'd have all day to get his questions asked before he went home and have time to get his blood drawn at the hospital if he wanted to.

"That makes perfect sense."

He sighed. "I just pray he doesn't have it."

"Me, too, Noah. Me, too."

Despite the blue skies, when Amelia set out for Noah's new house, she was filled with dread. She wanted to be there for him and for Will, but she hated being part of the conversation that would change the young man she'd come to care for, forever.

She and Faith pulled into the driveway. Noah was already there.

As she stared at the front door, Max and Jan pulled in behind her.

They made their way to the porch, and Jan put an arm around Amelia's shoulders. "I know you're nervous, just like Noah. It won't be easy, but I've done this many, many times. The anticipation that's hanging over Noah might be worse than the actual outcome. Regardless, I'll be there to help Noah and Will, every step of the way."

Amelia nodded, but her throat was too dry to make a sound. Jan's words comforted her, as did her confident but kind manner.

Before she could knock, Noah opened the door and led them to the patio.

She took one of the Adirondak chairs, as did Max. Jan sat with Noah and Will on the rock wall.

As she promised, she took over the conversation and explained that Noah had asked her to come to explain about his health condition and recent diagnosis. She explained the disease, without getting into the stages and what could come, but focused on that fact that Noah was healthy and had been diagnosed at the earliest possible time. She described the hundreds of patients she treated successfully and assured Will that she expected Noah to do well.

As she spoke, Will's face paled. He reached for his dad's arm and held onto it the entire time she talked.

He asked a few questions, and Max retrieved bottles of water from the fridge for everyone. Jan answered each of his concerns and explained how she planned to treat Noah via telemedicine along with utilizing Max and his office at the hospital for routine tests and consultations. "Your dad will need to have brain scans every six months, and he'll have to go to Seattle for that."

The poor kid was shellshocked but nodded his understanding.

After everyone had sips from their water, Jan continued. As gently as possible, she explained there was a chance Will could have inherited the same faulty genetic code. She went on to detail the tests he could have and was careful to explain their limitations.

She also went over the things to consider when making the decision on testing, reminding everyone that some people preferred not to know, while others wanted the information and pointed out the upside of knowing before Will had children. She stressed it was totally up to Will, and there was no rush to decide.

"It's something you have to decide if you want to do it. It's a simple blood draw that we can do here today, or you can do at another time if you want to think about it. The results take around ten days to come back. If you have a doctor you see in Virginia, I can forward them to him, or I can just meet you on video and give you the results."

Tears pools in Will's eyes and fell onto his cheeks. He kept shaking his head and saying, "No, no, this can't be happening."

He rose and ran toward the edge of the patio and onto the grass that led to the front of the house.

Max nodded at Noah. "I'll go. Don't worry. Just stay here, and I'll bring him back when he's ready."

Noah's shoulders slumped, and he put his head in his hands. He was a broken man. Jan reached over and rested a hand on his shoulder.

He finally lifted his head. "I hate this so much."

Jan nodded. "You remember how you felt when you

received the news. Will is dealing with the worry about you and his own fate. It's a double-whammy, and his reaction is perfectly normal. It's a huge shock."

Amelia suggested a walk, and she and Noah strolled along the patio, stopping to gaze at the water every few steps before Noah returned to his place on the wall. Almost ninety minutes later, Max returned with Will. He had more color in his face and looked less stressed.

Max placed his arm around Will's shoulder and led him back to the rock wall. Noah stood as Will approached, and his son rushed into his arms. "I'm sorry, Dad."

Noah held the back of his head against his chest. "I'm the one who's sorry. For so many things, but right now, for this."

Max took his chair and gave Amelia a reassuring nod.

Noah and Will took their seats, and Will sucked in a long breath. "I think it makes sense for me to take the test. I think not knowing might be worse than knowing."

Noah frowned at his son. "Do you want to talk to your mom, first?"

He shook his head. "No, I need to do this, and I'm not sure I can deal with her right now. That's one reason I want to take it. When I know more, I can tell her about you and then share whatever Dr. Jan finds out from my test." Will sighed. "You know her, Dad. She'll dog me with questions and if I don't have answers, it will only be more stressful."

Noah nodded and clapped his son on the back. "I agree, one hundred percent."

Max stood and said, "I've got my bag in the kitchen. We can do the draw here, and I'll get it down to the hospital and sent out today."

Will nodded. "That's what I want. I only wish I could get the results today."

Jan stood and led Will to one of the doors that led to the

kitchen. "I understand that and promise you the moment I get the results, I'll call you. I'm going to be on the island for a couple of weeks, so I'll be here when the results arrive. We can set up a video with you, and your dad can join us. Your mom, too, if that would be helpful."

They disappeared through the door, and Amelia rushed to Noah's side. She gripped his hand in hers and squeezed it "I know there's nothing I can say. Just know that I'm here for you and Will. Whatever you need."

He leaned his head against her and sobbed.

The next ten days went by at a snail's pace. Max checked on the results each day and texted to let Noah know he did. In turn, Noah texted Amelia.

Noah asked for Amelia's patience and understanding and wanted to spend the days waiting alone. He wanted to spend the time working. Amelia understood he needed to escape reality, plus she believed him when he said he would be terrible company. Being productive helped him, and she promised to include Goose on her walks.

Amelia did her best to keep busy with her remote work at the bookstore, her food bank work, and walking the dogs. Lunch and dinner invitations from all her friends rolled in, and she felt better each time she went and enjoyed the company.

Despite her distractions, the wait was excruciating, and she couldn't imagine the stress Noah was experiencing. She texted him updates on Goose and usually sent him a good night message each evening. He promised to stick to a more normal schedule and get rest like Dr. Jan advised, but Amelia doubted he was getting enough. She was having trouble sleeping, so he had to be.

Late in the afternoon, eight working days later, Amelia's phone rang and when she saw Noah's name on her screen, in her excitement, she almost dropped it before she could tap the green button.

"Amelia," he said, his voice serious. "Max just called, and the results came in. I'm heading over to his house to join in the video call with Will. I was hoping you could come, too."

Her heart fluttered. "I'll be waiting at the curb."

She left Faith with a promise she'd be back soon and hurried outside. As soon as she locked the door, Noah pulled up, and she ran to his car.

Noah pushed the speed limit, and they made it out to Max's place in fifteen minutes. Max and Jan were in the living room with the laptop connected and ready to go. Max pointed at the huge screen on the wall. "I've got it set so we can see Will on the larger screen."

Noah and Amelia took a seat on the couch, next to Jan and Max. She glanced over at Noah and smiled. Before she could say anything, Will's face filled the screen. He was dressed in a suit and tie, still at work. Like his father, Amelia suspected he escaped in his work.

He gave them a weak smile.

Jan put on her reading glasses and opened the file in front of her. "I know you're anxious, as is everyone. So, I'm just going to dive right in and explain these results to you. The result shows you will not develop Huntington's disease." She looked up at the screen. "So, Will, just to be clear, you don't have to worry about your future; you won't get the disease."

Everyone in the room let out a sigh of relief, and the look on Will's face was one of pure joy. Amelia wiped the happy tears from her eyes and when she glanced over at Noah, she handed him a tissue for his.

Jan smiled at Will. "As I explained to you when we talked about the test, there are four groupings of values that tell us about your likelihood to develop the disease and that of any children you father. Your result is in the second strand, which means you could pass the Huntington's genetic error to your child. Your values are in the low range, so there's a good chance you could not pass it on. It's not something we can guarantee either way."

Will nodded his understanding. "I remember you explaining that. Right now, I'm just happy I don't have to worry about it. I need to give some thought to the other. At the moment, I'm not really thinking about kids, but when that time comes, I want to talk to you more."

Jan removed her reading glasses. "I'm happy to do that, Will. We learn more about this disease each month it seems, so when that time comes, I may have more information or more tests that would help refine things for you."

He thanked her and addressed his dad. "I'm going to tell Mom about you if that's okay. Now that I know I don't have it, it will be a calmer conversation. I'll call you after I talk to her this weekend."

"Sounds good, Will. I'm so happy you don't have to face this."

"Me, too. I'm just sorry you do." He cleared his throat. "I also wanted to see if I could come for the holidays this year. I need to put in for the time off, but I'd like to visit you if that works."

Noah's leg rested against Amelia's, and she could feel the excitement humming through his body. "That would be more than okay. I'd love it. Just keep me posted, and I'll organize getting you from the airport to the island."

Will's smile returned, and he gave them all a wave. "Thank you. All of you. I really appreciate you being there for me and my dad."

Noah reached for Amelia's hand and brought it close to his lips. He kissed the top of it and met her watery eyes. "Now, there's the matter of the two of us."

CHAPTER TWENTY NINE

After thanking Max and Jan, Noah drove Amelia back to her house. As he pulled into the driveway, he grinned. "I think we deserve a celebration. Are you up for an outing?"

"Oh, am I. I need to burn off this nervous energy."

"Goose and I will be back within the hour. You and Faith be ready." He leaned over and kissed her.

She laughed and promised they'd be ready. It was wonderful to see him smiling again.

Amelia fed Faith her dinner and had just put her walking shoes on when Noah arrived. He took hold of both leashes in one hand and held hers with the other. He led the way to the beach and when they arrived, he pointed at a table, set up with two chairs facing the water. Votive candles flickered in the breeze atop the white cloth.

She frowned and said, "How did you manage all this?"

"It pays to have friends like Colin."

He dragged her chair through the sand and held it while she took her seat. Once he was seated next to her, he removed the covers from their plates. Hers held one of her favorites, a crab pasta, and his was some halibut with baby red potatoes and fresh veggies.

Amelia was starving and couldn't resist diving into the big plate of pasta that smelled delicious. As they ate, the sun dipped lower and kissed the top of the water, sending a sparkle of gold across it.

Noah raised his glass of iced tea and clinked it against hers. "First, I want to thank you for being there for me and Will over these last days. I know I've been less than companionable. I couldn't have made it through all of this without you. Second, I want to finish that conversation we started when Will was here. I know, now more than ever, I want you and need you in my life. I'm not sure what that will look like, but I think we can figure it out together."

She held her glass to his and smiled. "I feel the same way, Noah. Doris actually helped me grasp it."

He laughed and said, "Oh, do tell."

"She told me to imagine my life without you, and I can't do it. That's when I realized we can make this work. We're both smart people, we can figure it out. Henry also reminded me that Driftwood Bay is only a few hours away. I was thinking we could split our time between the two places."

"Funny you should mention that. When I talked to Will about you, before I told him about my illness and all the angst that came with that, he suggested something similar. He told me I was happier than he ever remembered, and he wanted me to stay that way. I like that idea."

They each took a sip from their glasses and reached out, clasping their hands together.

She took in a deep breath. "If you're okay with the idea, I'd like to take things slow, see how we do. I'm going to try to not get wrapped up in the future or worry about what's ahead. I want to hang onto this happiness we have now."

He smiled and squeezed her hand. "My thoughts exactly. I don't know what tomorrow will bring our way, but I can't imagine not having you with me when it arrives. With Will's good news, it's even clearer that I need to live for the present and embrace the chance at a life filled with happiness with the woman I love."

Tears leaked from her eyes as the sun dipped further into the ocean. "Like you said before, I think we both took the long way home, but it was worth it to find you and a second chance at happiness. I wasn't sure I'd ever find love again, but meeting you changed all that."

As the sun disappeared, and the first stars brightened the inky sky, they kissed and sealed their promise to each other.

EPILOGUE

Twinkle lights hung in the windows of *Books by the Bay*, along with a huge poster of Noah's new book. His publisher had shipped boxes of copies to the store, and they promoted the exclusive access attendees would get at Noah's signing. It was a rare event that offered customers a reading, an early autographed copy the day before the official release, and a reception with Noah after the signing.

The event sold out in less than a day, and people were coming from all over the Pacific Northwest. Amelia was giddy with anticipation.

She checked herself in the mirror one more time, adjusting her hair and making sure the black sweater she wore was free of lint. Noah was at her house, getting ready, and was due to arrive in a few minutes.

Mel was at the counter, ready to ring up what they hoped were additional sales, beyond the new release. They had stacks of Noah's other books positioned around the store and poised at the counter, ready for purchase.

The refreshment table looked gorgeous, thanks to Cyndy.

She and Lily were helping tonight and ready for the onslaught of customers.

Amelia made sure Noah's chair was in place and added one more marker to those already at his place. An author could never have too many pens. Bookmarks and promotional postcards with Noah's books were stacked on the table, and a copy of his new book was waiting on each of the chairs Amelia had rented for the audience.

She and Mel were armed with the ticket holder list and ready to check in the customers who were already waiting on the porch. It promised to be an epic night.

The back door squeaked, and Amelia turned her eyes toward the hallway leading to the kitchen. Noah stepped through the doorway and as soon as she saw him, her pulse quickened.

He looked handsome in the dark gray jacket he wore. He smiled at her, and she hurried to him, kissing him. "You look great," she said.

"As do you. I just got off the phone from talking to Will. He'll be here the Tuesday before Thanksgiving and doesn't have to go back until the week after Christmas. He's excited about visiting us."

This was their first attempt at spending time between the island and Driftwood Bay. They'd be at Amelia's for Thanksgiving. Actually, at Cyndy's. She invited them to join her family, and Amelia was looking forward to it. She wasn't sure she was up to hosting her first Thanksgiving without Natalie. It would be easier at Cyndy's, where they could make new memories.

The three of them would travel to the island in mid-December, where they'd stay at Noah's and spend Christmas with Georgia and Dale, along with all their friends. Georgia and Dale met Noah in September and like Amelia, they'd fallen in love with him.

Without Natalie, there were so many firsts, but Amelia was determined to make new traditions and take advantage of every moment with Noah. He felt good, and Dr. Jan was happy with his latest bloodwork. The disease wasn't progressing yet, which was the best gift she could have asked for this season.

Noah reached for her hand and jolted her from her thoughts. "Ready, sweetheart?" He pointed at the throng of people outside the front doors.

She nodded. "I'm ready. Bring it on."

She started to walk toward the front, and he tugged on her hand. He laughed and bent to brush his lips across hers. "Have I told you how much I love you?"

She shrugged and grinned. "Yes, but I'll never get tired of hearing it."

There was mention of the Lavender Festival in Lavender Valley, Oregon, in this book. Lavender Valley is the setting for Tammy's new *Sisters of the Heart Series*, where Georgia gets her own story. Read the prequel, GREETINGS FROM LAVENDER VALLEY, to learn more about all the women featured in this six-book series.

If you're new to the Hometown Harbor Series, you'll want to read the other books, each featuring a different heroine, starting with FINDING HOME, Sam's story. If you haven't yet discovered the Glass Beach Cottage Trilogy, you'll want to start with BEACH HAVEN, where you'll meet Lily, who is grieving and looking for a bit of hope and happiness in a new coastal community. If you're a lover of whodunits, check out the Cooper Harrington Detective Novels, with KILLER MUSIC being the first book in the series.

If you've missed reading any of this series, here are the links to the other books. All but the free prequel are available in print and eBook formats.

Prequel: Hometown Harbor: The Beginning (free prequel novella eBook only)
Book 1: Finding Home
Book 2: Home Blooms
Book 3: A Promise of Home
Book 4: Pieces of Home
Book 5: Finally Home
Book 6: Forever Home
Book 7: Follow Me Home

ACKNOWLEDGMENTS

When I mentioned Amelia in REUNION IN LAVENDER VALLEY, I had an inkling she needed her own book. I love writing this series because for me, it's the next best thing to a visit to the San Juan Islands. I'm long overdue for such a trip. Writing this one was like a quick vacation to the place I love, surrounded by my old friends. I hope you feel the same way when reading this new one.

If you haven't yet read my *Sisters of the Heart Series*, I hope you'll be inspired to try it after meeting Georgia in this book. I imagine Amelia and Noah will be taking a trip to Lavender Valley to enjoy the festival next year.

My thanks to my editor, Susan, for finding my mistakes and helping me polish *Long Way Home*. She does an awesome job, and I'm grateful for her. All the credit for this gorgeous cover goes to Elizabeth Mackey, who never disappoints. I'm fortunate to have such an incredible team helping me.

A special shout out to Aunt Jan, whose name I borrowed for Dr. Jan in this story. She's one of my favorite people and loves this series. I didn't tell her about using her name, so I'm excited to see how she reacts.

I so appreciate all of the readers who have taken the time to tell their friends about my work and provide reviews of my books. These reviews are especially important in promoting future books, so if you enjoy my novels, please consider leaving a review. I also encourage you to follow me on Amazon, Goodreads, and BookBub, where leaving a review is even easier, and you'll be the first to know about new releases and deals.

Remember to visit my website at http://www.tammylgrace.com and join my mailing list for my exclusive group of readers. I also have a fun Book Buddies Facebook Group. That's the best place to find me and get a chance to participate in my giveaways. Join my Facebook group at https://www.facebook.com/groups/AuthorTammyLGraceBookBuddies/

and keep in touch—I'd love to hear from you.

Happy Reading,

Tammy

MORE BY TAMMY L. GRACE

COOPER HARRINGTON DETECTIVE NOVELS

Killer Music

Deadly Connection

Dead Wrong

Cold Killer

Deadly Deception

HOMETOWN HARBOR SERIES

Hometown Harbor: The Beginning (Prequel Novella)

Finding Home

Home Blooms

A Promise of Home

Pieces of Home

Finally Home

Forever Home

Follow Me Home

Long Way Home

CHRISTMAS STORIES

A Season for Hope: Christmas in Silver Falls Book 1

The Magic of the Season: Christmas in Silver Falls Book 2

Christmas in Snow Valley: A Hometown Christmas Book 1

One Unforgettable Christmas: A Hometown Christmas Book 2

Christmas Wishes: Souls Sisters at Cedar Mountain Lodge

Christmas Surprises: Soul Sisters at Cedar Mountain Lodge

GLASS BEACH COTTAGE SERIES

Beach Haven

Moonlight Beach

Beach Dreams

WRITING AS CASEY WILSON

A Dog's Hope

A Dog's Chance

WISHING TREE SERIES

The Wishing Tree

Wish Again

Overdue Wishes

One More Wish

SISTERS OF THE HEART SERIES

Greetings from Lavender Valley

Pathway to Lavender Valley

Sanctuary at Lavender Valley

Blossoms at Lavender Valley

Comfort in Lavender Valley

Reunion in Lavender Valley

FROM THE AUTHOR

Thank you for reading the eighth book in the Hometown Harbor Series. If you enjoyed it and are a fan of women's fiction, you'll want to try my GLASS BEACH COTTAGE SERIES, set in Driftwood Bay, or my newest series, SISTERS OF THE HEART. You can even start this one by downloading the first book, GREETINGS FROM LAVENDER VALLEY, for FREE!

The two books I've written as Casey Wilson, A DOG'S HOPE and A DOG'S CHANCE, both have received enthusiastic support from my readers and, if you're a dog lover, are must reads.

If you enjoy holiday stories, be sure to check out my CHRISTMAS IN SILVER FALLS SERIES and HOMETOWN CHRISTMAS SERIES. They are small-town Christmas stories of hope, friendship, and family. I'm also one of the authors of the bestselling SOUL SISTERS AT CEDAR MOUNTAIN LODGE SERIES, centered around a woman who opens her heart and home to four foster girls one Christmas.

If mysteries are among your favorite genres, be sure to explore my COOPER HARRINGTON DETECTIVE NOVELS. Readers love the characters, including a loyal golden retriever and the plot twists that keep them guessing until the end.

I'm also one of the founding authors of *My Book Friends* and invite you to join this fun group of readers and authors on Facebook. I'd love to send you my exclusive interview with the canine companions in my *Hometown Harbor Series* as a thank you for joining my exclusive group of readers. You can sign up by following at my website here: https://www.tammylgrace.com/newsletter

I hope you'll connect with me on social media. You can find me on Facebook, where I have a page and a special group for my readers and follow me on Amazon and BookBub, so you'll know when I have a new release or a deal. If you haven't yet, be sure to download the free novella, HOMETOWN HARBOR: THE BEGINNING. It's a prequel to FINDING HOME that I know you'll enjoy.

If you did enjoy this book or any of my other books, I'd be grateful if you took a few minutes to leave a short review on Amazon, BookBub, Goodreads, or any of the other retailers you use.

ABOUT THE AUTHOR

Tammy L. Grace is the *USA Today* bestselling and award-winning author of the Cooper Harrington Detective Novels, the bestselling Hometown Harbor Series, and the Glass Beach Cottage Series, along with several sweet Christmas novellas. Tammy also writes under the pen name of Casey Wilson for Bookouture and Grand Central. You'll find Tammy online at www.tammylgrace.com where you can join her mailing list and be part of her exclusive group of readers. Connect with Tammy on Facebook at www.facebook.com/tammylgrace.books or Instagram at @authortammylgrace.

facebook.com/tammylgrace.books

twitter.com/TammyLGrace

instagram.com/authortammylgrace

bookbub.com/authors/tammy-l-grace

goodreads.com/tammylgrace

amazon.com/author/tammylgrace

Made in the USA
Monee, IL
11 February 2025

12092584R00173